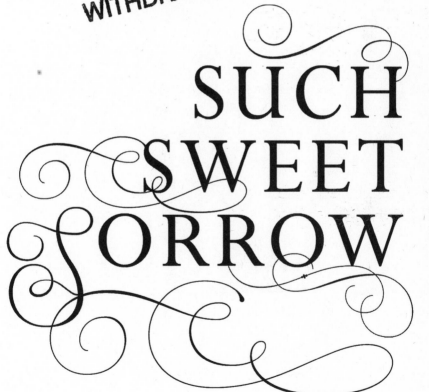

SUCH SWEET SORROW

USA TODAY BESTSELLING AUTHOR

JENNY TROUT

SUCH
SWEET
SORROW

Entangled Publishing, LLC
2614 South Timberline Road
Suite 109
Fort Collins, CO 80525

Visit our website at www.entangledpublishing.com.

Edited by Shannon Godwin
Cover design by Amber Shah
Cover art by Raquel Neira

Print ISBN   978-1-62266-158-9
Ebook ISBN   978-1-62266-159-6

Manufactured in the United States of America

First Edition February 2014

Thanks to Nick Harris, Miriam Kriss, and The Story Foundation. I had a really good time creating this book with you!

PROLOGUE

Two figures, both alike in stature and purpose, ducked beneath a bridge in Verona. The swollen river made mud of its banks. The men slid and fought against it, their torches flickering.

"Let's turn back, Romeo," Friar Laurence urged, pushing down the hood of his rough brown robe. "Can we not let poor Juliet rest in peace?"

The younger man fixed his friend with a critical eye. "Peace? My beloved Juliet knows no peace, only eternal torment. She took her own life, and that is my fault."

They pressed on, Romeo's steps becoming more determined the weaker his limbs grew. The poison that had incapacitated him, but not killed him, had ravaged his body. Tonight he traveled farther beyond his father's walls than he'd dared since the night he'd returned to Verona. Even though the prince had lifted his banishment, the streets still felt unfriendly. Although a truce had been called between Montague and Capulet, there were plenty of young men who would like nothing more than to avenge their kin by killing Romeo.

Their destination lay far from the city center, in a small encampment of hovels beside the river. Faces peeked from behind tattered curtains as Romeo and Laurence traversed the narrow lanes between the dilapidated buildings, coming finally to the very wall of the city itself. It was at this border that they found the *strega*.

Her door was painted red, surrounded by talismans on long chains that hung from the recessed arch. Romeo ducked beneath a dried and crumbling chicken's foot and brushed aside a crudely shaped metal eye.

"I go no further." Friar Laurence backed away from the threshold, crossing himself. "Romeo, I warn you, this is a fearful path you tread. Your soul will be lost to darkness. You will perish in the flames of hell. I beg you not to do this."

"I am already in hell." Romeo pushed open the door and stepped inside.

The interior of the witch's house was hot. It smelled of earth and the wood-like scent of herbs not used for cooking. A bent shape stood before the hearth, where a sulfurous cauldron bubbled. Romeo covered his nose and coughed.

"Ah, I was expecting a visitor this night." The strega lifted her head, the veil of coins that obscured her face tinkling like fairy bells. "Your man of God could not dissuade you?"

"Nothing will dissuade me." Even as he said it, his doubtful eyes took in the squawking black bird in the cage near the fire, the jars and bottles lining the shelves, murky objects floating in their slimy depths. "Benvolio told me you can communicate with the dead. He said you made him a charm to ward off attacks by ghosts."

The strega shuffled across the room, her coins and jewelry clattering. She pointed a bony finger at a chair, and bade Romeo sit. "You are unwell. Poison, was it?"

"Poison, yes." He could still taste the bite of it, still feel the stinging numbness in his veins. The physical evidence of it lay under his clothes, the dark stain of dying flesh spreading still, a little more each day. "Not enough."

"That's because you went to an apothecary," the strega sniffed. "If you want poison to kill a man dead, you must see a witch."

"I'll...remember that. In the future." Romeo clasped his hands and rested his elbows on his knees. "I came to you for knowledge of the dead. I will pay whatever it takes."

"The price depends on the knowledge." She rummaged through a trunk and produced a large, black bowl. Setting it on the floor, she reached into her clothes—it seemed she wore layers upon layers of tattered fabrics in all shades and thickness—and withdrew a vial. The sight of it winking in the light caused something to recoil inside Romeo. Too recently he had held a similar vessel.

Then everything had gone so wrong...

"What do you wish to know?" the strega asked, emptying the thick, black liquid into the bowl.

"My love, Juliet—" his voice trembled at her name, and he took a moment to repress his anguish.

"It was her you drank poison for." The strega swirled the liquid in the basin. "I see her."

"How do you know it's her?" He leaned forward, peering into the dish. He saw nothing but his own reflection.

"The same as you know the sun rises in the east. I simply know." She clucked softly behind her veil of coins. "Bound to you by the thread of holy matrimony. A secret wedding."

Romeo swallowed back unexpected tears. "Yes, she was my…she was my wife."

It still sounded strange to his ears. A wife was something an older man had, a man like his father. At only eighteen, Romeo could not imagine being so old one day. Perhaps that had been the poison's cruelest jest, to let him believe his life would end in the vigor of his youth, only to return him with none of that youth left in body or mind.

"The young are foolish and brash." The witch's tone softened. "Black of hair, brown of eye. As fair as any maid from Verona."

"Fairer," he corrected her, his hand clenching to a fist. His nails bit into his palm as he struggled to hold back his tears. "Is she happy?"

The strega considered a moment, drawing one finger across the surface of the liquid. When she brought her hand away, it shone wet and red. "No. She is in despair. That is all

I can see."

His heart squeezed tightly. He couldn't find his breath. He had hoped to hear that she was in a better place, as friar Laurence had assured him so many times. "There must be some way to assuage her grief. Some way to tell her—"

"Her eyes and ears are as closed as any dead woman's. Whatever torments her will torment her for eternity." There was no comfort to be had from the strega's voice. She reached out one gnarled hand, palm up. "If that is all—"

"It is not all!" Romeo shot to his feet, placing his hand on the dagger at his side. He did not have the strength to use it, but the witch couldn't know that. "You know dark magic. You can bring her back."

The strega slowly unhooked her veil, letting the net of coins fall to her lap. Her face was as aged and withered as her hands. One eye protruded grotesquely, a milky blue, while the other, shrewd and black, fixed on him. "I no longer do such magic."

"But it can be done?" Romeo asked, and when she nodded, he unsheathed his knife and prodded her knobby chin with the point. "Then you had better do it, witch."

The old woman did not tremble in fear of him. She grabbed the blade and pushed it away; it felt as though he cut himself instead of her. He dropped the dagger and stepped back, cursing as blood coursed down his arm from the slice that split his palm. Faster than he could have anticipated, the old witch grabbed his wrist and jerked his hand over the basin, letting his blood fall into it.

"I no longer work such magic," she repeated, swirling the blood in the bowl with her fingertip. "But there are others. To bring someone back, first you must find them. Are you prepared to walk with devils, boy?"

He nodded, his quick breaths flaring his nostrils.

"Are you willing to brave serpents and fire, to fight the keepers of the dead and hear ghosts speak?" She pushed his hand away. The blood on his palm stopped flowing at once, and the wound sealed itself, burning with invisible fire. He gasped and clutched his hand, watching with horror as the old witch's good eye rolled back in her head and she called out words he did not understand.

In the bowl, the liquid lightened, then glowed and turned an unearthly blue. A maelstrom formed in the shallow basin, and lightning crackled on its surface. All the while, the old woman chanted and howled, until the room filled with a spectral wind that seemed to originate inside the blue light. The bird screamed in its cage, and jars and bottles rattled and broke on their shelves.

The surface of the liquid rose in waves capped with frothy blue. As the peaks grew higher, the aquamarine light faded, leaving only a bubbling, roiling fount of blood rising as tall as Romeo himself. The burbling red took shape, into a form so familiar that Romeo at once recoiled from it and yearned to touch it.

His Juliet stood before him, or at least, the shape of her, frozen in blood, monochromatic crimson, but unmistakably her. Thick chains bound her across neck and waist; manacles clasped her wrists. Her eyes were the worst of all, open, bloody, blank and unseeing, yet somehow still accusing. Still hating him, for having let her go before him.

"I'm so sorry," he whispered, his throat raw with emotion. He reached for her, knowing it a foolish thing to have done before his fingertips brushed her bloody cheek.

The vision of Juliet opened its mouth impossibly, terribly wide and a bone withering scream burst from her at the same time the vision burst, raining blood over the room.

The strega braced herself with her ancient hands on either side of the bowl, and lifted her head, the blood running in rivulets down her face. "You must go north. You will find the man who can help you there."

"North?" He conjured up a map in his mind. "Grezzana?"

"Farther." The strega pushed up from the floor, righting herself. She looked smaller somehow, more fragile than fearsome.

"Erbezzo?"

The eyebrow over her good eye arched in exasperation. "Farther. Farther than you have ever traveled. Over the mountains, to a castle by the sea. The seat of a murdered king."

He opened his mouth to speak, but she cut him off. "I know no more. In payment, I ask only that you never darken my door again." She lifted the knife from the floor. He reached for it, and she threw it, so that the blade stuck in the lintel. At once, her terrible, craggy face transformed, her skin going smooth and youthful, her spider web hair turning to glossy black silk. She narrowed her eyes, no longer milky but deep black, and pointed to where the blade quivered in the wood. "Leave it. Let its absence remind you never to cross a sister of the fortunes again."

When Romeo emerged, Friar Laurence rose to his feet. The worry that creased his brow relented only a bit. "I heard such howling, I thought you must surely be in the grips of the devil himself."

"No devils here." Romeo made no mention of the dagger. It embarrassed him now, to think he had threatened a woman so powerful. "To find those, I must go north."

CHAPTER ONE

It was the perfect night to encounter a ghost. The stars did not deign to be seen in the moonless and cloudy sky. The crashing waves against the cliffs of Elsinore may as well have been the clawing fingers of a spectral sea hoping to catch an unwary soul and pull them down, down, into the depths.

And it was fantastically cold.

Hamlet, Prince of Denmark, bundled his cloak tighter around his shoulders and blew on his fingers to warm them. Above his hiding place against the earthen berm that surrounded the keep, Elsinore loomed, a darker black against the impenetrable night sky. In the daylight, it was a majestic castle, with ornate spires reaching toward the heavens. At night, it looked like a forest of daggers and sharp teeth stabbing and tearing deep furrows in the clouds.

"Are you about?" a voice hissed in the darkness. Wisely, it did not call out a name.

Hamlet answered, "Here," and waited for some sign of Horatio's approach. He hoped his friend did not slip and tumble off the tall berm. Hamlet had lived at Elsinore his entire life and still he found navigating the grounds in the dark a dangerous prospect.

When two hooded figures brushed close by him, he knew how his friend had made safe passage. "You were supposed to come alone."

Horatio pushed his hood back, his face a lighter blue than the blue-black night. The man beside him pushed his cloak down, as well, his chain mail haubergeon clinking softly.

"This is Bernardo," Horatio explained in low voice. "The man who first saw it."

Bernardo dropped to one knee, his hands clasped around the hilt of his sword. "My prince."

"Get up, get up." This wasn't the time for courtly manners or identification. "Show me where."

"Yes, your highness. Yes, this way." Bernardo gestured, but it was lost to the darkness. "Begging your pardon, but I've heard rumors about your affliction—"

"You shouldn't listen to rumors," Hamlet scolded. The kingdom had been rife with speculation about the prince's affliction lately. Some whispers, that Hamlet was mad, or in league with the devil had obviously come from King Claudius and were meant to harm Hamlet. Others were merely foolish, suggesting the prince had the power to read thoughts and control the weather, and linked the storms that raged over the seas to his tempestuous moods. Some held a stroke of truth, if not the entire portrait; that Hamlet possessed a rare gift that allowed him to see the souls of the departed.

It was not rare, he'd discovered, for others to see the spirits that plagued him. After all, this lowly guard had spotted a ghost during his nightly travails. But Hamlet had never met another soul who could hear the dead, though he doubted any would admit to such a thing, at the risk of sounding mad or being accused of witchcraft. When Hamlet saw a ghost drifting among the living, that soul could speak to him, and unfortunately they all seemed to recognize this talent.

Hamlet kept his gaze on his feet, or where he estimated his feet might be. This was not a night for secret doings. On the morrow, his uncle, the newly crowned king, would marry Hamlet's mother. The merry mood of the kingdom had not affected Hamlet; to the contrary, his demeanor grew more sour by the moment.

"Although, this rumor is one you may find proves true," Horatio supplied unhelpfully, to soothe his friend's surliness.

Hamlet tried to disguise his curse whenever possible—which had, so far, been his entire life. Only Horatio knew the truth. At the university, all manner of spirits had plagued Hamlet's wakeful nights, and he'd finally confided in his friend. Still, the ability to see and communicate with ghosts wasn't the sort of thing he liked to broadcast. Bad enough being a prince, everyone wanted something from him sooner or later.

But a prince who could speak to the dead, who seemed to pull specters from the abyss under his own power...

His father had once warned him that a king who ruled with fear would die in fear himself. How could anyone not fear a king who seemed to command spectral elements? When Hamlet was restored to the throne—the throne his uncle had stolen from him—he wanted to be loved for his good works, as his father had been, not dreaded by a resentful court who would find one way of replacing him or another.

The group of three made their way across a narrow wooden bridge that spanned the long, marshy drop. From there, they descended a short, rickety stair to a door so well hidden that even Bernardo could not find it on his first try. Once the watchman opened the door and ushered them inside, the sound of the raging sea was muffled by the thick bedrock of the cliffs.

"We met outside the castle, on a night like this, to go back inside?" Horatio muttered.

"I do not need my uncle's spies following me," Hamlet reminded him. Especially if the apparition they sought was who the guard claimed. The ceiling in the corridor was low, and dripping with moisture. Musty dampness scented the air, like the breath from some long-unopened tomb. The moonless night outside had been ink black, but the tunnel was darker. Hamlet groped along the sharp rock walls with clawed fingers, trying in vain to control his panicked gasps.

"Steady, your highness." Horatio knew of Hamlet's other affliction—his fear of close, inescapable places.

"There, your highness! There!" Bernardo whispered frantically.

Ahead of them, a light pierced the darkness. Only a mote of shimmering blue at first, it grew, swirling larger and larger, until Hamlet finally understood that his eyes had tricked him; the thing was not small at all, but far away. The tunnel wound on and on through the cliffs beneath the castle. The very thought of such a dreadful labyrinth made Hamlet's heart beat a frightful tempo, but he took a step forward, and another, as the apparition approached him.

"Your highness, you mustn't!" Bernardo warned, but Hamlet paid him no mind.

"This ghost is the reason you brought me here, is it not?" With one hand stretched out toward the specter and the other feeling along the rough wall, he forged ahead. "If it is my father, I will speak to it."

"And if it isn't your father?" Horatio warned, his voice sounding very far away in the dark. "You said yourself that spirits can deceive."

"Only if you let them." He drew closer to the apparition. The light took shape, a shroud of luminous blue falling over features that were at once familiar and strange. The high, pointed crown atop the king's noble brow was unmistakable, as were his strong profile and broad shoulders. He was like a bust carved of mist, for his chest ended in wisps of blue. His eyes, as blank and pale as a statue's, still stared, somehow, at his son, the prince.

"Hamlet…"

Hearing ghosts speak was one of Hamlet's least favorite parts of the curse. The sound was like the worst winter wind howling through a haunted night, mingled with the screams of the damned and chimes like breaking glass. He knew that behind him, Bernardo and Horatio would cover their ears. For the living not afflicted with Hamlet's strange ability, the voices of the dead were no more than the howl of a chill wind and a sensation of dire foreboding. Though Hamlet could make sense of the words, the rasping, sorrowful gasps still grated down his spine, filling him with dread.

One long tendril of glowing mist beckoned like a finger, and the apparition drifted away.

"Hamlet, don't!" Horatio called. "You'll be lost in the caves."

Hamlet ground his teeth. "If I am, then I suggest you and your man Bernardo come find me."

Putting aside all thoughts of dying trapped in the belly of the earth, Hamlet followed the shade, his rational mind warring with the grief that twisted his heart. His father had died only months ago. Until the last few days, the castle had still been in mourning for him. But by Claudius's declaration, the black shrouds and grim court dress had been banished. Though the courtiers were eager to abandon their sorrow and please their new king, Hamlet's grief for his father was so fresh that he woke in the mornings forgetting, only for a moment, that the king was gone.

The spirit drifted wordlessly, drawing Hamlet deeper and deeper into the cliff below the castle. The sounds of Horatio and Bernardo were lost now, and Hamlet hoped the men still followed at a distance. He'd lost track of the twists he'd taken, the turns when the opening of a new tunnel would make itself known with a blast of cool air and the stink of fetid sea water. Ahead, a glimmer of the same strange blue as the specter flickered in the darkness. He drew closer to it, and soon the shaft of eerie luminescence lit the tunnel like a cold sun, lengthening Hamlet's shadow and highlighting the absence of one where the ghost stood. With a tendril of mist taking the shape of a skeletal finger, the ghost of his father pointed, and Hamlet turned the corner.

There, crackling and spitting like blue hell fire, a huge stone portal, oval like an eye turned on its side, radiated with the promise of menace and salvation. A freezing wind that rivaled even the most bitter seaside winter blew through the surface of the portal, which rippled with waves of light like water. All along the stone frame, ancient runes covered in mold and lichen spelled out words in a language Hamlet doubted any living person could decipher.

Wetting his lips, Hamlet resisted the urge to plunge his hand into the beckoning void. "Well," he said to the ghost, unable to tear his gaze from the looming opening, "This is wondrous strange, indeed."

• • •

The kingdom was alive in celebration, from the lowliest peasant to the highest born lord. The king himself, the murderous, traitorous king, held a wedding gala that put every past celebration in the castle of Elsinore to shame.

Hamlet might have enjoyed it, if he'd bothered to attend. Instead, he hunched over his cup in the lowest, dirtiest alehouse in all of Denmark, far from the shadow of Elsinore's cruel spires, to forget all he had seen and heard in that fearful tunnel below the keep.

It was true that Hamlet had disliked the marriage between his mother and his father's brother, on moral and religious principles. That had been *before* the ghost of Hamlet's father had spoken such ghastly secrets. Things Hamlet could not put out of his mind, no matter how many taverns he visited, or how long he avoided his royal family and duties.

Revenge my murder, his father had said, the words hollow on the screaming wind of his spectral voice. *Protect the corpseway.*

The corpseway, the unearthly portal that divided the realm of the living and the dead, would be a powerful tool in the hands of a king with a noble soul. But in the hands of a vile ruler such as his uncle...

A devastating one.

Hamlet had been living atop it his entire life, with no notion that it existed; perhaps it was to blame for his affliction. Even if it wasn't, he finally understood his father's repeated warnings to avoid the caverns below the keep. If young Hamlet had found the portal, his curious nature might have rendered him dead Hamlet, the lost prince.

It was testament to his father's greatness as king that he had not used the portal to his own ends...but how King Hamlet had known about the corpseway remained a mystery that maddened his son. Had his father shared his gift? Why hadn't he told him? These were answers Hamlet sorely needed, but his father's spirit had vanished before he'd thought to ask them.

The existence of the corpseway did not trouble Hamlet half so much as his father's charge to avenge him. For though Hamlet had never believed his father had been poisoned by a snake bite—and as a result, he'd taken numerous and paranoid precautions against assassination in the months after the king's death—he'd also never suspected that the king's own brother could be implicated in a murder so foul.

Yet the spirit had insisted: *The serpent that did sting thy father's life now wears his crown.*

Not only was Hamlet charged with hiding the secret of the corpseway from his treacherous uncle, but he'd also agreed to regicide and treason. Though he'd fantasized about the joy he would feel in sending his father's assassin to hell, those fantasies had not ended with Hamlet's own neck on the block, an event that would certainly come to fruition should his uncle catch wind of Hamlet's oath to avenge his father's death.

And spirits, even familiar spirits, could not always be trusted.

The bench on which he sat rocked as new occupants

took up the space beside him. Someone brushed his arm and upset his cup.

"*Mi scusi.*"

Italian?

Hamlet lifted his head, squinting at the fellow. Young, about Hamlet's own age. Like Hamlet, he was tall and handsome, but his hair was black as a raven's feather, where Hamlet's was pale gold. The stranger's eyes were dark, and there they also differed, as they did in build; Hamlet wondered if the other young man's slenderness was a result of starvation or sickness.

"What are you doing here?" Hamlet asked, leaning his cheek on his hand, elbow propped firmly against the long wooden table he slumped over. "You sound strange."

"Because I am a stranger." The Italian was in a surly mood, despite his pretty appearance. Next to him, an older man in monk's robes with a monk's tonsure shorn into his hair cast his furtive gaze about the alehouse, as if waiting for sin or vice to assail them from every corner.

Figuring he might have better luck with a man of the cloth, Hamlet slurred, "Don't worry, father. No one would dare trouble you here. We may be fierce Northerners, but we do have religion."

The friar responded in a rolling babble that took Hamlet a moment to decipher. When he did, he replied in the same tongue, "Ah, Italians are you? I never much cared for the language myself, but it is terrifically easy to rhyme."

"We did not come here for a language lesson," the

handsome one snapped in his native speech. His hair was shorn quite short, and he ran a hand over it in a self-conscious gesture that suggested he might not be so surly and forbidding as he wanted people to think. "Kindly mind your own business."

"I'm not in the business of minding my own business. Not anymore. Bad things happen when people mind their own business." Hamlet had come to the tavern to drink away his dark thoughts, not invite new ones in. But the strangers were so intriguing, he could not help but think of them as a portent; after all, how many foreigners found their way this far north, with no clear purpose for being there? Speaking to his father's ghost had made him both suspicious and curious at once. "You didn't come here for a language lesson. What did you come here for?"

"Shelter," the friar spoke up, laying a warning hand on his companion's arm. "Shelter and something to eat, before our pilgrimage carries us far from here. We wish no quarrel."

In taking stock of the pretty man's appearance, Hamlet had already noted the spider's web of silver guarding the hilt of a sword beneath his cloak. They wanted no quarrel, but they had not come unprepared should one arise. Why did a pilgrim need so fine a blade? "I want no quarrel with you, either. Indulge a poor drunkard's curiosity. Where do you journey? You're Italian, that means you came from the South. Or perhaps you're traveling homeward? Where did you come from? There's nothing above us but sea, and beyond the sea, more Northerners. Worse than us, even."

"Would you kindly shut your mouth?" The younger man no longer masked his fury. The conversations around them quieted.

The priest was quick to calm his companion. "Now, wait, wait. You are tired and discouraged, that much is true. But perhaps this man could help us. We've come this far, Romeo."

With a pained sigh and a flexing of fingers into a fist that Hamlet deduced was meant for his face, the man called Romeo said, "I am on a quest."

"I suppose I didn't realize people went on quests anymore." The idea held a world of appeal to Hamlet. Striking out for an adventure, with a purpose, seemed far less dangerous than staying within his uncle's reach. "What kind of quest?"

Romeo's patience had worn visibly thin. "We came here because I was told to go north, to the seat of a murdered king, at a castle by the sea. Now we're here, where a *living* king sits in his castle by the sea, and I've no idea how to proceed. Is that enough for you, or would you like to sketch us so you'll have something to remember us by?"

The hairs on the back of Hamlet's neck stood. This Romeo spoke of a secret only Hamlet knew, and then only through supernatural means. Were they soothsayers? Did they suffer the same spectral affliction as he?

Or, perhaps, had Claudius sent them, to ascertain if Hamlet knew the truth of his father's death? Were that the case, the sword beneath Romeo's cloak would make all the difference in Hamlet's answer.

"You shouldn't speak about murder so openly here. Especially as it pertains to the king."

"Can anyone here understand Italian?" the priest asked quietly.

Hamlet checked about doubtfully, then called out in the same tongue, "The next round is on me!" When the other patrons paused to look incredulously at the man who spouted foreign gibberish loudly, he shook his head. "It doesn't appear so. How did you know the king was murdered?"

Some of the color drained from Romeo's sunburned face. "Call it a religious vision."

If the Italians would not share their true purpose, Hamlet could force the information from them. "Any charlatan could claim God spoke to him. But this vision seems too specific. You say you seek the seat of a murdered king...what assurance do I have that you're not here to kill the king? Perhaps my grasp of your language isn't as good as I thought it was. Should I find a royal guard and see if your religious vision can save you?"

"No!" The priest's face paled; even his sunburned pate lost a shade of red at the threat. "No, please good sir, I beg of you. You misunderstand. We are but two wicked pilgrims, sent here on a foul lie. We mean your king no harm."

That's a shame, Hamlet thought uncharitably. But if these men feared the king, perhaps they had not been sent by the king.

Or perhaps it was another part of their ruse. "Wicked? I don't care for the word. Isn't killing a king wicked?"

Romeo turned to the priest, who nodded and pressed the rosary clenched in his hand to his lips. His shoulders slumping in resignation, Romeo admitted, "A witch told me. I asked her how I could bring my beloved back from the dead, and the crone told me to seek my answer here."

"Did she?" *A witch?* That was no good at all. Hamlet had always believed in and feared witches, for it seemed unlikely to him that he was the only mortal afflicted with a supernatural curse. He'd never met a witch, so he had no clue if one would want to meddle with a corpseway. It was no coincidence that the Italians had shown up, eager to contact the dead, after Hamlet had been handed the awesome responsibility of protecting the portal. "Who have you spoken to here? How did you find me?"

Romeo straightened at the affront. "What are you blathering about? You're the only soul, besides Friar Laurence, to whom I have told this tale, and then only at his misguided urging." He scoffed. "What guard would believe a word of it anyway? You stink of ale and speak nonsense."

"And you just happened to come here, to tell a convoluted story of lost love and triumph over death?" Hamlet's mouth was thick, his thinking muddled. He'd had a point to make before, but now it slipped away, under the calm, soothing waves of intoxication. He struggled to keep his head clear, but it was futile; his earlier goal of oblivion had been achieved, but only after he'd changed his mind. These men had offended and confused him. Somehow. He wasn't entirely clear on how. "My god, you're probably not even Italians, are you? Just some peasant farmers come to torment me for curiosity's sake!" Hamlet slapped his palm on the table. "Oh, what that witch must have paid you. What vile favors did she bestow upon you? What does she seek? Power over the fates of men? Or is it something deeper? I'm sure she thought I would be moved by your story of love stronger than death. Well, you can tell your witch to go back to hell from whence she came, for she'll have none of my secrets."

Romeo's hand snapped to the grip of his sword, and the priest hurried to intervene. "He speaks madness, Romeo, stay your hand!"

"Mad, am I?" Hamlet rose, and downed his cup. "You'd be driven mad, too, if were suddenly forced to defend yourself from witches and wicked pilgrims! You would be mad if unquiet spirits tormented you in the night. Mad, you call me. We'll see how mad I am when I make you one of them."

He did not have a knife to draw, but Hamlet thought he'd made himself fairly clear. He intended to duel this stranger. Not now, with his limbs still unsteady from drink, but in a few hours. "Meet me, at dawn. On the public green in front of the castle gates. We'll see who is a mad man then."

He did not await a reply. He staggered from the alehouse, not certain if he'd settled up with the barman or not. Horatio would take care of it tomorrow, if Hamlet were to meet his death in the duel. Horatio was a good friend that way.

"A good friend," Hamlet burped, addressing the specter

of an old man who slumped against the alehouse doorway. "A good friend, and the best of men."

. . .

Romeo stared after the figure departing the tavern, a sense of understanding creeping over him. The exchange had been so bizarre, like falling into a tossing ocean and not knowing which way to swim, but with the confusing man departed, small pictures stood out. The cut of the man's clothing, the fine silver buttons on his doublet…he was a rich man. A rich mad man, perhaps.

"Laurence," Romeo said slowly, his tongue thick in his mouth. "I think mayhap divine provenance has lit the way to my Juliet."

"Do not put too much stock in the words of a lunatic, or you may be disappointed." The friar bent his head as though he would withdraw into his scratchy robe.

"No… this man knows something. Madman he may be, but a drunken one. Tomorrow morning, he is sure to be sober." Romeo chewed his thumbnail and hunched his shoulders, avoiding the stares of the other patrons. "Did you see how he reacted, when I told him the strega's words? He seemed nervous."

"Because you were speaking treason freely," Laurence scolded. "It means nothing, Romeo. Let it be."

"I could meet with him tomorrow. Ask him what he meant by his words, and tell him all that I meant by mine."

"You'll win the confidence of a madman," Laurence said with a lift of his eyebrows and the tone of Pontius Pilate washing his hands. "I believe I've made my objections known, so I won't waste my breath objecting further."

"Beer loosens men's tongues," Romeo said, shaking his head. "Any information he might have given us tonight could be lost to sobriety. And if he insists upon dueling, I shall have to kill him, and then it is lost for good."

Laurence grew thoughtful. "Do not kill him, Romeo. There is already a stain on your soul from your past deeds. Tybalt? Paris? Or have you forgotten your life before this sacrilegious quest?"

"Why did you come with me?" Yet Romeo knew why. Because Laurence could not have considered letting his young friend take up such a dangerous journey alone. Because he felt guilty that his plan to save Romeo's marriage to Juliet had instead doomed her to hell, and Romeo to a living one. Because he had regretted the antidote he'd administered from the moment Romeo had opened his eyes.

Laurence's spine straightened, his chin lifted. "You know why I am here. And you know that I will follow you into the underworld itself if I must. But I will not stand by idle while you send yourself there. What good is recovering Juliet, if only to separate yourself from her in the hereafter with your earthly deeds?"

"You make a good point."

Romeo paid a wench for a pitcher of ale and two suppers, but he was not inclined to eat or drink. His heart no longer rejoiced in living, not with Juliet still cold in her tomb—yet the traitorous organ still beat within his chest.

After several ravenous spoonfuls of the muck the barmaid had returned with, Laurence looked up, then cast his gaze down again to hide his worry. "I doubt dry bones will be able to complete this quest as ably as a living body. I beg you, Romeo, sustain yourself."

"You are too good a man to refuse." Romeo tried not to smell the greasy stew as he lifted his spoon to his mouth. It was better to ignore the scent. The taste was diminished that way. He remembered the days when he and his friends existed only to laze in the sun, rising at night to drink their fill and feast like kings. So many of them were gone now, lost to foolish feuding. Mercutio had died in his arms. His beloved Juliet had forsaken her own life. It was all so senseless, and so he had to try to bring it to right, no matter the consequence.

Even if it cost him his soul.

"I will go," he said at last, wiping his mouth on the back of his hand. "To duel with the madman. If it proves a false end, if that witch has tricked us, then I say we turn for home."

Laurence stared in open-mouthed disbelief, a pity, for he had not finished chewing. "You can't be serious."

"Why not? We've been at this for months, and we've found nothing." It made Romeo feel foolish to admit it now, when they'd traveled so far from home. "We came all this way on the word of an old woman who had no stake in any of this."

"When you emerged from the witch's house, you told me

of strange sights and terrible rituals. You believed then. Why does your trust in her words falter now?" Laurence raised one bushy eyebrow. "If you have forsaken your faith in God to confer with witches, what do you have left when you cast those sinful beliefs aside?"

"Nothing." Romeo had taken stock all along the difficult journey. Yet every day that passed without even a glimmer of hope that Juliet would be returned to him, he longed for that cold tomb and for just a drop more poison.

His body ached, unaccustomed still to the weakness the vile potion had left in its wake. Though he boasted of skill and the certainty with which he would kill his opponent, he doubted his chances of besting the man at dawn, be the young Dane mad or drunk or both. "Do you really believe our answer lies at Elsinore?"

The friar considered. "*You* seem to. Have you taken my advice yet on this journey?"

Romeo rubbed the stubble on his chin. "I will meet the madman at dawn, then."

CHAPTER TWO

"You're doing what?"

"I'm going to duel an impertinent Italian," Hamlet repeated calmly, taking a few clumsy thrusts at the air with his sword. He frowned at the inelegant swipe that left the heavy blade quivering comically before him. He should have kept up his fencing studies while at university.

"Where did you meet an Italian?" Horatio closed the dusty tome he'd been studying. The small desk he sat behind swayed dangerously with the motion, laden down with too many books to remain upright for much longer.

Hamlet mimed a parry and knocked over a history of Caesar's exploits in Gaul, seven volumes that turned into a landslide. "At the ale house."

"Of course." Horatio rubbed his hand over the close-fitting linen cap he wore. His pale blue eyes rolled heavenward. "Are you certain they were even Italian? They might have been just as stinking drunk as you were."

Hamlet winced, and even that small motion made him feel the wrath of last night's demons fighting it out inside his head. "They were Italian. Trust me."

"I trusted you to be in the hall for the banquet last night! 'I have a headache, go down without me, I just need a moment to rest my eyes in the dark.' I didn't realize that you meant you were going to rest them in a dark tavern and leave me to make your excuses all night."

"If it makes you feel any better at all, I have a headache *now*." With a sigh, Hamlet tossed the blade aside. It clattered onto the floor. He paced across his chamber, his boot steps echoing hollow off the stone. He resolved to be kinder to Horatio in the future. After all, the man had left the university to accompany Hamlet to Elsinore. His friendship had kept Hamlet from withering away in total despair while he had watched his father die a slow death.

A death that was not natural, Hamlet reminded himself angrily. He strode to his wardrobe, reaching for the key around his neck. Slipping it into the lock, he opened the doors and selected a loaf of bread and some hard cheese, then, securing the lock behind him, he turned and raised the food in silent offering.

"I'll pass." Horatio rose and carefully navigated the slowly narrowing path across the long room. He stopped at the pile of clothing on the floor beside the wardrobe. "You know, clothes can be poisoned as easily as food."

"No, not as easily, actually." Hamlet sat and cut into the cheese with the knife from his belt. "I'm not taking any chances. Not after what my father told me."

"Your father's ghost," Horatio corrected. "Hamlet, I know you put faith in apparitions, but I do not. There must be another explanation for your father's death."

If anyone else had suggested such a thing, Hamlet would have had them thrown in the dungeon. This was Horatio, gentle Horatio, who cared only for his best friend's well-being. Perhaps Horatio felt Hamlet's doubt. It was an uncomfortable possibility, but Hamlet wouldn't discount it. Horatio had an uncanny ability to see what Hamlet would never confess to another soul. Gently, he observed, "You saw him too."

"I did," Horatio admitted, after a time. The war in his rational mind would not be won over a meager breakfast of cheese.

So Hamlet changed the subject again. "What would you have me do about this duel?"

"I would have you choose someone to fight in your stead," Horatio suggested, then quickly, with both hands held in the air before him, said, "Not me. Someone competent."

"No, no one competent. I don't want this fellow to die." Hamlet had, the night before, when he'd been confident that he would murder the fiend in a single, glorious blow. The morning light had brought him clarity. Searing pain, as well, that had eventually dulled to a throb behind his eyes—he might never touch a drop of ale again—but clarity, foremost.

The specter of death, always around Hamlet, had intensified tenfold once he'd ventured through the glittering corpseway. What could his uncle, the new king, do if he gained knowledge from the world of the dead? Hamlet didn't know, and that made the prospect of Claudius discovering the gate to the underworld all the more terrifying.

"These men claimed to be on a quest," Hamlet confessed, looking away from Horatio. It sounded almost too absurd. "I thought they might be my uncle's spies."

"What kind of a quest?" Horatio seated himself on the mass of clothing. It was almost as tall as a chair and would do nicely in the role.

Hamlet hesitated. He did not fear ridicule, for Horatio had mocked him many times, and Hamlet always took it for an expression of love through sarcasm. He feared the possibility that Horatio, upon hearing the strangers' tale, would agree that they were spies. It would make his uncle's treachery that much closer.

"They were sent by a witch, to the seat of a dead Northern king. The young man, Romeo, believes he can bring his lost love back from the dead. A bit dramatic, but touching, really. A love stronger than death." Something crucial twisted up from the broken pieces of his drunken interlude. "No. They did not seek a *dead* king. They sought a *murdered* king."

Horatio took a long, deep breath, but said nothing.

"You see, then, why I might find their story suspect. Of all the ale houses, and in Denmark, of all places, they find the one man who knows the king was murdered?"

"Not the only man," Horatio reminded him. "King Claudius almost certainly knows it as well."

"Then you see my dilemma." Hamlet shook his head, a rueful smile tugging the corners of his lips. "It seems too coincidental."

"Perhaps it is fate?" Horatio shrugged. "Stranger things have happened in the course of human history, I'm sure of it. But as you say, it is very convenient. The night after you learn the true circumstances of your father's death, these strangers appear?"

"And yet that information may also prove their tale without any connection to my uncle. Suppose a witch really did tell him to seek the seat of a murdered king. No one else on earth, save vile Claudius, could possibly know that. No rumor doubting the nature of my father's death could have flown south, without our hearing." Hamlet took a deep breath, nostrils flaring. "You're clever. What do you suggest?" It was a common, albeit surly, way for him to concede he was out of his depth and—grudgingly—that his friend was the smarter of the two of them.

"Your curse is proof enough that stranger things exist than we have dreamt of in our philosophies." Horatio scowled and shook his head, scratching at his nape as he pronounced, "But it is an awfully big coincidence."

It was a terrible thing for a scholar to be confronted by that which he could not explain with his rational mind. Hamlet pitied his friend, for Horatio did not have seventeen years of experience reconciling the rational and supernatural, as Hamlet had.

The more Hamlet ruminated on the solution to this puzzle, the more he recalled the sadness in Romeo's eyes, the hopelessness that some might mistake for the weariness of a tired traveler.

"There was something about him," Hamlet began slowly, "A melancholy. It was far too genuine to be a forgery. I could believe that he was truly grieving his love."

"But could you believe he came all this way to try and raise her from the dead?"

Hamlet considered. "I could… if you did."

"Let us speak with them. Proceed with caution, Hamlet, but I do not believe these men could be your uncle's spies. After all, his majesty believed you to be in your bed last night. Why send an assassin to an alehouse, when he knew you to be asleep in your bed?" Almost the moment his sentence ended, Horatio's shoulders sagged in defeat. "You cannot give up sleeping Hamlet, please don't try."

"Just not sleeping in the castle." Hamlet rubbed his jaw. "It is decided then. We will go and meet these Italian fiends and speak to them with words instead of steel."

Hamlet's chambers were in a long gallery on the eastern side of the castle. He'd abandoned his place in the family quarters when his uncle had announced his intention to become king in Hamlet's stead. Uncle Claudius had called him a "boy" and suggested that he "wait to come of age" before inheriting the throne. Hamlet's mother, the queen, had turned on him, quick as the viper he'd believed had poisoned his father. She had been so eager to marry Claudius, she'd barely worn a scrap of black for King Hamlet. She no longer seemed all that concerned with Hamlet the younger, either. That had been proof enough that his place had been unfairly usurped. His uncle had not only stolen the throne, but Hamlet's own mother, as well.

In the intervening months, he'd made his new room a home for himself and his friend, and they'd spent many long hours in study and drink, content to be left alone by the rest of the castle. He would occasionally forget his sorrows and think himself back at the university with Horatio. In those moments of blissful denial, Hamlet would imagine his parents in Elsinore, his father stern but proud of his son the scholar, his mother loving. That woman had disappeared when the king had died, and Hamlet had become an orphan. He could not be blamed for savoring the past.

Without the bustle of serving maids stripping beds and kitchen boys bringing breakfast to the royal family's quarters, Hamlet and Horatio were free to sleep as late as they wanted, and as a consequence, the castle had woken hours before they had. Servants had broken their fast and now hurried about, sweeping the floors, beating the tapestries. Hamlet squinted one eye into the sunlight shining in a narrow shaft across his path as he realized his error. "I...may have told them to meet me at dawn. Do you think they're still here?"

"Do I think a man waited five hours for a chance to kill you?" Horatio's disbelief changed mid-thought. "Actually..."

"That's enough from you, peasant." Hamlet stalked ahead, through the dark corridors and down a curling stair. At the bottom, he nearly collided with a figure swathed in golden velvet.

"Hamlet!" Ophelia's eyes, greener than any blade of grass Hamlet had ever seen, grew wide as he clasped her arms to steady her. Her waist-length ringlets bounced beneath the linen veil she wore, and the copper circlet over it matched the color glinting off her curls. She frowned as she searched his face. "You must be feeling better, then?"

"Better than what?" Hamlet asked, before Horatio elbowed him sharply in the ribs. Ophelia had a strange power about her, possibly stranger than Hamlet's own curse, wherein she seemed to muddle a man's brain by mere proximity. It seemed to only have grown worse as the years went on.

"I was so worried for you." She placed her hand on Hamlet's arm and continued their walking for them, gently pulling them along in the direction they had been heading, though Hamlet was certain both he and Horatio had forgotten where they'd been going in the first place.

"Oh, because of the headache, yes," Hamlet feigned a grimace. "Too much reading by candlelight, I suppose."

She clucked her tongue. "So much studying lately. Hardly any time at all to speak with your uncle on matters more… personal."

Ah, so it was that again. Hamlet's father hadn't been keen for his son to grow too close to the daughter of his advisor. Somehow, Ophelia had gotten it into her head that the king had been the only impediment to their love, and now that he had passed away, there might be hope for them.

It was not that Hamlet didn't find her pleasing. He did and enjoyed her company immensely when she was not set on matchmaking. It wasn't that he never planned to marry. He would have to, at some point, but not now. Not at eighteen, when he hopefully had an entire life ahead of him for such drudgery. He would not resign himself to the prison of marriage at such a young age, no matter how Ophelia might wish otherwise.

Certainly not now when there were other mysterious matters of murder and quests with which to contend. Though he could not openly express it to Ophelia and risk misleading her further; he liked her too well to draw her into danger with him.

"I fear you would find my uncle's answer much the same as my father's," Hamlet told her, hoping his sincerity covered his relief at having put her off a little while longer. "As long as I am heir to Elsinore and all of Denmark, I find myself at the mercy of my uncle's political maneuvering. But never fear, dearest Ophelia, my heart is ever yours."

Though she blushed and fluttered like the sweet maiden that she was, she was not a foolish girl. No doubt her mind calculated furiously behind her pretty face.

Nothing was more fearsome than a young lady plotting marriage.

"Are you going out this morning?" she asked sweetly.

"I am. To fight a duel." *Why*, Hamlet scolded himself, *do you persist in desiring her attention when you mean to discourage her?*

"A duel?" Her free hand flew to cover her mouth. "I cannot bear to watch."

"Thank God for small mercies," Horatio muttered. Then to cover his gaff, "You would not wish to see a duel. They are messy, violent things."

Hamlet eased Ophelia's hand off his arm and raised it to his lips, like a knight in a story book. "If I die, know that I will carry your memory with me, and it will be all the heaven I need."

She jerked her hand back coldly. "You said that last week, after you slipped on the stairs."

As they watched Ophelia storm away, no doubt lamenting her poor taste in insincere men, Horatio said, "What has got it into her head that she could marry a prince? Her family may be noble, but your father largely improved their status. People won't have forgotten that."

"She's been planning our wedding since we were five. She believes our great love will triumph the will of a king." He shrugged. "Can I help it if I'm flattered? I'm rarely set upon as a romantic hero."

Perhaps that was for the better. If Romeo was not a spy sent by Claudius, but was indeed lamenting a love lost to the grave, Hamlet did not envy the man. If love could wreak such misery as had been written on the poor fool's face, then Hamlet would do well to avoid it.

As they made their way onto the wide lawn before the castle gates, Hamlet wondered if the Italians had already left. It had been rude of him not to at least send someone ahead at dawn. He hadn't had the foresight, in the pounding aftermath of his inebriation. But there, just beyond the guard's post, two cloaked figures waited. They caught sight of him at almost the same moment he'd noticed them, and they started toward him.

A guard stepped into their path at once, and Hamlet called ahead, quickening his pace, "No, no. Let them through, by order of Prince Hamlet."

"*Un principe*?" Romeo spat on the ground. "Is this a trick? I've come to fight you, and you choose here? So a guard can stick a sword into my back after I stick mine into your belly?"

"Horatio, this is Romeo," Hamlet responded in the travelers' language, which both he and Horatio had studied at university. Hamlet searched his vague memory of the night before. "And his friend here is a friar."

"Friar Laurence," the holy man said, his eyes still on the guard at his post. "I beg of you, your highness, forgive my companion's impertinence. His thoughts are much confused, shrouded as they are in sorrow."

Romeo shot the friar a glance, as though he objected to the apology.

"Don't worry," Hamlet said, managing a cheerful smile. "I didn't come here to fight you. Or punish you for your impudence, though it has been noted. I seem to remember that the two of you were on a quest?"

"I am," Romeo answered, nodding past Hamlet to the figure of Horatio behind him, silently demanding an explanation.

"Romeo, Laurence, this is my closest friend and advisor, Horatio." Hamlet tilted his head, studying the paleness of Romeo's face, the deep circles beneath his dark eyes. He suspected it was more than just fatigue from travel that weakened the Italian...more than just sorrow for his lost love. "For example, he just now advised me not to duel you, for fear that I would not win. Looking at you, I think you got the better end of his advice, wouldn't you say?"

A muscle in Romeo's cheek twitched, but he did not flare to angry threats, as Hamlet had supposed he might. Instead he pushed down the cowl of his cloak. The sunlight set deep amber in his short black hair, and it seemed unusual for a body so frail looking to be crowned with such color. "I am ill. It is not a plague, do not fear for yourself. I was poisoned, and I am long in recovering."

"Poisoned?" Hamlet filed this strange coincidence with the others. "Who poisoned you?"

It might have been too personal a question, for the young man made a face like someone biting into a particularly bitter fruit. "I did."

"Excuse me?" Hamlet was certain he had not heard correctly. Young noblemen—and Romeo's impudent bearing and fine sword testified to his nobility—rarely took up poisoning themselves as a sport. If Romeo had willingly drunk poison, he'd been mad, or truly despondent.

The young man was looking less like Claudius's spy by the minute.

"I poisoned myself," Romeo admitted through clenched teeth.

With a glance at Horatio, Hamlet smiled at the two Italians. "Gentlemen. I welcome you to Elsinore. I believe we have much to talk about."

CHAPTER THREE

"I do not like this," Laurence remarked for the third time as they treaded across a checkerboard floor.

"This way, this way," the prince called over his shoulder as he cut a swath through the courtiers who assembled there.

Romeo kept his eyes straight ahead, ignoring the groans of disgust he and Laurence left in their wake. The courtiers were all finely dressed and heavily perfumed, and the only thing that had perfumed Romeo's long-worn travel clothes had been the alehouse floor where he and Laurence had slept.

"Be calm, Friar. Who would harm two pilgrims in a strange land?" Romeo crossed himself quickly, hoping their piety would be noted by the people turning up their noses all around them.

He'd come too far on his quest to reunite with his true love to be done in by a group of courtiers.

The man who walked with the prince spoke rapidly, close to the Prince's ear, and Romeo could not make out what they talked of. The barriers of language and volume made it too difficult, but Romeo believed he understood what was happening in front of them. The prince had invited them inside, and his advisor didn't like it.

Well, that set him on equal footing with the prince, didn't it?

What kind of a prince spent his nights in ale houses, utterly unprotected? There had been no guards around him, no elaborate disguise. He hadn't covered his pale blond hair or obscured his face, which bore what seemed to be a permanent expression of disdain. Perhaps everyone in the north looked that way, and they couldn't tell each other apart.

Furthermore, what sort of castle was kept in the disarray the prince had brought them to? In the room they entered, books and papers covered every available surface. Some stacks stood waist high, and precious volumes splayed open on the floor. Trenchers of untouched food lay rotting beside the door, and half-eaten loaves of bread grew stale sitting about on desks and chests. There was a pile of clothing beside the wardrobe, and rivulets of candle wax had frozen beneath their sconces on the walls.

"Pardon," the prince's advisor said in halting Italian. "The prince was not expecting company."

"The prince himself invited us," Romeo said pleasantly, but he narrowed his eyes.

"Yes, I did," Hamlet interrupted, brandishing a sheet of parchment, which he handed over to Romeo. "I wanted to hear more about this quest of yours. Specifically, the poison."

Frowning, Romeo quickly scanned the page. "I don't understand—"

"It is a list of poisons commonly used by assassins in Europe and as far away as China. If you could so kindly point out to me what you poisoned yourself with, and tell me the antidote—"

"That's what this is about?" Romeo snapped angrily. "The poison?"

Hamlet blinked his icy blue eyes.

When he did not speak, Romeo crumpled the parchment in his fist. "I'm no apothecary, I know nothing about poisons."

"Neither did the apothecary who sold you your poison, or it would have worked." The prince rubbed his chin. "This is troubling. I thought I might be able to help you in your quest, but if you cannot help me—"

"How the hell would you help me?" It was wrong to speak to a prince that way, Romeo knew well enough. The prince of Verona would have had him flogged for such impudence. But they had come so far, and for nothing. All the while Juliet was trapped in a dark and lonely death. They stood at the seat of a dead king, as the witch had told them, and still they'd received no answers. Now this spoiled, heartless cur was making a game of his quest?

A change came over Hamlet's features. A moment before, he'd been a pompous, irritating boy. He now looked a dangerous man, with dangerous thoughts and the wealth and status to back them up. Romeo wished he had not spoken so rashly.

Though he expected that the prince's next words would be something like, "take him to the dungeon," instead, Hamlet gestured to a chair piled high with books. At once, Horatio swept them onto the floor, and Hamlet lifted his chin, saying, "I have been rude. Please sit down, Romeo. I would like you to tell my friend Horatio the tale you told me last night."

It was not a story he wished to share, not in front of this young man who would likely mock it, but he'd already been impertinent, and he did not wish to offend the prince further. "I was heartsick, and I wanted to die."

"Heartsick?" Hamlet made a sharp noise that Romeo supposed served as a laugh. "A man who looks like you? I doubt you want much for feminine company."

"It was not lack of feminine company, in general, that made me heartsick, *your highness.*"

Hamlet's eyes flared in recognition. "Oh, yes. Your beloved. You mentioned that last night."

Friar Laurence stooped down close to Romeo's ear. "Please. You need this man's help. Be cautious. Tell him what he wishes to know."

Faced with the wisdom of his friend and the prospect of another dead end, Romeo could see no other option than to acquiesce. If he was going to tell his tale, he should start at the beginning. "I was banished from Verona for killing a man."

The advisor, Horatio, went wide-eyed and pale. Perhaps he'd never been in the presence of an actual murderer before. Romeo ignored him. "He was a kinsman of my bride, Juliet."

Just speaking the name sent a stab more deadly than any blade through his heart. It seemed wrong, that he should share this story with strangers, when Juliet did not live to protect her half of it. Would she want these men to hear it? "We had married in secret, and she would have been forced to forsake her vows to me to marry another, but…"

"She killed herself?" Hamlet finished for him.

That was so much simpler than what had happened, it seemed an insult not to tell the rest, the foolish coincidences that had conspired against them. There was no way to make these young men understand the brilliance of the light that had been extinguished with Juliet's death. They could not miss the joy of her smile, or her soft breath against their skin. Perhaps a skilled bard could weave such magic from simple words, but Romeo was far more skilled with sword than pen. When Friar Laurence started to speak, though, Romeo covered him with his own voice. "Yes, that was the way of it."

"And you poisoned yourself in your grief." Horatio was taller and leaner than his royal companion, with golden hair and a nose that was just slightly too large to be handsome. He'd been tapping his lips with steepled index fingers as he'd listened, but now he crossed his arms, studying Romeo's face intently. "But someone saved you?"

"It didn't take." Romeo could still taste the bitter poison on his lips sometimes, at night, when he lay in darkness like that of the tomb. "I appeared dead for a few hours, then, as my mother wept over my body, I began to stir."

"Why did you kill your wife's kinsman?" Horatio asked in the silence that fell over the room like a shroud.

Hamlet waved a hand, indicating Romeo's act of murder didn't concern him. Somberly, the prince spoke almost to himself, "That is the beloved you speak of bringing back from the dead. What do you think, Horatio?"

"I don't think he's lying."

"Lying?" The word left Romeo on a barren whisper. "Who would lie about such a thing?"

"Italian spies," Horatio suggested.

Before steel could be drawn, Hamlet stepped between his advisor and the chair upon which Romeo sat, ready to spring. "I thought before that you were a spy, sent by my uncle. You see, last night, when you spoke of seeking the seat of a murdered king... you have found it. I thought perhaps my uncle had sent you, to test my suspicions."

"Why do you believe differently now?" Although Romeo bristled at being branded a spy and assassin, he also felt relief and elation at the confirmation of the strega's promise.

Hamlet leaned down, his hands braced on the arms of the chair Romeo occupied. "In my life, I have seen all manner of performers, from traveling minstrels to the bawdiest playhouse players, and never once have I believed a declaration of love as I believe in the story you've just told. If you have been sent here by my uncle, then your art of deception is truer than any I've ever seen, and I should not feel the smallest amount of shame at being drawn in, should you ultimately prove false and murder me."

If Hamlet had been anyone else in the word, he would have had a stiletto in his gut already for accusing them of being spies and insulting Romeo's honor. But looking into the prince's eyes, Romeo saw a mad desperation he could not help but pity. Whatever had happened to this young man, it had been severe enough that he would invite two suspected assassins into his quarters for...

What had he called them here for?

"You said you could help us," Laurence reminded Hamlet, his gentle voice a thunderclap that broke the quiet tension of the room. "Perhaps you could tell us how? And why on earth you would wish to?"

"I wish to," Hamlet began, slowly straightening, "because I have recently been called upon to avenge a murder, and to protect a doorway separating the land of the living from the realm of the dead. I'm not entirely sure how factual either of those statements are, as they were told to me by the ghost of my father."

Romeo's heart thundered against his ribs so furiously he was certain his bones would break. "A doorway—"

"Between the land of the living and the realm of the dead," Hamlet repeated wearily. "I understand how mad it sounds. I wasn't sure I could trust the apparition that came to

me in my father's face. I was told—as was all of Denmark—
that King Hamlet had been bitten by a viper and died. Then
my father's ghost appeared to me and warned that he had
been murdered by his own brother, Claudius, who sits on my
throne in my stead."

"You want to be king?" Romeo wondered how much
of *this* story was false, and his doubt turned to shame. The
prince had believed a tale of witches and convoluted suicide.
Romeo owed it to him to take him at his word.

"No! That would be horrible. Far too much responsibility.
What I want is for my father to be king. As I can't have that,
though, I must either accept his murderer on his throne,
or take on the crown myself." Neither choice sounded
appealing, the way the prince spoke of them.

"That still doesn't answer my question, your highness,"
Laurence reminded them both. "With deepest respect, I
must ask… why would you help Romeo seek his beloved?"

"Because I don't know what's beyond the doorway."
Hamlet shrugged as though it were perfectly clear, and he
was astounded at the foolishness of the strangers before him.
"I'm supposed to protect it, and that's all very well. But I
don't know what it is, and I'm not certain how I can protect
it without that knowledge. I can take you to it, you can go
through, save your Juliet, bring her back through the portal
and report back to me."

"How do you know it works that way?" Horatio asked.
He had been silent for a long time, and it occurred to Romeo
that the prince's companion rarely spoke, unless it was to

impart something crucial. He went on, "You've never been through the portal. How do you know Romeo can come back? How do you know he could bring back the girl?"

"I stuck my head in," Hamlet argued. "It came out again. And my father's ghost was able to traverse the corpseway. I see no reason that it might not work exactly as I've described."

All the while they had traveled on this quest, Romeo had desperately wished to hear just such an offer laid out so neatly for him that it would be impossible to resist. But considering the source, the slightly *mad* source…

Laurence had asked him where he would put his faith once he lost it again. It seemed he had only one choice; this strange prince who'd spoken at length about spirits and death in an alehouse, and who now offered help so nonchalantly in matters of raising the dead.

Anything to save Juliet.

Hamlet's voice lowered, and his posture became very severe indeed. "You must swear a vow of secrecy, upon your very heart's blood. You must swear that you will never tell another living soul what I show you. Your friend the good Friar too. And you must swear to me that you will report back all that you see and hear after you've fulfilled your quest."

"I make no oaths but those I swore unto my God." Laurence drew himself up stiffly. "But you may trust my discretion."

"And mine, so long as you promise that no harm will

come to my friend while I am gone." Romeo glanced to Laurence "I would not ask you to put your mortal soul in peril by testing the laws of nature."

Hamlet stared at them in stony silence for the space of a breath, then a too-bright grin transformed his face. "Excellent! Then you must follow me!"

. . .

Under normal circumstances Hamlet would have waited for nightfall to venture back to the tunnel. Though, on second thought, he wasn't sure there were "normal circumstances" for raising the dead.

Hamlet was relieved that it was this Italian, and not himself entering the corpseway to investigate. The spirit had warned Hamlet of dire powers and secrets no mortal should know, and those warnings were very troubling. But they didn't give Hamlet very much to go on. How was he to protect the corpseway? Could it be destroyed? Where did it lead?

He'd looked through it only briefly, before his father's ghost had pulled him back with a mighty wind and the roaring fury of a tempest. He'd loomed over Hamlet, an unearthly version of the earthly king's anger, and made Hamlet swear he would never step foot though the portal.

But what if something beyond the shimmering blue gate would help to overcome King Claudius? How was Hamlet to protect something he knew nothing about?

Now he had Romeo, the Italian murderer, to find all this out for him. If he returned, that was. If he did not, Hamlet reasoned, it was surely better to be trapped in the beyond with the love of one's life than separated from her by the mere act of living.

"You cannot seriously be contemplating sending him through the portal!" Horatio hissed in the torchlight. "You have no idea what you're doing, or if he is your uncle's spy. This entire proceeding is a farce, and you're leading them directly to the corpseway that your own dead father told you to keep secret!"

"What I saw through the portal was confusing and very disturbing," Hamlet replied in a low voice, checking over his shoulder that the Italians still followed. "But it didn't look dangerous. I need to know why my father's spirit could cross the barrier between worlds. I want to know what exactly there is behind that doorway that is so dangerous he would return from his grave to tell me about it. This is the safest way I could think of, and it suits both of our purposes.

Horatio stopped, and with him, the circle of torchlight stopped as well. "Can you name one person who has ever crossed over to the other side and lived to tell the tale?"

"Can you name one person who has ever been given the chance?" Hamlet let that challenge hang between them, before glancing back to the two men that followed, and said, "This way, not much farther.

"If you are so inclined, he could wear a rope around his waist, and you could hold the other end. Then, if necessary, you could pull him back." Hamlet gave his friend a reassuring smile, all the better to misdirect him.

It worked for a moment too. Horatio breathed a sigh of relief and replied, "That *would* make me feel better, thank you," before his face fell and anger smoldered in his eyes like the tip of the pitch-soaked torch he bore. "We don't have any rope with us."

Hamlet did not let his reassuring smile fade.

They reached the convergence of tunnels that would bring them to their destination. Cold blue light already flickered against the walls like water shadows. Hamlet turned to the Italians and tried his best to reassure them. "The corpseway is quite intimidating. Don't let it fool you. It's not as terrifying as it seems it will be. What is beyond is very much like our own world, from what I have seen."

"From what you have seen in your less than one step into death?" Horatio grumbled. "You might as well admit it, you don't know what you're doing. You only found the corpseway two days ago."

"I don't like this, Romeo," the friar said, his thick black eyebrows shooting up as he shook his head. "I have stood by while you confer with witches. I have chased about with you on this fool's errand, but I will not stand by and watch as you defy the will of God! You cannot just traipse between the realms of the living and the dead without consequence."

"Orpheus went into the underworld to rescue Eurydice," the young Italian countered.

Romeo's quiet determination was a sight to behold, and

Hamlet found himself grudgingly impressed. He'd thought the man a common brute; he'd mistaken true honor for a quick temper. It made Hamlet feel a bit guilty that the poor young man might yet die on the other side of the portal.

Clapping his hands and rubbing them together briskly, he suggested, "Friar, you may stay here if you wish, and wait for him to return. Horatio, I expect you'll want to do the same, and I'll let you. I will anticipate brave Romeo's return at the alehouse."

They followed the curve of the tunnel until it bent and brought the corpseway into sight. Romeo's steps halted, and Hamlet stopped too. The light looked like water as it shimmered in the oval doorway. He knew what Romeo was thinking. *Would it be wet?* Hamlet knew already that it was not wet, in fact, it had a disturbing lack of feeling as one passed through it, as if to intentionally remind the unwary traveler how insubstantial the line between life and death really was. On the other side there had been only another tunnel, cobblestones all around it so that it was impossible to tell which way was up or down. Little round doors had been set at all angles into the walls. Hamlet had obsessed all that night as to what could be behind those doors, but had not had the courage to look again.

"What do I do?" Romeo asked, his tongue darting out to nervously wet his lip. "Do I run at it, or go slowly…"

"You step through, that's all it takes." Hamlet moved closer, feeling the pull of the light, the silent urging to abandon life for the mysteries of death. He put one hand out, anticipating the warmth that would not be there, the tactile sensation that would not touch him to warn him away.

"Try to remember everything that you see," Hamlet reminded Romeo. "I do not know how you'll find your Juliet, but I know you have the courage to do so."

Romeo stepped up to the edge, took a breath, and looked to his friend the Friar. The pair exchanged something Hamlet did not understand; a steely nod from the Friar, a grim resolve etched in Romeo's face. It was a truly poetic moment between friends, a bond Hamlet felt honored to have viewed.

Then Romeo grabbed the front of Hamlet's doublet, and they both tumbled through the corpseway.

There was no dark, silent tunnel of doors beyond, but the smell of blood and the shouts of battle. Steel rang off steel, and an inhuman roar shook the ground they stood upon. Hamlet stumbled, then fell to his knees, tripping over a disembodied arm. Romeo fell to his back beside him, breathing hard and pushing a dead man away, blood seeping red-black into his doublet. "I thought you said it wasn't terrifying!" he shouted, his eyes wide with fear.

Hamlet looked up into the jagged white face of a merciless frost giant as it raised its glittering ax for a blow that would cleave them both in half. He could only think that something had gone very, very wrong.

CHAPTER FOUR

Hamlet shrugged. The bastard actually shrugged as he lay there on the stone. Romeo would have punched him, but there were more pressing matters at hand than the prince's maddening attitudes. For example, the looming form of what appeared to be a living mountain towering over them, holding an axe.

"Move!"

Romeo turned toward the voice, just in time for another axe blade—the largest he'd ever seen, and gleaming gold instead of steel—to pass so close to his face he swore he felt the wind on his nose. A man with arms the size of wine casks wielded the weapon, and he buried it deep in the goliath's huge…well, Romeo supposed it was a leg, really, though it looked more like a tower of stone and ice. The thing was tall and angular, owing to the fact that its body seemed to be made entirely of frozen water as blue as the sea. Its head was pointed and capped like the peaks Romeo had seen on the journey, but those hadn't had eyes like icy caves bored into their faces. As tall as the goliath was, his head did not brush the ceiling of the long hall he stood in. The scents of wood smoke and blood and battle filled the air, and red stained the rushes beneath their feet.

The burly man bellowed a fierce battle roar from behind his braided gray beard and made to remove the axe from the giant's leg.

"Frost giant, I expect." The prince had gotten to his feet and for a moment, seemed more awe-stricken at the vision before him, than angry at Romeo for pulling him through the portal and into harm's path. "My mother read those stories to me."

It seemed to Romeo that it might be possible to die from choking on one's own anger. "I'm not really concerned with mythology right now!"

"Well you should be. It's probably going to kill us." Gaining his senses, Hamlet stabbed the air furiously in the direction of the lumbering ice creature, his face twisted in rage. "It'll kill him first, though. Oh, and I'd like to thank you very much for pulling me into this mess!"

It was true, Romeo supposed, that the prince had a better reason to be angry with him than the reverse. But Romeo was not a fool. He'd known all along the he was being sent on a dangerous errand. Hamlet didn't care one bit whether or not Romeo found Juliet. He cared only to know what was beyond the portal, what he was too frightened to see for himself.

It had been Laurence's idea that Romeo take the reluctant prince with him. *"The prince's desire for your return will be far greater if his own survival hinges upon it as well,"* Laurence had said, and though it had made sense at the time, it seemed mercenary now that it was clear that Romeo had put Hamlet in real danger.

The warrior charged the monster, leaping through the air at a height no mortal man could hope to match. He would drive that golden axe right into the giant's hollow black eye, but the monster swung one large, square hand and caught the entire head of the axe in the palm of his hand. The warrior dangled from the haft, helpless, feet kicking in the empty air over Romeo's head.

Romeo ducked out of the way and looked up. A twinkling, crackling rime of frost slithered down the handle of the axe and over the warrior's fingers. Romeo expected screams of terror, but all the huge man uttered was an exhausted, "I'll never get the hang of these," as his head froze solid. The giant released the axe, and the warrior shattered into frozen chunks on the ground.

"*Now*, it will kill us. I hope it kills you first, you damned Italian!"

Romeo could have sworn that the prince sounded maliciously cheerful. There was a time Romeo would have been happy to die, but that time was not now. Not when

Juliet was so close. He scooped up the golden axe, but the moment he swung it, he knew his error. He was not as strong as he had been before the poison, and even in those days he'd never wielded a weapon so clumsy as an axe. A rapier or a stiletto, certainly. Elegant blades all, but most importantly, light. He tried to bring the axe up, but his arms would not let him, and he stared in dismay as the frost giant fixed his hollow gaze upon him and raised a jagged finger to point. Snow slid from that admonishing finger and onto the ground, a flurry of flakes rising between them.

It was possibly the most ineffective barrier in the history of man.

The giant twisted his enormous body, and every movement sounded like the stone lid of a sarcophagus scraping as it opened. All around, the shouts of other warriors and monsters locked in battle beneath the arched wooden beams of the hall carried on, and Romeo wondered if he'd found himself in some undocumented circle of hell. Still pointing, the frost giant roared, a tremendous noise that shook the ground from beneath Romeo's feet. Hamlet's as well, for they both fell back. When the stars of pain stopped whirling in Romeo's vision, a girl stood over him, with yellow hair and pretty pink lips twisted in anger. On her head she wore a golden, winged helm, and over a flowing white toga she bore a breastplate of matching gold worked to resemble rows upon rows of delicate feathers. Her arms were roped with lean muscle, and the calf that peeked from a slit in her garment was thick and strong. Her forearm flexed above the thick, gilded bracers at her wrists.

"What in the nine worlds are you doing here?" Around her neck she wore a short, slender flute and a pendant shaped like feather. She lifted the flute to her lips and blew a high, shrill note. "Back to your positions, men! We fight once more!"

"You're always fighting once more," Hamlet said with a proud grin as he rose to his feet. "I know you. You're a Valkyrie. You're Hildr, leader of the Valkyrie."

"Mortals." She reached over her shoulder for the spear strapped against her back. "You are not allowed in halls of Valhalla."

"Where's Juliet?" Romeo got up and pushed Hamlet aside. The prince's all-too-nonchalant attitude about the battle they'd stepped into betrayed his true purpose for sending Romeo though the corpseway. It was a childish lark for the prince, nothing more. "I demand to see Juliet."

"So go see her," the Valkyrie said with the slightest arch of her fair brow. "She is not here, and you cannot remain in the Afterjord."

"We were just leaving." Hamlet walked backward, each step bringing him nearer to the portal that had deposited them in this place. "Romeo, come on."

"I'm not going." Not when he'd come all this way, when the place he stood was certainly hell. He would find Juliet in hell, he knew that much already. After her suicide, she'd been removed from the Capulet family tomb and buried in unconsecrated ground. As he would have been, if he'd died.

Suicide exacted a price after death, it was what he'd always been taught...and Juliet was now tasked with paying it.

He couldn't allow it. "If I go through that portal—"

"You won't." The Valkyrie blew into her whistle once more, and the air around them shimmered. Another Valkyrie appeared behind Hamlet, blocking his path. Yet another held the tip of a spear to Romeo's throat, before he even saw her materialize beside him.

The first Valkyrie stepped toe to toe with him and looked into his eyes. Her own were a pale blue, like the frost giant that stood patiently by, crackling and freezing. As the Valkyrie stared, seemingly into Romeo's very soul, he thought he might have preferred the frost giant. It had a warmer personality.

"You don't understand," Hamlet began, the uneasy tremor of his voice mirroring Romeo's own trepidation. "I've been charged with protecting the corpseway—"

Hildr's nostrils flared before she bellowed, "No mortal man has been given such a divine destiny! On whose authority do you come here?"

"On the authority of Hamlet, king of Denmark, murdered months ago by his wicked brother, Claudius. It was he who—"

"Mortal men hold no sway here, be they king or peasant." Hildr sniffed regally. "Out. You are banished from Valhalla."

"Banished?" Hamlet's voice held a note of panic. "How will we get home?"

"Mortals aren't allowed to travel by corpseway."

"But I wasn't even supposed to be here!" Hamlet argued.

"No. You weren't." With that, Hildr turned her back on them, lifted her snowy white wings, and flew away.

The Valkyrie with the spear at Romeo's neck pulled her weapon back and gestured to him. He turned and came face to face with the warrior that had frozen. Only, he wasn't as dead anymore. He was, remarkably, in one piece.

"My axe," the man growled, and Romeo was not proud of the way his own hand shook as he pointed across the stone floor.

The man bared his teeth, but his expression did not look much like a smile. "Thank you."

• • •

As two Valkyrie marched them through the cavernous battle arena, Romeo wondered at what he saw and thought he must certainly be going mad. All around, impossibly huge men, in various states of mortal injury dripping gore, wearily rose from the stones and righted themselves, as though it weren't all that terribly unusual to wake from death.

What must it be like, to exist in such a state? If this was not hell, then what did Juliet suffer?

"Vikings," Hamlet said as they passed one warrior diligently poking his innards into the wound in his gut. "Only the very best get in here. The *Einherjar*, they're called, and they spend their every waking moment preparing for

Ragnarök."

"I didn't understand a word of that." The ceiling was an endless sea of shimmering golden shields, and Romeo watched their shapes distort in the curved, reflective surfaces.

"The end of the world," Hamlet clarified. "They're practicing for the battle that will decide the destiny of the gods."

"Gods?" Romeo scoffed, not caring if he did sound like Friar Laurence. "You mean God. There's only one."

"What a lack of imagination you have." Hamlet clucked his tongue. His steps slowed as they passed another giant, this one formed of what appeared to be molten metal. Its feet were stuck to the stones, and it groaned impatiently as three Valkyrie worked to free it. "Although, I must admit, it's terribly clever what you did. Taking me as hostage, pulling me through the corpseway after you. I must remember to return the favor some time."

The two guarding Romeo and Hamlet gave them sharp prods with the shafts of their spears, moving them along the seemingly endless arena.

"If there is only one God," Hamlet continued, his voice rising queerly as the butt of the spear poked him in the back, "then explain this. Explain why we would be suddenly transported from the world we know, only to be thrust into a rehearsal for the battle that will determine the fates of these gods that don't exist? How could we currently be marching through ranks of men impervious to death but dying all the same, led by an army of demigods who right this very moment have weapons jabbing into our backs? I ask you, Romeo, where in all of this"—he waved his hands about, nearly slapping Romeo's face as he did so—"do you find room for such a rigid interpretation of divinity?"

A great deal of sense could be made from the prince's words, and Romeo found himself agreeing. He couldn't let that happen. "Perhaps this is hell after all?"

"Don't be stupid. There's no such place."

The idea of there being no hell—although what he'd witnessed so far in what the Valkyrie had called the Afterjord certainly resembled it—gave him a slight twinge of comfort. If there was no hell, then perhaps Juliet's fate wasn't a dire as he'd imagined.

Yet a fate less dire was still dire nonetheless.

Romeo, lost in his own dark thoughts, barely noticed that Hamlet had stopped walking. There were two doors, each one as wide as the river that ran through Verona. Huge, rusted rings were set into them, far higher than any man could reasonably reach. Even if he could, they would be too heavy. They were as thick around as Juliet's frumpy nurse had been.

His grief proved as opportunistic as a carrion crow, and it thrust sharp talons inside his chest. With every day that passed since he'd left Verona, he'd forgotten a little more what had led him to where he stood. Ever seeing Verona again, the people who had once lived there—the flushed red face of the fat old nurse, the bright eyes of his beloved as she smiled at him— seemed even more impossible now that he stood upon the threshold of supreme impossibility.

The doors scraped open of their own accord, just wide enough to admit a piercing shaft of light. Romeo shielded his eyes, and saw Hamlet do the same.

There were no final threats or proclamations. Romeo had been ejected from taverns with more pomp than the Valkyries displayed, shoving both Romeo and Hamlet through the doors to sprawl on the smoothly polished steps outside. The stairs were twice again as broad as the doors, and not a soul stood upon them. A few steps down, the staircase split in two, to encircle a towering tree wrought in gold. A breeze stirred the leaves, and a few fell, ringing like merry bells on the stone.

"If it were Hell," Hamlet said calmly, after the enormous doors had scraped shut once more, "They wouldn't have magnificent feasts."

Romeo turned, intentionally slowing his breath in an attempt to calm himself. "I don't care about your theology—"

"Mythology," Hamlet interrupted cheerfully.

"I don't care!" Romeo could not hold back his anger any longer. "You're mad, and I'm a fool for letting you lead me here."

"I believe it was you who led me here," Hamlet pointed out quietly. "You wanted my help, and when I offered it, you endangered my life and brought me here. I'm sorry if my *theology* offends, but you're not really in position to be offended by anything I may say or do."

"We are both trapped here now!" Romeo ran a hand

through his short hair in frustration, though he felt a twinge of guilt at Hamlet's words. He hadn't expected the mad prince to argue so logically in such an illogical place. Not that he was ready to concede the point.

They were still virtual strangers, after all. His mission was Juliet's rescue, not Hamlet's friendship. No matter how he worried he'd need it.

His anger had given him the strength to embark on this mad mission, so he drew from that now by striking out. "You had no idea if I would come back. You, *your highness*, were meant to be my assurance that I would return to the mortal world. You know more about this place than I do. The dead sought you out specifically to care take this place. You must have an idea of how to get us home."

Hamlet raised his hands helplessly. "Perhaps if you'd asked these questions before you jerked me through the corpseway…"

"Then we are lost." The taste of failure was bitter on Romeo's tongue. It had never occurred to him that his own impulsiveness where Hamlet was concerned would result in a failed mission.

Hamlet groaned. "Oh, stop pitying yourself. You were desperate and unhappy at home, you're desperate and unhappy now. Nothing has changed, except that now we're closer to your goal."

"And if we do find her, what then?" Romeo raised his eyes to the bleak horizon. The stairs descended to a long, shimmering bridge, made seemingly of glass that rippled in glittering waves. Colored light glinted from it, only to be lost in the dark chasm that lay beneath it like an ugly wound in the ground. But was it ground? Or some mirage? There was no hint of the familiar about the place, no way he could begin to imagine living the rest of his life in this bizarre underworld, much less eternity. "That harpy in there said we couldn't use the portals. So how are we going to get home?"

"I wouldn't say harpy too loudly here," Hamlet advised, flicking his nervous gaze to the vast emptiness above them. "Besides, she said we weren't allowed to use the portals, but we clearly did. It might be forbidden, but the corpseways don't seem to know that. It let us through the first time, didn't it?"

Hamlet's words were but a slight balm to Romeo's despair. "I cannot imagine what Hell is like, if it is not like what I have just seen." Romeo jogged down four steps, then realized the futility in forward motion. He had no idea where to go or how to proceed. Staying in one place would be far safer. He sat and lifted one of the golden leaves that littered the steps.

Hamlet joined him, his gaze fixed on the gold tree as he spoke. "I imagine you know well enough what hell is like. How did you lose your beloved?"

"I told you, she died, and I tried to poison myself." Romeo did not know this man, not enough to share so precious a secret with him. And yet, there was a dark intelligence beneath the prince's obnoxious prattle. The man Romeo had been before losing Juliet would not have hesitated to trust Hamlet. In fact, Romeo suspected that had he met the prince under other circumstances, he would have deferred to Hamlet's station and simply expected wisdom from him.

That Romeo had been a much simpler man…and much happier.

But hadn't the witch told him to seek the seat of a murdered king? It seemed only Hamlet and his father's ghost knew the truth of that. Had that been the witch's way of giving him a sign he could trust? Romeo had never been in the business of trusting strangers. The company with whom he surrounded himself in Verona had been the young men he'd grown up with. There had never been a doubt that he could trust them.

Resigned, he tried again to share the story. "That's not the whole truth of it. When I killed Juliet's kinsman, Tybalt, I was banished from Verona."

"Seems to be a lot of that going around," Hamlet interjected, gesturing to the doors of Valhalla behind them.

"Juliet did not mean to kill herself. Not at first. Friar Laurence gave her a drug intended to help her feign death. He sent a letter, instructing me to meet him outside the city walls, and he would bear Juliet from her crypt to my keeping. Once she awoke from the potion, we would be reunited.

"But the message got mislaid, and the news of Juliet's death reached me before the truth of Laurence's plan." An hour hadn't passed since Juliet's death that Romeo did not torment himself with the serendipitous consequence that had left his heart in ashes. That tantalizing promise of what could have been, if only the message had reached him on time, haunted his every waking thought. To speak of it only intensified his despair, and he paused to control the emotion in his voice. "I was mad with grief. Still am. I went to be with her, to drink poison and go to my eternal rest at her side. Instead she awoke on her bier, and me, cold and seemingly dead beside her. So, she took my dagger, and my place in Hell."

Hamlet said nothing at first, and Romeo treasured each silent moment. If the prince did not speak, then the prince could not annoy him.

"It's not really Hell," Hamlet said after a time, and when Romeo did not respond except to raise an eyebrow at him, he continued, "the place where we'll find Juliet. It's Hel, one l. Sounds quite like Hell in name, but it's very different. I've studied it."

The indignation that rose in Romeo's chest was apt to choke him. "Have you listened to a word I've said?"

Hamlet nodded. "I've listened, but I cannot think of words that will ease the pain of the past for you. What would be the point of trying?"

"Is it also pointless to rescue your father?" Perhaps this was a step too far, a question too cruel for the small peace they had made between them. In an attempt to soften it, he added, "Perhaps I could help you. As long as we're rescuing loved ones from death, that is. We could find your father and get him out too."

"My father was murdered by his own brother and

betrayed by his wife. A return to Midgard would likely be a worse version of hell." He picked up one of the golden leaves and flicked it off his thumb with his forefinger. It jingled merrily down the stairs. It seemed rather a peculiar sound to exist in the underworld. "Have *you* listened to a word you've said? You're miserable without your true love, and you've come here to find her. You are closer to rescuing a loved one from death than any man has ever been, and now all you're doing is complaining."

"Because we can't get back!" Romeo threw his hand toward the tall doors of Valhalla. "You've gotten us lost here, and we're never going to find the way out again."

"*I've* gotten us lost here?" Hamlet snorted. "I don't recall anyone shoving you through the corpseway. I remember being pulled through against my will, but I don't believe you were forced to come here. You wanted to."

Those allegations were true, and they shamed Romeo into justifications that sounded hollow even as he spoke them. "I had no idea what I would face here. I needed someone who had a passing acquaintance with the myths and lore of the underworld. You have that. It may come as small comfort to you, but if we are trapped here, and if we can't save Juliet… at the very least, you might be able to save *me*."

"Our chances of being trapped here are not certain. It's quite likely, but it's not certain. But does it matter?" Hamlet faced him finally, his ice blue eyes even more unnatural in the golden light that lit the pale brown sky. "You were willing to go into the abyss for your love before. Now you're here. You had nothing to lose, and you still stand to gain everything. If we find your Juliet, we might not be able to get back to Midgard, that's true. But at least you'll be together."

It spoke well of the prince, that he could have hope for a man he had every reason now to hate. "You think we can find her?"

"I think we have nothing better to do, if we're exiled to death so prematurely. But you can't give up now." Hamlet shrugged elegantly. "If you did, you'd be literally wasting your life, wouldn't you?"

"Where do we even begin to look?" They hadn't seen another soul, save for the fearsome creatures and Vikings in Valhalla.

Hamlet considered. "You believe that by killing herself, Juliet has damned her soul to hell. Would she believe the same?"

"She was a pure and devout girl," Romeo said with pride, thinking again how miraculous it was that such an angel had deigned to love him. "Of course she would believe that hell awaited her. Her religious beliefs would have dictated it."

Hamlet stood, his gaze fixed on the pathway in front of them. "Then perhaps we should begin there."

CHAPTER FIVE

As the radiant waves of rainbow-hued light pulsed and vibrated all around them, all Hamlet could think was, *it's all real. Down to every last detail.*

"I thought you said there wasn't any hell," Romeo argued beside him. "Now you believe we should look for Juliet there?"

"I don't believe there is a hell. But nearly every religion dictates that there is a place for good souls, and a place for bad ones. If Juliet believed her soul would be damned, the Afterjord may have agreed with her."

Hamlet should have been more worried at their dire predicament, or more furious with Romeo for dragging him through the corpseway, but Hamlet could honestly say that for the moment, he didn't mind that he wasn't in Midgard.

He was almost grateful to Romeo for pulling him throughout the corpseway. This was a chance to explore the truth behind his childhood bedtime stories, the vast pantheon of ancient lore that people of the modern age dismissed as fairy tale.

Every night he had listened with rapt attention to his mother's stories. He would lay his head on her lap while her fingers danced over his hair, and she would tell him of giants and gods and Fenrir, the huge, ravening wolf held by chains no thicker than ribbon, but stronger than iron.

She'd told him of the Vikings too, and their mighty warrior kings, Hamlet's own ancestors. Their pride and courage was legendary, and Hamlet had just seen one completely obliterated by a Frost Giant. Being trapped in the Afterjord forever seemed a small price to pay to witness such an amazing feat. Perhaps he was driven by a longing for the mother who'd existed before Hamlet had come of age and realized all her faults. Or perhaps this misadventure simply gave him an escape from a life that had been recently turned upside down. He knew that he should be worried about what was happening on the other side of the corpseway. Would Horatio do something completely mad, like run for help? What about the Friar? How was Hamlet to keep the corpseway secret if he was trapped beyond it?

But he had to concentrate on the situation at hand, if he was to escape and avenge his father's murder and protect the corpseway.

"Do you wonder if this place changes from soul to soul? That is, does it change its appearance and structure to suit what an individual believed in life?"

Beside him, Romeo grumbled in response. "You don't have to speak that way, you know."

Hamlet waved his fingers through the blue, then violet, then pink light that rose from the rainbow bridge, Bifröst, if he remembered the name correctly. "Speak what way?"

"As if you were trying to sound too smart on purpose. Like you don't want me to understand you." There was a note of hurt frustration beneath Romeo's rough tone. "I'm not stupid. I know what you're saying, and no, I don't think it does."

"You don't think it does what?" Of course, Hamlet knew what Romeo referred to, but he couldn't help himself. The Italian was an easy mark for vexation. Hamlet much preferred him in that state, rather than weepy, sentimental, and utterly useless on their quest.

Romeo rolled his eyes. "The Afterjord, as you call it. If it changed to suit everyone individually, why am I seeing all the trappings of your odd Northern ways?"

"They're not our ways." Hamlet took a strange sort of offense to the mockery. Though he'd never been able to profess a disbelief in the supernatural—he'd been plagued by spirits for as long as he could remember—he'd refuted any notion of God with a methodical sort of detachment. After all, no priest had ever been able to explain to him where spirits roaming the physical world had their place in a dogma that spoke of Heaven and Hell and Purgatory. No, they fit so much better with his mother's stories of trolls and strange beings lurking, awaiting the end of time. He didn't appreciate some foreigner poking fun at the closest thing he had to religious beliefs. "They're the ways of the people before us. Perhaps the geographical location of the portal has something to do with it? Or the people who put it there? If we went through a corpseway beneath the Vatican, I'm sure we'd be surrounded by incense and men in frilly dresses."

"So, in all your vast knowledge of your ancestors, is there anything that will help us find Juliet and get us home?" Romeo's jaw was set quite stubbornly.

Hamlet considered, watching his feet make disrupting waves in the colored light beneath them. Bifröst was a far longer and wider bridge than he'd imagined when listening to mother's stories, but not nearly as sturdy. The glow they walked upon was a thin haze, and beyond that a yawning chasm of blackness. With every step, the bottoms of his feet tickled, pricked by fear of falling. But they would soon reach the end. A stone arch was visible through the rainbow-hued mist. "I do believe you will see her again. Spirits have been coming to me since I was a child, and most of them want to see their living relatives as much as their living relatives wish to contact them. My own father appeared to me, after all."

"That must be a great comfort, to be able to communicate with your loved ones after death." Romeo's voice was strangely gentle. "And a terrible burden, as well."

"Yes, I suppose it is. The dead always want something, Romeo. Otherwise, they would be here. They only come back to our plane of existence if they have unfinished business."

"Your father was a king, with an heir. What unfinished business would be left?" He paused, and Hamlet let the man puzzle it out himself. "I still don't understand why you're not king, if your father was."

"Oh, you noticed that, did you? That I am not King of Denmark?" Bristling at the man would do him no good. Hamlet forced aside all the feelings of anger that had plagued him in the months after his father's death, a considerable feat that would not hold for long. "No, I am not. We do things differently in Denmark. The people preferred Claudius's succession to mine. One can hardly blame them. I had been tucked away at school for so long, they barely knew me. My uncle was far more familiar to them, and with the approval of my mother, the queen, well…he was a good enough replacement for my father in her eyes, so why not in everyone else's?"

"You said your mother betrayed your father. Do you believe she plotted with your uncle to secure the throne?"

Hamlet arched a sardonic brow. "She married Claudius practically before the mortar sealed my father's crypt. What conclusion do you come to?"

He looked to Romeo and saw the other man's face light in recognition.

"Of course," Romeo said slowly. "The state of your room, your caution upon meeting me…You prove no challenge for your uncle if you are dead."

"That is why my father came back to warn me," Hamlet finished for him. "That, and to charge me with avenging him. Which I will do, once I make a plan for it."

"Have you ever killed a man?" Romeo asked, as though he were asking about the weather. "It's a terrible thing. Do you think you could live with yourself, after?"

"Have you ever raised the dead?" Hamlet asked back, and he felt that answer was far more pressing. "You know how it feels to lose Juliet. Can you live your life with her, dreading that feeling every day?"

Romeo took a long time to answer. "I had not considered it."

Hamlet sighed. "Right now, however, we have something greater to worry about."

"And what is that?" Romeo asked warily.

Hamlet pointed ahead, to where the mist around them seemed to clear. "We're almost at the end of this bridge, and we have no idea what is on the other side."

They moved from the terrifying suspension of Bifröst to solid stone beneath their feet, and Hamlet could not deny his relief. He'd never liked heights.

Overhead, a cavern stretched long, pointed formations toward the ground. Mingled among the stalactites, tall windows of stained glass let in light that didn't quite reach the crowd milling in the sandstone plaza below. There was no sky here, just an encroaching darkness.

"These trees aren't gold," Romeo said, reaching up to pluck an apple. The plaza was dotted with fruit trees of all earthly varieties, and some Hamlet couldn't be sure were earthly at all. They rose from tall stone urns and seemed to be thriving despite the lack of sunlight.

Hamlet let Romeo raise the apple nearly to his lips, the fool, before he smacked it away. "Never eat anything in the underworld. Haven't you ever heard of Persephone?"

The Italian had the grace to look at least a little embarrassed by that. "Of course. I don't know what I was thinking."

There were other people in the plaza, all kinds of people, milling about together in what appeared to be mass confusion. The babbling of many languages filled Hamlet's ears. A man draped in a toga stood there, a Roman senator by his garb. Over there, a woman with tangled hair full of leaves and swirling designs tattooed on her skin could have been some prehistoric child of the forest. Hamlet's eyes widened at the sight of a naked man dyed blue with woad and an Egyptian Pharisee strolling side by side, attempting to speak to each other.

"My God," Romeo said, and crossed himself as naturally as breathing. "*Purgatorium.*"

"Is it?" Hamlet glanced about. It certainly didn't seem like any Purgatory he'd read about. "I'd assumed there would be fire…scourges…"

"Look." Romeo pointed straight ahead. The souls wandering beneath the lush green foliage seemed out of sorts, but calm enough. Their gazes would meet, and they offered each other hesitant polite smiles before turning their attention back to their strange surroundings.

All but one, a young woman in a blue velvet gown

who seemed to move a bit faster, to show more panic the other souls about her. She pushed between two of them, murmuring frantic apologies as she turned this way and that.

"She knows where she is," Hamlet realized, and a sick feeling gripped his stomach. "My god, she…she knows she's dead."

"And all the others don't seem to," Romeo continued, pointing to an old man who rested against a potted lemon tree. "They're waiting. But she knows."

The woman grew more frantic now, racing down the neat rows, shoving others aside. "Help me!" she screamed, clutching the front of her torn dress. Golden curls spilled down her back from an elaborate braid coming undone, a tower of hair falling to a ruin in time with her own slipping sanity. "Please, someone, you must help me!"

Something detached itself from the darkness above, drifting down slowly like cloth sinking in water. The woman in blue looked up, and her face contorted in terror. She ran from the thing, which now took a vaguely phantasmal shape. Long, drifting tendrils of arms, a hood of darkness for a head, the thing was not so much terrifying as unsettling, but the woman seemed to take a far different view of it. She ran from it, pleading, screaming.

"I had no choice!" As she fled, another dark form appeared to pursue her, and she begged it in turn, "He had to die! I had to kill him! He was the only one who knew!"

"They're herding her," Hamlet observed, watching as the two specters moved purposefully toward the woman, backing away to let her escape them in one direction, then closing her off from another.

Romeo gestured forward. "Come on."

Hamlet had no choice but to follow him. If they became separated in the Afterjord, there was even less chance of either of them getting out. "Wait! I wasn't finished, when I told you about my father. I believe spirits can return to Midgard only when they have unfinished business. My father has involved me in his…Did Juliet ever charge you with hers?"

Romeo's eyes widened slowly.

"You won't be able to return without me." Hamlet knew it as certain as he knew they should not interfere with the shades' pursuit of the woman in blue. "That's why the Valkyrie blocked your way. You're not allowed to use the corspeways, because you don't have unfinished business. Avenging my father, that's mine. If we're parted, you may never make it back to our world."

Romeo's eyes were still wide, his hand on the hilt of his sword. "Look out!"

Hamlet turned as a flurry of black materialized behind him. This shade was far different from the ones pursuing the woman in blue. Smoke-gray teeth, long and pointed as needles, dripped liquid that turned to noxious vapor as it splashed on the stones. He stepped back, barely missing a long, clawed appendage as it flashed out to grab him.

Romeo drew his sword, and the shade shrieked, the piercing cry startling even the calm souls around them.

"Put that away!" Hamlet shouted. "Everyone is already dead, what good will it do?"

"Then what do you suggest?" Romeo snapped as they continued to back away from the advancing ghost.

Two large stone archways stood at either side of the plaza. At their peaks, they bore symbols; one depicted a chalice spilling its contents, the other the same chalice being filled. The shades pursuing the screaming woman drove her toward the gate with the spilling cup.

Hamlet considered the other gate for only a blink of an eye before he dismissed it. He pointed in the direction of the fleeing woman. "I suggest we go that way. And I suggest we run."

CHAPTER SIX

Hamlet ran toward the gate before Romeo could relay the words to his feet. The shade behind him slashed out, and Romeo hurried away, pushing through a crowd of souls to follow the prince.

They couldn't be separated. Well, that was just lovely, wasn't it, considering Hamlet appeared to be the fastest man alive. Romeo watched in dismay as Hamlet grabbed the woman in blue and fell with her through the stone arch. Both of them seemed to snuff out like the flame of a candle, and the shades turned on Romeo, going all drooling acid and terror in a heartbeat.

If the choice was to stay with the angry shades or follow the only man who could get him home, Romeo chose the prince. He rushed at the two shades guarding the arch, straight toward their grasping hands and gnashing teeth, and dropped to the ground as they snatched at him. He rolled beneath their floating forms and spilled through the arch.

The air around him crackled, then changed, and he collided with Hamlet as he rolled to his feet.

"Where's the woman?" Romeo demanded. They stood in a long, round hallway. Overhead, doors of all shapes, sizes, and colors nestled in the curve of the ceiling. None of them were accessible from where he and Hamlet stood.

The prince held out his empty arms. "I don't know. She was here a moment ago. We went through the arch and she just…vanished."

The hall stretched before them, empty and mostly dark, with an occasional shaft of stark white light leaving large circles on the floor. Romeo and Hamlet moved toward one cautiously, and passed their hands through it.

"Seems safe enough," Hamlet said with a shrug. "I think this was what the corpseway showed me the first time."

"Where do we go, then?" Romeo asked. If they had a ladder, they might crawl through one of those doors, but ladders seemed rather thin on the ground at the moment.

"I don't know. I never stepped completely through the corpseway." Hamlet's thought trailed off as he moved through the light, sliding his feet cautiously along the floor. "Seems safe enough. Come on."

A chillingly familiar shriek sounded behind them.

"It's found us." Hamlet backed slowly away from the direction they'd come. "It knows you're not supposed to be here. It knows *we're* not supposed to be here. Stay with me. Don't go through any of those doors. Just keep running, and don't look back."

A cold chill raced down Romeo's spine. Until now, Hamlet had seemed so certain of himself, despite their odd circumstances.

But now…

If he was afraid, Romeo felt he definitely should be, as well.

The shade whipped out of the darkness, its horrible, formless mouth gaping wide, lined with its needle-like teeth. Romeo kept up with Hamlet for a moment, but all too soon the fatigue set into his legs and lungs, and he fell behind.

"How will we know when we've outrun it?" he called, praying the creature would give up its pursuit. Romeo almost lost track of Hamlet racing ahead of him.

"Keep running!" the prince shouted back.

As though Romeo needed incentive to run. Behind him, the shade's cries echoed off the walls. For all the doors overhead, just out of reach, there seemed to be no egress from the tunnel, and the shade came ever closer. A black tendril of smoke lashed in front of Romeo's eyes, and he ducked it, but only barely. His heart pounded hard enough to burst, and it might, he feared.

Had Juliet faced these otherworldly terrors? Had she run from them, pleading, as the woman in blue had? Romeo knew his own fear, as the shades shrieked their pursuit, and he would not wish such horror on anyone, let alone his love.

For a brief moment, he imagined Juliet running the same, fearsome corridor, and he felt her beside him. She awaited him, and that lent him the strength to continue, though his breath was ragged and his limbs weary. For Juliet, he could run across the earth without stopping.

His next step did not land, nor the one after that, and he tumbled, his still pounding heart floating into his throat. The fall was endless, through a darkness so encompassing he couldn't tell which direction he'd come from or where he was going. He might have landed on his head and broken his neck, if not for happy circumstance. They had fallen into blackness, and it was blackness they landed upon, hard, though not as hard as he might have expected.

Hamlet lay motionless a few feet from him, unmoving but for the heaving of his chest. One hand lay limp there, and he lifted a few fingers as if testing that they still functioned. "Ah. Here we are."

Though every bone was certainly broken, Romeo forced himself to his knees. "The shade!"

"Would have gotten us by now, if he wished to." Hamlet didn't even bother to open his eyes. "You saw what they were doing back there."

"Preying on helpless victims?" Romeo stared into the darkness above, certain it would sprout claws and teeth at any moment.

"They were sorting them," Hamlet replied calmly. "You were the one who introduced the idea of Purgatory. You were wrong, though. It was Sheol. I saw it written on the arch as I passed through it."

"Sheol?" Romeo did not like the taste of the word on his tongue.

"From the Old Testament. You could call it Hades, or Tartarus, if those are more familiar. An underworld. We have entered the realm of the wicked dead."

"Does it matter what this place is called? It's hell, no matter where we are!" Romeo raked a hand through his hair. His legs trembled from fear as well as exhaustion, and he fell heavily to his side, gasping. He'd wanted to undertake this quest. He desperately wished to find Juliet. To save her and build the life they had hoped for. He'd just never imagined it would be so difficult.

It's as though you don't want to find her, he scolded himself. It wasn't that, not at all. He wanted to find Juliet more than anything. He'd been living in a nightmare world since she'd died, but when he compared it to the nightmares of the world he currently stood in, he began to doubt. Perhaps Juliet was better off dead than living. If they escaped, she would be left with the memories of these horrors. He hadn't even found her yet, and he'd gotten her into a terrible predicament.

"The shades are sorting the souls, sending them where they belong. They seem mainly concerned with that central area." Hamlet pushed himself up, groaning as he did.

"How do you know that?" Romeo snapped. "Did you read it off another arch?"

Hamlet titled his head, and a loud pop issued from the vicinity of his neck. "It's not chasing us anymore, is it?"

Once again, the prince was irritatingly correct. But Romeo preferred smug knowledge to none at all. Without Hamlet, Romeo would have been lost.

"And only one pursued us. The other two stayed behind. I think you just made that one mad with your sword nonsense." Hamlet got to his feet and gazed into the vast blackness like a man looking for a ship on the horizon.

"I don't suppose there's a particular direction we should go in?" Romeo asked, failing to keep his annoyance from his words.

Hamlet turned to him and indicated straight ahead. "That's as good as any, I would think. How about you, are you able to make the journey?"

The question set Romeo back. His weakness would have been obvious to a child, but he would never have expected a prince to worry about his well-being. "I'm as able as you. Well, perhaps not as able as you, but I am able. For Juliet, I am able."

Hamlet clapped him on the back. "Excellent. Lead the way."

Romeo did as the prince commanded, and they ventured forward into the blackness.

• • •

One strange thing about the dark void they'd found themselves in, Hamlet mused, was that despite the lack of walls or paths, there seemed to be a general sense of direction to their travels. An urgency propelled them forward in the darkness, even though there weren't any landmarks to gauge their progress by.

Stranger still, despite the absence of light, he didn't have trouble seeing Romeo beside him, limping through the blackness with a determined expression that had really begun to irritate Hamlet.

At some point, the Italian was going to have to accept that they may have doomed themselves. Or more succinctly put, that Romeo had doomed Hamlet the moment he'd pulled him through the corpseway. Seeing Valhalla had seemed a fine reward for his troubles, but now they would spend their days endlessly wandering in an undefined space. Hamlet found it rather difficult not to feel the pressing need to return to his own purpose, now that the newness of the adventure had worn off.

"We're close," Romeo said, for perhaps the thirtieth time in the last…well, Hamlet had no idea, really. It was, unsurprisingly, difficult to get a sense of time or distance in an utterly blank space.

"You keep saying that," he observed dryly. "Do you think saying it again and again will make it true? Or are you merely hoping to say 'I told you so' on the unlikely chance we'll find something out there?"

"No, look. There's something out there." Romeo pointed in front of him.

It took Hamlet a moment to trust his eyes. After all, when isolated in a completely silent, completely dark environment, the mind tended to play tricks. He knew as much from the ravings of his uncle's prisoners in the dungeons below Elsinore.

He knew it from his own psyche as well, the clawing evil that gripped him with terror in the night. In his desperation he often saw clawed hands, flickering visages of the long dead. He'd never been able to separate these false torments from his terrible gift, and that made them all the more terrifying.

But Romeo's eyes weren't deceiving him, unless he'd gone precisely the same shade of mad as Hamlet. There *was* something out there in the distance, a glittering, pale thing that took shape by unnatural degrees with each step. Though the vision had appeared quite some distance away, like the horizon over the sea, it took them only a few steps to get close enough to comprehend what it was.

A river sprouted up at their feet, moving swiftly, the caps of the occasional wave rising with red foam as it rocked and raged at its invisible shores. For where there should have been a bank or earthen slope containing the water and directing its flow, all that lay on either side was the ever-present dark.

The gleaming white they had seen was the form of a woman kneeling beside the stream, wrapped from head to toe in white. A winding shroud, Hamlet realized with horror as he watched her lift the tail of her own garment and dip it into the bloody water.

She raised her face, and Hamlet recoiled from the sight. Her eyes and nose were covered by strips of her grave shroud, which were befouled by seeping pink. Her skin was pale as watery milk, her mouth a black hole that opened to release a torrent of maggots as she shrieked a chill, despairing cry.

"What is that?" Romeo reached for his sword hilt, and Hamlet stayed his hand.

"A washer." Hamlet licked his lips, his mind placing the taste of grave worms and rot upon his tongue. "They're portents of death and appear on the eve of a battle."

"What does it want with us?" Romeo whispered, as the sobbing wraith bent to scrub her shroud.

Her lamentations almost inspired pity in Hamlet, if he hadn't known that she wasn't a person, but an embodiment of pure regret and sorrow. He'd read about the Washer at The Ford as he'd studied the death myths of the world. He knew her place was to warn of deaths to come. He hoped she wasn't washing his garments, or Romeo's.

"It doesn't want anything, it's here to warn us." He turned around, and a sudden, sick feeling of motion was upon him. Romeo staggered beside him, and they both turned as a burst of light, violent and blue, illuminated the darkness behind them.

"A corpseway!" Romeo shouted, and he charged for it.

Another strangely dizzying sensation gripped Hamlet, and he closed his eyes to endure it. Romeo blundered into him, and they both sprawled to the...well, it wasn't ground exactly, but they fell.

When Hamlet dared to open his eyes again, they were on the other side of the river. Or the corpseway was. In either case, the washer and the river were both now between them and their salvation.

"Witchcraft!" Romeo roared, drawing his sword.

Hamlet rolled his eyes. Would the fool never learn?

The creature looked up, bared its blackened, needle-like teeth.

"Put your blade away," Hamlet hissed. Then, to the washer, he called, "Good day, fair lady. Might we…cross?"

She considered them with a jerky tilt of her head, then resumed her scrubbing and wailing.

"Is that a yes?" Romeo asked, his fingers wriggling on the grip of his sword. He ached for combat, Hamlet knew. Still, there were more things on heaven and earth than could be found in the philosophy of some war-hungry Italian.

"For God's sake, keep your temper until we find out." Hamlet inched forward, putting one foot cautiously into the water. The depth might be as bottomless as the black void around them, but he did not fear. Though nothing could be certain in the Afterjord, Hamlet had no choice but to trust the unfriendly water.

The moment he waded in, the washer lifted her head, and then her hand, a long, bruised finger dripping bloody water as she pointed at him. But she made no move, only shrieked her rage as he stepped another foot in, and then another, in the surprisingly shallow water.

Romeo followed him cautiously. Hamlet turned, was about to say something like, "It isn't deep," or some other foolish thing, when he plunged entirely below the surface. The metallic tang of blood filled his mouth, bloody water flooding into his nostrils. He fought the current, trying to stay afloat.

As his head broke the surface, then sunk below the water again, he saw the world narrowed into slices of time between bouts of drowning. He saw Romeo struggling against the current. For a man supposedly weakened by a near lethal dose of poison, he was a suspiciously strong swimmer. He caught the front of Hamlet's doublet and tugged him toward the opposite shore.

The washer woman screamed again, but this time the sound changed, bent into something even more horrifying than Hamlet would have thought possible. The current tugged him down again, and when he lifted his head this time, the washer's winding shroud had lengthened, filling the river, growing plump as a drowned corpse's swollen flesh. The cloth fell away from the thing's face, revealing no eyes, no nose, just the sightless, round countenance of a maggot and a circular mouth full of teeth in endless rings.

If ever were there a time to learn to swim, it was perhaps at that very moment, Hamlet decided, and he made for the other shore. But the monster, now a bloated, white serpent, a giant grave worm seeking to destroy them, swatted him to the opposite shore. He drew his dagger—for all the good it might do him against an undead creature—and lunged at it, grappling for a hold on its body.

The worm's flesh was gelatinous and insubstantial. Everywhere Hamlet laid a hand upon it, thick mucus enveloped his skin. Bile rose in his throat, but he clung to the giant maggot as well as he could as it thrashed and bucked. Its upper body retained its horrible, clawed arms, and they windmilled about, trying to grab him.

"Romeo!" Hamlet shouted. The Italian stood before the corpseway, staring into the glimmering blue void as if in a trance.

"She's there!" He shouted, over the shrieks of the monster and the smack of its flailing tail on the water.

The creature lunged forward, and Hamlet plunged his knife into its back. A gush of rotten black blood spurted from the wound, but he clung to the hilt of the blade as a handhold. He plunged into the spectral river on the maggot's back, and when it surfaced, screaming its rage from its horrible, rotting mouth, he saw through the portal.

And he knew Romeo would not save him.

CHAPTER SEVEN

His Juliet was there, his love, beyond the surface of the corpseway.

Romeo braced his hands on either side of the portal's silver frame, plunged his head through. Beyond lay a fierce chasm and a blue-gray sky. He looked down into deepening blackness, felt the wind on his face, heard its mournful howl. There, just out of reach, his Juliet.

She was chained, as were the other souls around her. Her eyes closed as if in sleep, thick iron manacles around her neck and wrists. Her gown, the blue color of a clear Venetian sky, covered her ankles, but the man beside her boasted thick shackles above his bare feet. His yellowed white hair blew onto Juliet's shoulder, but she did not stir. Below her, another soul, its sex indeterminate, had been reduced by the wearing wind to nothing but scraps of leathery skin clinging to bone.

They were everywhere, the souls, shackled together, suspended by nothing in the empty chasm. They clustered in inverted cones that hung like arrow tips from the sky.

He pulled back, recoiling from the vast emptiness. The screams of the maggot-like horror in the river pierced his head, confusing his thoughts.

"Romeo!" Hamlet had scaled the monster's back, and he clung to it as it plunged below the surface.

The prince had brought him this far. Romeo owed him a debt for that, at least. But to come so close, and then fail...

He looked back to the portal, at Juliet's dark curls stirring against her skin, once deep brown and burnished gold, now as ashen and gray as the souls around her.

He pushed his face through again and screamed her name, but the wind swallowed it up, and she did not wake.

Breaking free of the portal, he staggered back a few steps. Hamlet still held on to the creature, or more accurately, onto his dagger hilt, which protruded from the demon's back.

It was dishonorable to leave the prince this way, after the assistance he'd given Romeo. Hamlet would be fine, Romeo reasoned with himself. The prince was far better equipped to navigate the Afterjord than Romeo was, so at least he had a chance of escape.

But without Hamlet, Romeo had no chance of escape.

Without Romeo, Juliet had no chance of escape.

Though the guilt at leaving Hamlet behind would plague

Romeo until the end of his days, it was not a difficult choice to make. If he were to live the rest of his mortal life in the Afterjord, he would do so with Juliet at his side. The prince had gotten him this far, and no power on hell or earth could stop Romeo from rescuing his beloved now.

He took a breath, willed his weakened body to remember its lost strength, and ran at the portal. The tension on the surface of the glittering light held him back just a bit. As he broke through, he swung his arms, moved his legs to run across nothing. He collided with Juliet, grabbed on to her, stood on the crumbling finger bones of the soul below her.

"Juliet." His heart could have stopped beating, and he would not have cared. Here she was, at last. The year of suffering that had felt like an eternity melted away. And yet, she did not open her eyes.

"It's me," he tried again. "Juliet, it's me. Your Romeo."

She did not stir.

"My love, my wife," he whispered. He pulled himself up to brush his lips across her cheek, repeating the words he'd said to her as she lay upon her bier. "Death, that hath suck'd the honey of thy breath, hath had no power yet upon thy beauty."

Her eyelids fluttered.

"Juliet?" His arms ached from holding himself up. He looked down, and wished he hadn't. The blue-gray void stretched endlessly below, rows upon rows of the floating soul islands he could fall into.

He again called upon strength he did not really have,

kindled embers of hope that had grown cold, then flared again, only to be snuffed by this heartless place.

"Juliet, please," He whispered into her ear. His arms were limp as soggy bread. The wasted muscles of his shoulders quivered. "Juliet, please. You must wake. Please."

Why, he did not know. The corpseway was out of his range now. He'd made a fantastic leap to reach her, but there was nothing to push off from, no place to take a step back and gather speed. They could not leave the way they had come.

Not to mention the iron bands securing Juliet. Even if he could get his sword out and hack at them, they would sooner break his blade than crumble beneath it.

He had come, and failed at his quest. Hamlet now dead. Juliet still trapped. But he himself could not die without looking into her eyes once more. "Please, my love. My wife. Open your eyes."

Slowly, her eyelids lifted. Her lips parted, and she frowned. Her forehead creased, and she squinted as she looked at him. "Romeo?"

The shackles at her throat and wrists gave way before he could answer, and she fell heavily forward. With nothing to prevent himself from tumbling backward into the abyss, he grabbed Juliet in his arms. Together, they plummeted, screaming.

Romeo held onto Juliet, clung to her for both of their lives, which would not be much longer. The jagged finger bones of wind-tattered corpses caught at his back. Frail though he was, practically a corpse himself, Romeo shielded her with his body.

They never struck one of the ghastly floating islands, though, and when it seemed too lucky that they had not, he opened his eyes. He would rather look upon Juliet's form, though her face was buried against his chest. He would rather enjoy the last few moments they would have together before he died, when they would no doubt be cast to opposite ends of this hellish afterworld.

He had rescued her soul, only to dash it to pieces on the jagged teeth of a raging river at the bottom of the chasm. He saw it above them? No, below them, for they had tumbled midair and now plunged headfirst at the water. He held her tightly, afraid the current would drag her away when they went under. They crashed into the waves and through them, surfacing suddenly in another river, without ever swimming up.

"What is this place?" Juliet screamed, her eyes showing wide and white as she fought above the bloody surface of the river of gore.

"The maggot," Romeo sputtered, droplets of blood fighting their way past his lips no matter how he tried to puff them way. "Make for the shore!" Then, in desperation, he shouted, "Hamlet!"

This was what he wanted, Romeo reminded himself. *It was Hamlet that wanted to go on, when I would have given up.*

That rationalization did not erase the memory of the

prince's cries for help as Romeo abandoned him.

"Hamlet!" Romeo roared again, demanding this time, but the prince did not come.

What did come was the pale, bloated shape of the graveworm, rising from the waters beneath them, meeting their feet as though they'd fallen on it through air. It forced them from the bloody water, sent Juliet sprawling on the black void of the shore.

Romeo clung to the thing, grimacing at the texture of it under his hands. It felt like undercooked fat on a piece of greasy meat, all slime and gelatinous membrane. He pulled his dagger and sank it into the creature's back for a handhold, as Hamlet had done. "Juliet, watch out!"

The monster had already made a meal of Hamlet. It would not feast upon Juliet, as well.

The maggot lunged at her, its bizarre, human arms reaching out to pull her toward the leech-like mouth with its rows of horrible teeth.

"Romeo!" She screamed, rolling away as it grabbed for her. The creature swiped both arms, suddenly longer, and ropey, but they came up empty.

"We must kill it!" Juliet shouted. "Your sword, Romeo! Your sword!"

No doubt she wondered why he didn't simply kill the beast and get it over with. She didn't know yet that he was not a wraith as well, that she had been far more effective than he at ending his life. His strength was still constrained by the limits of his mortal body.

Still, he had to fight it, even if the battle was over before it began. He unsheathed his sword, ducking the reach of the monster's arm as it tried to wipe him off its back. The maggot screeched its fury and lashed its body like a whip. Romeo fought to hold on, but his arms were too fatigued from his attempt to hold on to Juliet. His hand slipped, and he slid down the creature's back, only to encounter Hamlet's knife still protruding from the monster's side.

The sight was a fist to Romeo's chest, shattering bones inward to pierce the place where his heart would have been. But he had no heart, he'd proved that when he'd abandoned the prince. There was no other way to describe it. Romeo had pulled Hamlet through the portal, he'd brought him to this place, and he'd left him to die.

Romeo gripped the hilt of the dagger and pulled himself up, climbing the monster's thrashing back. He withdrew his sword from its sheath and sank it as deeply into the beast's hide as it would go. Gouts of black blood thick as tar poured from the wound, and Romeo swung to the side, wrenching the dagger from the worm's flesh with one hand to hang suspended from the creature's disgusting body.

On the shore, Juliet backed up a step, then another step, her gaze never leaving the creature as she waited for it to strike.

Despite the sheer, blood-pumping terror coursing through him, Romeo felt some admiration at that. She was not a delicate flower to wither and die from fright. She would not let the beast take her.

The maggot jerked its upper body from left to right, and Hamlet's sword came loose. He spun through the air, a dagger in one hand, the sword in the other, and he would give up neither. He landed awkwardly beside the river. It hurt, and it didn't seem like it should, when all he'd fallen upon was darkness.

Juliet ran to his side, and that was both a mistake and a blessing. A mistake, because the moment Juliet took her eyes off the horrible creature's sightless head and greedy mouth, it lunged at her. It tracked her, a foul slime issuing from its evil mouth, and she dodged it as she ran. Romeo struggled to his feet, put himself between Juliet and the thing, and it was by the good will of fortune that he'd managed to get between them just in time. He hacked at the worm's head with all his might, splitting down the center, his blade parting the creature's swollen body like rotten cheese. The two halves wobbled, then split apart, a large, foul chunk sheered off at an angle by Romeo's blade. It fell with a wet, bouncing smack on the black ground beside them.

Panting in fear, Juliet fell against his side. He would have liked to take her into his arms, to give her the strength of his body, but he had none left. His hand on her shoulder, he steadied himself against her, and they both crashed down.

"Romeo, are you hurt?" Juliet rolled him to his back. She dragged the backs of her fingers across his forehead; her palm cupped his cheek. Her large, brown eyes searched his with frantic worry, then moved to follow her hands down his chest. "Are you hurt, did it bite you?"

"No." He captured her delicate hand in his and brought it to his lips. Then he pressed it against the bony hollow where his ribs met. She recoiled, feeling his thinness beneath his doublet, but he held her palm against him. "Do you feel it?"

"Romeo…" Juliet's gaze darted from his hands holding hers, to his face. He knew he appeared different to her now, but his heartbeat would leave her no choice but to believe the truth. Her lips parted in surprise. "You're alive."

"I am." He did not add, "for now." He did not want to ruin his heroic triumph with further proof of his feebleness. "I came for you."

"Came for me?" She frowned at him. "But where was I?"

"You were here. In the Afterjord." Romeo studied her expression as it changed subtly from confusion to relief and back again.

"The Afterjord?" She snorted in disbelief. "No, I've never heard of such a place. The last thing I remember—"

Her eyes went wide, and she pulled her hand away from him. She brushed it off on her skirt, as though she'd touched something diseased.

He sat up with effort, and reached for her.

A chill crept over his thinking. When he looked at her now, she did not seem quite like the Juliet he remembered. There had been something to her, a spark of life this Juliet did not have.

What a stupid thing to think, he scolded himself. Of course she was not as lively as she had been. She wasn't alive.

But she would be, when they got back to the corpseway,

back to their world.

Wouldn't she?

His guide through all of this had been Hamlet. The prince had brought him here, and he'd known little of the place when they'd arrived, but he thought quickly and was more educated than Romeo. Juliet was smart as a whip, but confused, and rightly so, upon waking to a nightmare world.

"Romeo, I don't like this place," she said, still backing away from him. She looked down and screamed, and Romeo saw that the monster he'd slain had dissolved into thousands of wriggling maggots at her feet.

"Don't look at them!" he ordered her, reaching out and pulling her to him, away from the cursed creatures. The river beside them was no longer a torrent of blood, but a pool of crawling grave worms that swelled and burst, flinging the tiny, wriggling white bodies onto their clothes and hair with horrifying puffs of weight. But when he looked up, Romeo saw nothing but his sword, his dagger, and Hamlet's as well, lying in the blackness.

Juliet sobbed against him, as disconsolate as the night he'd been banished.

How she'd raged at him for his part in her cousin Tybalt's death. It had been their wedding night, and rather than spending it in joy, they'd consummated their love in desperate fear and consuming grief; her, for her cousin, Romeo, for Mercutio.

He wondered if either man roamed this bleak void. He hoped they would not meet them, for what could he say to

Mercutio, a better man who'd met a crueler fate than he? Would there be anything Mercutio wished to hear, given his parting words to Romeo of a plague on both houses, Montagues and Capulets? And Tybalt, would he still bear the mark of the sword Romeo had plunged through him? The image haunted Romeo's nightmares; he did not wish to see it again with his own eyes.

Kissing Juliet's forehead, he murmured comfort that was woefully inadequate for the situation. But what did one say to one's deceased wife, who did not remember how she came to the land beyond death?

He leaned back a little, his arms still tight about her. "Juliet, do you remember how you came to be here?"

She nodded, and swiped at her face. "I was in the piazza," she began, and a frown creased her forehead. "There was no one I knew. No one. And I couldn't find my way home. Everywhere I turned…blackness."

Romeo thought of the terrified woman he'd seen fleeing the shade. If Juliet had experienced just a fraction of that panic…but he could not think of that now.

"Do you remember how you got to the piazza?" he asked gently.

She smiled—a part of her that had remained unchanged by death, untouched by the underworld. How he had missed her smile, so wide and bright, each perfect tooth like a pearl, her eyes shining like dark jewels flecked with gold. "Don't be stupid, of course I know! I've walked the same way every day with my nurse, since I was a child. Down the Via Palermo, across the bridge, unless it's market day, then we take the via Francessa…"

As she spoke, a troubled veil fell over her features. "But no…that seems so wrong."

He'd thought that facing her and admitting to his part in her cousin's death would be the most difficult conversation of their lives. He could never have imagined this one.

"My love. My heart," he began, taking one of her hands in his and squeezing it tightly between them. "Do you remember Tybalt?"

"My cousin?" the smile returned, slightly dimmed, no less brilliant in Romeo's eyes. Then it froze, all the beauty turning to sadness. "But he's dead. Isn't he dead?"

"Yes. He is dead. For that I am so terribly, terribly sorry." He waited for some indication that she remembered the circumstances of her beloved cousin's demise, but she only looked more confused. He had to continue. "You remember how it happened?"

"You killed him."

He had hoped to never again see the horror in her expression that he had seen that awful night. He'd thought nothing could ever hurt him so.

"Is that why you're in hell with me?"

He'd been so wrong.

"Walk with me, Juliet," he said, his throat parched and dry. "We have much to discuss."

CHAPTER EIGHT

"So this place is not hell, then?" Juliet's voice held a plaintive mixture of terror and disbelief that she didn't like the sound of. But everything he'd told her as they'd walked through the darkness had muddled her head. Valkyrie? Corpseways? A Danish prince? It had sounded like the ravings of a maniac. "It's as though I've awoken from a dream into a nightmare."

No, more than that, she felt as though she'd woken from death, into hell, no matter what Romeo might have called it.

His hand found her sleeve, then her fingers, and he squeezed them to reassure her. At least, she thought it must be Romeo. He looked so different than she remembered. He looked older, gaunt. His hair was shorn close to his scalp, and silver threads jabbed up here and there, like short needles. Had the world beyond the grave done this to him? He'd been all of seventeen years old when they'd met, two years older than she…how long had passed since then?

"I still can't believe you're real," she admitted, reaching out one had to touch his pale, drawn face.

He flinched from her touch, her fingertips managing only to graze his cheek. "Come on. Our work is not half yet done."

"Who is this that we're looking for?" she asked, trailing along in the darkness. She supposed it was rather silly to object to finding this friend of his. After all, she was dead; there was precious little for her to spend her time on. But some of her happiest times had been alone with Romeo, and now they were alone together, possibly for eternity. Did he not see it for the paradise it was? Why would he wish to fetch someone to share it with them?

"Hamlet. He's the prince of Denmark, actually." A flush rose to Romeo's cheeks, and for a moment he reminded her of the youth he'd been when they'd first met. "He came with me. He didn't want to. If there is any chance he might still be alive, we must find him. Otherwise, we may never get back."

"Get back?" To the racks, and the cold, howling chasm she'd been captive in?

"To Midgard. The real world." He paused, looking this way and that in the darkness, but there was as much nothing on either side of them as there was ahead and behind. "Home."

Return to the real world? The thought made Juliet doubtful and sick. Every moment she remained in the afterlife, she felt more a part of it. Being dead had only just begun to feel right. Ridiculous as she knew it would seem to him, death seemed comfortable and safe in comparison to the haphazard order of living.

"I don't belong there," she reminded him softly, pleading with every fiber of her soul, the only thing she had left to herself. But she knew it was a plea that would go unanswered, as she could not put it into words and she doubted he would allow himself to hear it. "It can't be good for the natural order of things for a once dead girl to suddenly spring back to life. Where is my body? How long have I been away?"

He would not meet her eye. "A long time. Months. Your body has rotted away by now. But I believe you can step through the corpseway and rejoin me in the mortal world."

"How do you know this?" She wasn't sure she even wanted a body. Her old one had given her so much trouble. She had been beautiful, but her beauty had drawn men who'd had wrong intentions. Her figure had blossomed before she'd understood the difference between childhood and womanhood, and she'd been ill-prepared to defend herself from the boys she'd once played with as friends. If that was all her body could do for her, she might as well remain a spirit.

A memory, nebulous and watery, swam to the surface of her mind. Everything was fuzzy and out of focus. She saw the ceiling of the crypt, heard the weeping of her mother.

"Where did they bury me?" she asked, though she suspected the answer.

"Just outside of the cemetery walls, in unconsecrated

ground." His voice was choked with emotion. "I was so weak, I couldn't do anything. I would have tried, Juliet. I thought I might move you back to the tomb some night, but I lost my nerve every time. I didn't want to dig you up and see you that way."

Buried in unconsecrated ground. Perhaps that was how she'd found herself in the hell she'd been confined to. "Are you still banished from Verona?"

Romeo shook his head. His voice was hoarse with fatigue and sorrow, but they walked on as he answered. "Upon my recovery, the prince of Verona lifted the banishment. He said that in my state, I was a threat to no one."

That would have hurt her prideful beloved more than any blade could have. She did love him, but her love was not blind. There was a streak of childish bravado in him that could not be denied. It had been the aim of all Montagues to be intimidating to the other citizens; anything the family had ever gotten, they'd claimed through fighting.

Still, his fighting had brought him here, beyond the gates of hell, and all for her. Juliet's eyes filled with tears. "How does my nurse fair?"

"Poorly," Romeo admitted reluctantly. "She grieves you and blames herself for her part in this. But she could not have known the outcome when she delivered you to the church that day."

"And my mother? My father?" Juliet's parting with them had been bitter, but she had not meant it to be. She'd quarreled violently with them, when her father had decreed she marry Paris. She'd thought that someday, perhaps years after she'd faked her demise and been reunited with her banished love, she might return to Verona and make peace.

"They are...subdued." There was a curl to Romeo's lip as he spoke. He had nothing but disdain for her parents, for her entire family, a disdain that had been bred over decades of feuding. "The prince of Verona declared peace, and our families seem content to abide. For now. But it has only been a few months since the declaration."

"So it was the poison, and not time, which has done this to you?"

"The poison aged me as well as time ever hoped to," Romeo responded with a rueful chuckle that died on his lips. "The days I have left will be filled with you. I will cherish every one, even if they're all spent here."

If she'd had a heartbeat, it would have stopped at those words. He had come to this bleak and dismal place to stay with her, if he could not return home. Though she could not clearly imagine what that home felt like, or why it should be important to her now, she did appreciate the depth of that sacrifice.

A sound drifted to them through the darkness, an insubstantial whisper like a coil of smoke on the air. In the soundless black, the faraway tune amplified with each step. It was a nursery rhyme, in a language Juliet didn't understand. As she listened, the words took shape, melding one unknown word into a known one, until she took their meaning clear as day.

She clutched her head and doubled over, a dizzying sensation momentarily putting her off her balance. But that was absurd! Souls didn't have balance.

They probably didn't have a language, either, she reasoned to herself. Perhaps that was why she understood the song.

"Juliet!" Romeo gripped her wrists and pulled her up, concern welling in his dark eyes. "Are you all right?"

"I'm going mad," she said with a shake of her head. "Forgive me, I think a bit of madness can be excused, given the state I'm in."

"Listen, it's coming from that direction." Still holding one of her wrists, Romeo pulled her after him. With every step, the voice came closer, the words of the song pushing Juliet toward the precipice of insanity.

And will a not come again? And will a not come again? No, no he is dead. Go to thy deathbed, He never will come again, His beard all flaxen white with snow, All flaxen was his poll. He is gone, he is gone. And we cast away moan, God ha' mercy on his soul!

"It's me."

The voice came from behind them, and Juliet shrieked, clutching Romeo's doublet. The man who'd crept up behind them was fair of hair, his eyes wide and haunted. For a moment, Juliet had mistaken him for a ghost.

"Hamlet." Romeo reached out to him, his excitement for the man's appearance evident in his features, but the pale man shrank violently from his touch as if burned by fire.

What had occurred between them, she wondered, to inspire the brotherly concern in Romeo's eyes?

He turned back to her. "Something is wrong with him."

Juliet studied the prince, willing her death-clouded mind to take in anything unusual about him. In her experience, the more powerful a man, the more soft and old he was. This was not the case with Prince Hamlet, who was as fit as Romeo — or, as Romeo *had* been, before the poison had made him leaner —, with a handsome, straight nose and eyes as blue and glittering as...

As nothing Juliet had ever seen before. There was something unnatural in them, a presence that would have made Juliet cold all over, were she not deceased.

"She's talking about me, in her songs. She's telling me something...something I don't want to hear." He covered his ears, his eyes still swirling with eerie blue light.

Like the corspeway. Juliet tugged Romeo's sleeve. "Some spirit has possessed him. Look into his eyes."

Romeo wetted his lips, his expression still and grave. "Hamlet...something has happened to you. You have to come with me. I have Juliet. We can leave now."

"I can never leave," Hamlet moaned pitiably and covered his eyes. "Not having seen what I've seen. Not knowing what I've done."

"What have you done?" Juliet asked.

Hamlet dropped his arm, his eyes meeting hers. Slowly, the glittering blue in his unfurled into water shadows that slowly reached for Juliet and Romeo. The shadows became claws of woven light, reaching out to swipe at their eyes. Romeo dodged, but Juliet stepped into the misty hands, letting the power wash through her.

Her vision went over all watery, as though someone had dumped a bucket over her head. As Nurse had done, during her baths as a child. Something in Juliet's soul pulled oddly at that memory. The remembrance of her mother's weeping hadn't stirred anything in her, but somehow the feeling that Nurse was near, caring for her, made her feel...safe, until her vision cleared, and she remembered she was not a child having a bath in her warm, safe room, but a shell, a broken soul drifting through Hell, lost for all eternity.

"Do you see her?" Hamlet asked, pointing to the figure of a woman standing in a pool of black water. Her voluminous white gown fell heavily from her shoulders, as though it were pulling her down. She seemed unconcerned by it, holding out a length of her skirt as a basket for a heaping mound of wildflowers. As she sang, she tossed the blossoms onto the surface of the water. A time or two, she reached up to pat a bloom into the copper curls that framed her face and cascaded down her back.

"Ophelia," Hamlet said, the name almost a prayer on his lips.

Beside them, Romeo looked about, his forehead creased with confusion. "I see no one."

"There's a girl," Juliet explained, taking a step toward her.

"Don't!" Hamlet restrained her with a hand that gripped

Juliet's arm like a vise. "You can't go near her. I've tried. Over and over again, I've tried. She drowns. Every time you touch her, she drowns."

"Do you know her?" Juliet had dreamed all manner of horrible dreams as she'd slept in Sheol. Was this another? Or had the blue mist brought her into Hamlet's dream, as well? "Is she someone you knew, who died?"

"No, she cannot be dead. I saw her only just…" he shook his head. "She is in Midgard. She is safe. This is just some witchcraft, made to drive me mad."

"What is this sorcery?" Romeo wandered around them. "What are you seeing, that I cannot?"

"The source of the song," Juliet explained patiently. "Hamlet, what happens after she drowns?"

"I tried to save her," he babbled. "But she's too heavy. Her clothes drag her down, they… they would drag me down too. I have to let her go."

"I cannot fight an enemy I cannot see," Romeo told Juliet, his helplessness evident in every word.

"Perhaps she's not your enemy." Juliet took a step toward the girl, then another, and another. Her feet touched the water, and the depth beneath the girl's feet changed. Ophelia plunged down, clawing at the water that swallowed her and covered her face.

"Save her!" Hamlet pleaded, for he didn't see the trick that it was.

He'd helped Romeo, and in doing so, he'd freed her. For that, Juliet owed him this, no matter how unpleasant the act might seem.

As she approached the mad girl, Juliet's dead heart and fractured soul saw the true intent of the apparition. She was meant to drive the prince insane, to prevent him from leaving the Afterjord. That made it easier to reach into the water for the drowning girl. Juliet followed her down, held her firmly under even as she thrashed and struggled to keep her head above water.

"What are you doing?" Hamlet shouted, his hands balled to fists he beat against his thighs as he doubled over. He screamed, despondent, while Romeo backed away a step, two steps.

Juliet knew what he saw; his two companions driven to madness by a force invisible to him. But to Juliet, it seemed so simple. Romeo and Hamlet were real, living beings. They felt fear, projected it. It brushed across Juliet's soul like a cat's tongue, rough and clammy. But this thing before them was only a shade. A trick, playing on their earthly thoughts like so many harp strings.

When she straightened, her arms did not drip with water. "None of it is real, Hamlet." She turned to Romeo. "It's a trick."

"But how did you know?" The mist was slowly lifting from Hamlet's eyes, and he gripped her upper arms with an intensity that would have caused her pain, could she have felt it.

"I just...knew." She shrugged off his touch. "I could see the emptiness around her, just as I can see the souls in the two of you."

Hamlet turned to Romeo, who still looked bewildered. "Your beloved is a valuable tool, blessed with insights to which neither of us are privy."

"She isn't a tool." Romeo's jaw jutted forward as he ground his teeth. "She is my wife."

"Wife?" How had she forgotten so significant a detail? A memory stirred, still attached to her soul by golden threads that wove tighter as she concentrated. "Oh yes. Yes, the man, with the tonsure…"

"Friar Laurence," Romeo prompted, a queer expression on his handsome face. "Juliet, do you truly not remember?"

"If I may," Hamlet interjected, coming to stand beside the slight space between them. "The circumstances of Juliet's death were traumatic. I've spoken to ghosts who remember nothing of their past lives, who they are, where they came from…and some who remember the moment of their birth, but not the month that they died. It is possible that in the sorrow surrounding her demise, your Juliet's soul was so wounded that somehow, she lost her memories."

Romeo's hand came up to cup her cheek. His touch, warm and full of life, made her shrink from him. "You truly do not remember me?"

"I remember…" she frowned. "I remember that you care for me. That you love me. It's what helped me break free from the fetters in Sheol. But I can't remember how any of it came to be."

His dark eyes filled with pain, and he looked away from

her. Juliet turned to Hamlet. "I do remember my nurse. I remembered her giving me a bath. I remembered being in my tomb, unable to move, but not dead. Is that what happened to me? Did they bury me alive?"

She might have vomited, if she'd had a living physical body. She'd had nightmares as a child waking in a dark room, ever since she'd seen the inside of the family crypt after the death of an uncle. She had been terrified of dying then, and being left alone in that room full of dead strangers. It had taken such courage to swallow the potion...

"The potion!" She gripped Romeo's doublet in both fists, not sure whether she wanted to tug on it or slap her palms against his chest. "I took the potion for you!"

"I didn't know it was a potion." He swallowed. "I heard only that you were dead. I came to the tomb...I killed Paris..."

"Paris?" She searched her memory. Yes, she had argued with her parents. They had fought, bitterly. She would be forced to marry. "They were going to make me marry him. But then, I was already married. They didn't know. I never told them?"

"You thought I would send for you," Romeo reminded her. "You thought Friar Laurence would pass me the message."

"And he did not? He failed me?" How could she have been so stupid? "I should have told my father, immediately. I should have relied upon Friar Laurence to prevent the wedding, to go to the bishop, something...What have I done?"

Romeo tried to hold her, but she wrenched away. She couldn't stand for him to touch her, now that she was a dead thing and he still so full of life. They had chosen death over being kept apart in the land of the living, and now they were kept apart by the strongest force of all.

Hamlet said quietly, "You must remember that what has passed has passed. You cannot undo it now, no more than you could have seen the consequences of your actions then. The only way now is forward."

She didn't want to face him, or Romeo. She had been blessedly absent during her imprisonment in Sheol. There had been no pain, no confusion. Merely a blank peace, a long void of time without end. It should have been a torment, with the vivid nightmares that had sometimes gripped her, but compared to what she had seen of this place, she preferred it.

"How do we go forward, then?" She opened her eyes. Her beautiful blue gown was vibrant with brocade flowers and delicate white lace. Her wedding gown, or it had been meant for that purpose. They had buried her in the dress she would have worn to marry Paris.

She lifted her head and met both of their gazes. "How, then? How do we go forward?"

"I don't know," Hamlet admitted. "But it seems far more sensible to venture on as one, than risk perishing alone. You may not remember your connection to him now, but would you really want Romeo to be lost in the Afterjord forever?"

"No." This was no place for anyone, living or dead.

"Then I suggest we continue walking. Juliet, your help

will be invaluable in spotting the traps this place might lay for us. Will you help?" He slowly tilted his head down, a lock of pale hair falling across his eyes.

"Yes." She gritted her teeth. There was nothing she disliked more than being treated like a child.

She remembered that, at least.

CHAPTER NINE

The blackness had an end.

Before them loomed a triptych, like the altar screen in a church, but seemingly miles long, and painted with scenes of horror. Demonic visages devouring human flesh, rivers flowing red.

"More rivers of blood. I suppose one can't have enough of those lying around," Romeo observed with a curl of his lip.

Hamlet did not respond.

It had been one thing for Romeo to have grabbed him and tumbled him through the corpseway; Hamlet had almost forgiven that. He'd ascribed the Italian's actions to nerves, and reasoned that he might have been frightened enough to do the same thing, in his shoes.

But when Romeo had left him behind, left him to drown in a wriggling, bloody river of maggots, Hamlet's understanding had taken a sharp toll. They may not have been fast friends, but it seemed a cowardly and cruel thing to leave a man behind in the situation Hamlet had been left in. He could barely look at Romeo.

Juliet wandered apart from them, and Hamlet called to her, "Don't go far. We don't want to be separated."

"There's a door," she answered.

"A corpseway!" Romeo rushed after her. Without hesitation, he plunged his head through the pointed arch of blue light. When he emerged, he whooped in victory. "It's a castle! It's home!"

"Are you certain?" Hamlet jogged to their side and looked through, himself. The scene on the opposite side of the corpseway looked familiar, indeed. It seemed a normal feasting hall. Fresh rushes covered the floors, and they smelled almost sweeter than the aroma of the food on the long, polished table.

He stepped back. "I think you're right. I think this is our world. But…"

How would he explain to Romeo and Juliet that they might once again be parted? How did people, in general, feel about these things?

Hamlet had never done well where emotions were concerned. When he'd seen the vision of Ophelia, he had wanted to dismiss it out of hand. When he'd last seen Ophelia, she had been full of life and a bit annoying. Not on the brink of suicidal madness. Still, his feelings had overwhelmed him, completing the Afterjord's trick, and now his heart mourned for her a bit, though he knew the vision had been false.

If something horrible *had* befallen Ophelia, Hamlet would feel responsible, just for having seen the vision. How would Romeo feel if Juliet stepped through the corpseway and met a second death?

Hamlet decided the best way would be to say everything as plainly as possible, so there could be no misunderstanding. "We don't know that Juliet will have a body on the other side. So prepare yourselves, both of you. Her soul could be destroyed. Let's go."

Romeo grabbed him and shoved him against the triptych, beside the portal. "What do you mean, her soul could be destroyed?"

"Romeo, let him go!" Juliet shouted. The enraged Italian ignored her.

Since Romeo was the one who had such a violent hold upon Hamlet's person, it was Romeo whom he addressed. "Well, how should I know? I saw my father pass through the portal, but he was a ghost. A wraith of blue light that could barely pass for human. I don't know what will happen to Juliet."

"You don't know? And yet you brought me here to find her?" Romeo could display surprising strength when angry, for someone as frail as he was. He shook Hamlet and slammed him against the wall again.

"*I* brought *you* here? You manhandled me through

that portal against my will!" Hamlet huffed. "May I remind you that just on the other side of that corpseway, you could be executed for laying your hands upon my person in this impudent manner?"

"You're not helping!" Juliet scolded and forced her way between the two of them. "Now both of you, calm yourselves for one moment. Hamlet, what makes you think my soul could possibly be destroyed?"

He shrugged. "I was trying to prepare you for the absolute worst case scenario. I was trying to be helpful."

"As helpful as a stick in the eye," Romeo muttered, but a single stern look from Juliet silenced him.

"If your father's soul could pass through the portal, it stands to reason that mine should be able to as well." Though she addressed Hamlet, she appeared to be speaking more to Romeo. "We have no reason to fear. If I cannot remain in corporeal form in…Midgard," she struggled visibly with the term, "then I can come back through the portal."

"I will not leave you here," Romeo vowed.

She sighed her resignation. "We'll cross that bridge when we come to it, much as my nurse used to say on our walks."

Hamlet blinked at her.

"There are a lot of bridges in Verona," she explained, and paused again. Then she dropped her gaze and muttered, "I thought it was very funny."

"Hamlet, you go through first," Romeo suggested, a muscle in his jaw flexing. His eyes darted to the portal. "Then Juliet. I will stay behind, lest we become separated."

"And what?" She frowned up at Romeo. "I'll come back through and you'll stay here?"

He glowered. "I won't leave you behind. It was my love for you that brought me here, and it is my love for you that will keep me here, if I must stay to be at your side."

"I'll go through then? To spare myself having to listen to any more of this," Hamlet said, cheerfully, to buy him time before they comprehended the biting sentiment.

He stepped through, his breath held. If it was Midgard he entered, he wanted his first breath to be free from the stain of the Afterjord.

Hamlet's boots touched stone and rushes. The warmth from the fire burning in the hearth at the end of the hall made him suddenly aware of the lack of temperature in the void. It had been neither cold, nor warm, lending more of a feeling of unrealness, wrongness, than he'd noticed at the time.

He took a few cautious steps. The hall had a low ceiling, intricately carved with indistinguishable scenes that did not reveal themselves in the flickering of the firelight. The long table was heaped with food, but no one seemed to be present to eat it. Whoever lived in this castle would no doubt be along at any moment, and it seemed vital that the three of them be gone before they were noticed by a servant, or the lord of the manor himself.

Hamlet stuck his head through. "Quickly, we haven't much time."

Juliet looked at Romeo, the briefest glance, before

stepping through. She slid through the portal with a gasp, and looked about herself with wonder. She lifted her hand, turned it this way and that in the firelight. "Did it work?"

Hamlet reached out and pinched her shoulder, hard. She slapped his hand away with a shout of indignation, but that affront changed to joy in a heartbeat. "It worked, didn't it? I feel more...alive."

Romeo came through. He did not blink before he reached for Juliet. He wrapped his arms about her, and she went easily into his crushing embrace. "Praise God. Praise God, you have returned to me."

"She came through the corpseway unscathed," Hamlet agreed. "But we do not know where we've come to. And I am not in a position to be kidnapped. If this castle belonged to an ally of my uncle, or an enemy, it would not matter. They will seize me upon sight."

"They might not know you," Juliet said in a whisper, her gaze searching the room. "They might be able to help us get back to Verona."

"And they might murder us on sight for breaching their walls." Something bothered Hamlet, pricked at the back of his mind like the tip of a knife. "The corpseway remains."

Romeo looked over his shoulder. "That it does, the evil thing. Do you think this might be the domain of a sorcerer?"

"Do you believe in sorcerers?" Juliet asked, leaning back in Romeo's embrace. "The boy I remember did not believe in such nonsense."

"Says the dead girl," Hamlet muttered under his breath.

He did not begrudge the two their happy reunion. Something had indeed taken place when Juliet had stepped through the portal. There was more life to her, more warmth. Having not known her when she was alive, he could not say whether she was back to normal or not. Romeo seemed satisfied that she had been restored, and she did, as well. But something wasn't right.

He hated to cast a pall over their joy, but he could remain silent no longer. "Whoever possesses a corpseway in Midgard is a formidable enemy, indeed. We should proceed with extreme caution."

Footsteps sounded beyond the two carved doors on either side of the fireplace.

"Hide!" Romeo whispered fiercely.

The only source of egress seemed to be the doors that now creaked open, both at the same time.

Guards, Hamlet reasoned, sent to find the cause of the disturbance. They had been found out.

"Under the table," Juliet mouthed frantically, rushing to the narrow end, where no trestle bench would block them. She ducked beneath the tabletop and scrambled forward on her hands and knees, and Romeo followed.

It was the first place a guard would look, Hamlet lamented, but he had no other choice. The doors were opening, and he would be spotted. He climbed beneath with them, wishing for a tablecloth to conceal them. Perhaps the darkness and the long, low benches would do well enough.

Feet plodded in, slapping against the floor. Wet, white

feet, like those of a drowned corpse. Hamlet wondered at that. What kind of guard wouldn't wear boots?

Then he saw the expressions of Romeo and Juliet beside him, her eyes wide with fear, his mouth in a grim line.

Someone had to see what was happening. He motioned with a finger toward the tabletop above them, and slowly lowered himself flat to the floor. He pulled himself forward as silently as he could, but the horrible wet, smacking sounds of the seemingly hundreds of feet thundering in the room would have covered the peeling of church bells. Worse still were the sounds that followed, worse than the sloppy eating of the most uncouth noblemen at a celebratory feast. Hamlet gagged as a bitten plum bounced off the rushes and a slimy white foot crushed it. More food fell, chicken skin and chunks of masticated fruit, great globs of spittle-covered pastry crusts, as though the men feasting were merely chewing the food and tossing it down. Without dogs to gobble up the scraps, the disgusting banquet remained splattered on the floor and the feet, and Hamlet could no longer stand not knowing to whom those feet were attached.

He rolled to his back, looked up, and dodged a falling lump of thoroughly chewed beef and glistening fat. He retched at the sight before him. The creatures were a mockery of the shape of a man, two rubbery feet on long tubes of legs that rose up in an arch. Two arms, reaching and grabbing at the food on the table, were connected beneath a long, horrible oval of a head. Where the eyes should have been, only two empty holes, like thumbprints in dough, gaped sightless above the wide, formless mouth. As the creatures devoured their food, it fell out. There were no parts to swallow it down to.

Hamlet quickly slid beneath the table again and mouthed, "Don't look."

Of course, the other two did not heed them. He may as well have cautioned them not to touch a hot dish. Romeo drew his sword and caught the reflection of the creatures in his blade, and Juliet covered her gasp with her hand.

"Do you think they'll eat us?" she whispered.

"I don't know. It is certainly nothing I would wish to test!" Hamlet hissed back.

Romeo's chest rose and fell rapidly, his jaw tight, eyes ticking from side to side as he watched the rows of feet and spindly legs swaying like a demented forest beyond the bench. "I can cut a path for us."

"Don't be foolish, Romeo, there are too many of them!" Juliet's hand came up to cup his cheek.

Hamlet almost looked away. Open displays of affection always made him uncomfortable. Perhaps because he could not think his way around the emotions, or convince himself to feel them.

Then he thought of Ophelia, how it had been to watch her drown, and he thought perhaps he felt a little of what they did at the moment. "No. I'll do it."

They both looked at him as though he'd turned into a giant maggot serpent. Romeo sputtered, "Hamlet, you'll die."

"You're not the only person alive who can wield a sword,

you know. I've been taught by the best fencing masters in all of Europe," he argued.

"Fencing, yes!" Romeo shot back, straining to keep his voice low. "But have you ever fought in a melee? In close combat with other men who want to kill you?"

"No, because I'm not a brutish thug!"

"Will the both of you shut up?" Juliet admonished, putting a hand on Romeo's chest, as if to hold him back from lunging at Hamlet. "You're arguing about which one of you is better suited to be torn apart by those things!"

"I can clear a path through," Romeo snarled. "To the corpseway. We can get through it. It's no better on the other side, but we could at least wait until they leave."

"What if they come after us?" Juliet asked. "If I could pass through the corpseway, they might be able to as well."

"We'll stand a better chance out there. There were no physical restraints in that place, and there are here," Hamlet admitted. "He has a good plan. Godspeed, Romeo."

Giving Juliet a quick, hard kiss, Romeo put one hand on the hilt of his sword and slowly, clumsily crawled to the head of the table. There was a large chair there, like a throne, and he heaved his weight against it to knock it back. It clattered to the floor and the ring of legs around the table widened. Everything went suddenly quiet, as though the creatures had been shocked at Romeo's sudden appearance. Then, a deafening shriek went up, and the things skittered away, their moist soles slapping against the stones.

"I think that answered our question," Hamlet told Juliet

with an arch of his brow. He climbed out, reaching down to take Juliet's hand and help her up.

Romeo walked to them, sheathing his blade. "They ran away."

"Then they must be fairly harmless," Juliet said with a smile of relief. "But now where do we go?"

"Out the doors after them?" Romeo suggested. "I don't think the answers lie through that corpseway. We've made progress."

"No, we believe we've made progress. For all you know, we've gone backward." Hamlet frowned at the table. None of the food was missing. Everything had returned to the way it had been. "Don't touch anything. It could be a test."

"What do you mean?" Juliet asked. "I knew you were being tested with the girl in the water. Why wouldn't I see that this was a test, as well?"

"Because you're different here than you were in Sheol," Romeo said softly. "You weren't yourself there. A part of you was missing."

"That's impossible, I don't remember any bit of me going missing," she argued. "I feel as normal as I ever have."

"But there was something…" Romeo looked almost ashamed. "I owe you a debt too large to ever repay, Hamlet."

That took him aback. It was rare that anyone thanked him for anything. Perhaps because he'd spent so much time worrying about his own concerns, rather than the concerns of others.

"We aren't in Sheol anymore," Hamlet announced, only

partially for the change of subject. When the other two regarded him with quizzical expressions, he gestured around them. "This place is different, so you're different. You're dead, so your soul will be affected by the Afterjord in a way we will not."

Romeo put his arm around Juliet's waist and pulled her to his side, looking hopefully to Hamlet. "What if you're wrong? What if she's just getting better, becoming more alive the closer we get to Migard?"

"Better than what?" Juliet pressed her hand to her chest, her shoulders slouching forward as though she would become as empty as the hollow souls they had seen but a moment before. "I don't remember being any different. I cannot bear the thought of another corpseway stripping away a piece of me, without me knowing the absence of it. If I go through another portal, what will happen? Will I become someone else without ever knowing?"

"We can't tell." Hamlet met Romeo's despondent gaze. "I warned you that this journey would be difficult. Did you imagine it would be only fording rivers and traversing deserts? I told you that I didn't know what would happen when you got here."

"Was there no way to find out, before you did this to me?" Juliet asked, her large brown eyes full of hurt. "The two of you never thought that a bit more preparation might have been required before tampering with the forces of life and death?"

Neither Hamlet nor Romeo supplied an answer. It

seemed they both felt foolish, confronted with their oversight. It was a dire thing to unite them, Hamlet thought grimly.

Romeo tried to comfort her, his hand rising to touch her shoulder, but she pushed him away.

"I can't go back to Shoel. We can't go back to that, not now that I know the difference." She pointed accusingly at the corpseway. "There will be another way out of this room, we simply must find it."

Her gaze dropped to the table, and Hamlet followed the line of it to an apple gleaming red and bright on the dark wood. Juliet snatched it up, and Hamlet shouted, "No!"

She paused, clutching it in her hand.

"Don't eat that. You don't know what will happen. You might become one of those things. We don't know what the test is. Juliet, this isn't the way," Hamlet warned, stretching his arm toward her, trying to look unthreatening. They didn't know what the test was, that was true, but it seemed unlikely it had nothing to do with the banquet laid before them. He could not let her take a single bite.

"Eat it?" She frowned at him. "I was going to throw it at you."

He gaped at her in disbelief.

"I'm not stupid." She rolled her eyes in exasperation. "Just…angry."

Hamlet laughed. He couldn't help himself. It was true, he and Romeo had been tampering with forces they knew nothing about, and Juliet had every right to be furious with them. But the idea of vengeance for cosmic transgressions coming in the form of a tossed apple was simply too amusing for his exhausted mind.

Juliet's frown relaxed, and she laughed as well. Not as hard at first, but soon her mirth grew, and Romeo was the only one among them still angry. Or worried, it seemed, as he looked between Hamlet and Juliet as though they were both utterly mad.

But even he could not resist a break from the tension that continued to drain their hope and sap their wills. He snickered, then said, "All right, we've had a bit of fun," but he couldn't get through his sentence in seriousness.

It was not an easy peace they had found. Hamlet had not entirely forgiven Romeo for trapping him in this place and abandoning him in a time of dire need. Still, it seemed a far better plan to remain a whole than fracture apart.

At least Romeo could be amusing with his insults.

The thunder of slapping feet reverberated through the floor, and they all turned their heads towards the doors at the end of the room.

"They're coming back." Romeo unsheathed his sword.

"They were harmless," Juliet reminded him. "Maybe they're just over their fright and coming back for their food."

She looked at the table and screamed.

The heaps of fruit and roasted meat were gone, replaced by mounds of putrid, glistening organs. Ropes of entrails hung in rotting loops spilling off the tabletop. Arms and legs, unmistakably human, lay among the livers, hearts, and lungs in the festering feast.

"Perhaps not," Hamlet said under his breath.

"Take this," Romeo ordered Juliet, pressing the stiletto from his belt into her hand.

Hamlet drew his blade. A true leader should be both a scholar and a warrior, his father had counseled him shortly before his death. He should rely on his mind as much as his sword.

It didn't do him much good now, Hamlet reflected, to have ignored the latter part of his father's advice in favor of the former.

The doors burst open, and the hollow souls flooded in. Their appearance was not so benign now, if Hamlet could have called it so before. He did much prefer the toothless, eyeless horrors to these creatures. Their shape was much the same, but in the empty sockets, burning red lights glowed for eyes. Their mouths had become ringed with predatory fangs, seemingly made of steel, like knives that gnashed horribly as they rushed toward them.

Romeo was the first to strike a blow, cleaving one in half as easily as cutting an overripe pear. It fell to two pieces, shrieking and writhing, then burst into a wisp of smoke as it hit the floor.

"They can be killed!" Romeo roared over the commotion of shrieks and stamping feet.

Hamlet plunged his blade into the face of one, slashed at the throat of another. Or, where its throat might have approximately been. While their bodies were insubstantial, there wasn't much space to attack.

One grabbed Juliet by the wrist, and she plunged the stiletto into its eye, bending over it to follow it to the floor as she stabbed it again and again.

"Watch out!" Romeo warned her, cleanly beheading one of the swarm that had gotten behind her and made to lay its rubbery arms around her.

"There are too many," Hamlet shouted, thrusting his blade into another, and another, until he lost count of the number he'd killed. They kept coming, more and more of them, until it was clear to Hamlet that the only choice was to fight until he grew too exhausted to fend them off any longer. Then, he supposed he would become a part of their hideous feast, as well.

Juliet proved tireless with her blade, to Hamlet's surprise and delight. He could not imagine the ladies of his uncle's court taking such bloodthirsty delight in defeating monsters. Though his arms ached and their doom was imminent, he had a grudging admiration for her.

"Will they ever end?" Romeo puffed with exertion as he wielded his sword. The long, thin blade snicked and swooshed through the air, destroying one creature before him in the same motion as one behind him. There, too, Hamlet had to have some admiration. He may have trained with the best teachers, but Romeo had clearly learned his fighting skills from real world application.

A roar, loud as thunder, trembling as an earthquake, rent the air and shook dust from the ceiling overhead. The dreadful creatures screamed, their nail-less fingers raking down their faces as their mouths contorted to horrified ovals. Once again, they fled, tripping over each other, shoving in their stampede toward the doors.

"What was that?" Juliet pushed back her hair, which had come undone from her long braid and now plastered against her perspiration-damp face. She looked weary, more than frightened.

"Something worse," Hamlet warned.

The three of them took up stances beside each other, weapons at the ready.

CHAPTER TEN

The heavy wood door to the left of the hearth exploded off its hinges in a shower of splinters, and in its wake, the largest warrior Hamlet could ever have imagined tore into the room, an axe brandished above his head.

Flame orange hair cascaded back from a deep widow's peak on the beast-man's forehead, and a shaggy orange beard hung over his bare, bloodied chest. Inscribed on his flesh in blue paint, runes smeared with dirt and sweat shined greasy in the light. A finger bone was tied at the point of his beard; a necklace of them clattered as he stomped in his huge, heavy boots toward the gruesome table. He lifted his axe and roared, and the windows of the hall exploded inward in a spectacular spray of glass.

Hamlet covered his ears and saw the other two do the

same, as the berserker brought the axe down, right through the center of the table and its disgusting bounty. Pieces and parts flew everywhere. Hamlet sidestepped a rotting head that bounced toward him and maintained his grip on the hilt of his sword.

"There are three of us," Romeo said bravely. Stupidly. "We can take him, if we hit him from all sides. I'll fight from the front, Juliet, you and Hamlet try to strike his back."

"He can hear you!" Juliet snapped. "Would you like to draw him a map detailing how we plan to kill him?"

There was no time to bicker further. The berserker came at them, charging across the broken table, the axe over his head. Hamlet dove to one side, Juliet to the other. Only Romeo stood his ground, dodging the axe at the last second to bring his sword down on the warrior's arms. He cleaved one hand off, but the berserker didn't seem to feel its loss. He roared again and swiped his bleeding stump through the air, catching Hamlet in the chest and toppling him backward.

"Get up!" Romeo shouted, as encouragement, not an order. Did the Italian actually think Hamlet was capable of fighting?

Jumping to his feet, Hamlet rushed at the berserker from the side and slashed at his face. The warrior only whipped his head away from the blade and whirled on Juliet.

"Hey!" Romeo shouted, stabbing his sword into the warrior's stomach. It sank to the hilt, but did not protrude from the back. Hamlet boggled at the size of the berserker, and the fact that having a surely mortal wound didn't seem to bother him. Nor did he trouble himself with the man who'd just given him that wound. He seemed intent upon Juliet, baring his teeth and swiping for her with his remaining hand.

Hamlet tried to trade his sword for the berserker's axe, but he couldn't lift it.

Juliet struck out at the warrior with her stiletto, but she was hampered by the short length of the blade in comparison to the awesome reach of the berserker's arms. She could not get close enough to stab him without risking him closing his grip on her. As she backed away from him, she had the presence of mind to knock over a bench, to kick some rotted bones at his feet. But none of it was enough to stop his pursuit. She grew more panicked with every swing of his great axe, and though Romeo hacked at the berserker's muscled shoulder, he could not cleave his arm or distract him from his pursuit of Juliet.

Hamlet saw the skull that lay in her path, but could not shout his warning before she set her heel upon it. Her feet went out from beneath her, and she fell onto a pile of innards. A groan of disgust pulled from her throat as the berserker toppled onto her, his bared teeth sharp points that snapped at her face. Romeo shoved at him. Hamlet raced to his side, tried to sink his blade into the warrior's head, but the shock of the impact with the berserker's skull radiated down his arms.

Juliet's hand reached out blindly, and she came up with a splintered femur. When the berserker opened his mouth to let out another mighty roar, she stabbed the bone forward, driving the jagged point into the roof of his terrible mouth. She pushed and pushed, her hand going into the cavern of teeth to the wrist. It was Juliet's own roar that remained as the berserker's died away.

"Juliet!" Romeo shoved the dead berserker aside, and Hamlet helped him to pull her free from the huge body.

"I'm all right," she assured them, though she was trembling, and tears shone in her eyes. "I'm fine."

"Why was he so fixed upon you?" Hamlet wondered, stooping over the corpse. He poked at the necklace of bones, pulled it this way and that, examining. In addition to the finger bones were ears and a nose in varying states of decay, as well as a feather carved of bone, so delicate it seemed impossible that it had survived even passing association with a creature such as the one who wore it. That was strange enough that Hamlet gave the necklace a tug to break it and pull that charm free.

"Perhaps he likes the taste of female flesh better than male?" Romeo suggested with contempt. "Or perhaps he was a coward."

"Yes, I'm sure that's it," Hamlet said with a roll of his eyes. He got to his feet and slipped the feather carving into his doublet. "The enormous berserker with a giant axe and host of ravening hollow souls was too cowardly to face a nearly dead Italian and a prince with a shortsword."

He cleared his throat. "I'm referring, of course, to this sword and not—"

"Enough!" Juliet shook her head. "It's my fault. I did

something stupid. I...tried to keep the apple."

She reached into the folds of her skirt, withdrawing something red and round from her pocket. When she looked upon the object, she gasped. The fruit had become a human heart, red and slimy with blood. She dropped it to the floor and wiped her hands on her dress.

"Why would you do that?" Romeo asked gently. "We knew it was a test."

"You're still alive," she explained sheepishly. "I thought that later you might need to eat, and as long as there was all this food..."

"It's good that you didn't think to steal a chicken, I suppose. Imagine what that could have transformed into," Hamlet mused, pushing a disembodied leg with the toe of his boot. He looked up at both of them, staring at him horrified. "I fear our celebration may have been too soon, Juliet. I am sorry, but this is not Midgard."

"Thank God for that!" she exclaimed. "I couldn't live in a world where these creatures existed."

"Speaking of creatures, we should go, before those others come back." Romeo sheathed his sword and took Juliet by the hand. "Let's go."

There was no question now that they should attempt the doors the monsters had come through. Romeo and Juliet didn't give the corpseway a second look.

Hamlet let them go a few steps ahead, and paused beside the gleaming portal. He pulled the bone carving from his doublet and held it up to the blue illumination. The plume softened and waved in the touch of the light, as though it were not made of bone at all.

He frowned and tucked the relic inside his doublet.

• • •

They had been prepared to find anything beyond the doors, and charged through with blades drawn. To Romeo's great relief, they found nothing but empty hallways.

Beside him, Juliet kept her head low, like a fighter, and Romeo's heart swelled with pride. Gone was his frail, flowery Juliet, locked away behind her father's walls. Indeed, vile Capulet would have blamed his treasured daughter's sudden change on the influence of those outside his family, and perhaps it really was this place that had changed her. But Romeo had seen this fire in her from the very instant they'd met, though it had been only a small spark then. Set among the tinder of conflict, she was now ablaze.

"Is it true, what he said?" she whispered, though Romeo had no doubt Hamlet had heard her. The hall was wide and echoing. "Did you really pull him through a corpseway against his will?"

Romeo bristled at the judgment in her voice. "He seemed to know more about the Afterjord than I did. He professed to speak with the dead. I didn't know what I would find here, so I thought it better to bring him with me."

"And you abandoned him in Sheol?"

"To save you!" he hissed, his patience fraying. Could she

not see that he'd had no choice? Rescuing her had been his only goal, and now she was free of her deathly chains. Could she not celebrate that?

"But in saving me, you've likely damned another," she said, her large, dark eyes filled with hurt in the torchlight. "Romeo, my beloved...we cannot keep hurting people to defend our love."

Ahead of them, Hamlet took a crude torch from the wall and held it up to examine a tapestry. Romeo caught the flash of an embroidered berserker, shocking orange hair flying as he devoured a screaming body. The prince quickly moved the torch away. "It appears this place is a castle, that's all. Though not one I'd like to live in."

"If it's a castle, there are bound to be servants. More of those things must live here, as well." Romeo ducked beneath the ragged edge of a torn curtain. He was happy to abandon his conversation with Juliet, would be happier still if he never again saw such disappointment in her eyes reflected back at him. "Did you see how they scattered when the berserker came at us?"

"Yes, and now he's not here, and we are," Hamlet murmured, stopping again to pause in front of a tapestry. This one was decidedly normal, depicting a square courtyard with a fountain and toga-draped maidens.

"Then perhaps we shouldn't be here when they return and find him gone," Juliet suggested.

Hamlet paused before a door and reached into his doublet.

"It's locked," Romeo observed as he took hold of the handle.

His perpetual scowl deepening, Hamlet produced a thin, surprisingly rigid feather. He pushed the pointed shaft into the lock, turned it this way and that, muttering.

Romeo put his hand on the prince's wrist to stop him. "Where did you get that?"

"It was on the necklace of bones around the berserker's throat," he replied, as though it were the most obvious answer in the world. "I thought it might be useful."

"Why did you think that?" Romeo looked doubtfully at the feather.

"Because it was on the berserker's necklace," Hamlet repeated unhelpfully. With a sigh, he continued, "Look, he kept it with all those bones and ears and things rotting around his neck. That means it was a prize of some kind. When I held it up to the corpseway, it changed."

"Let me see." Juliet held out her hand, and Hamlet grudgingly dropped the feather into her palm.

"Be careful with that, we don't know—" Hamlet warned, but the moment it touched Juliet's hand, the bone seemingly melted away to become a life-like feather once more.

"So, we know it's not just a key, then, not a simple carving." Juliet held it by the quill and turned it this way and that as she inspected it. "And it's clearly affected by things that belong in the Afterjord."

Romeo flinched at that. Juliet didn't belong in the Afterjord any more than himself or the prince.

"That makes no sense." Hamlet took the feather back. At once it stiffened, returning to the sharp bone carving it had been. "I have a gift! I can see the dead, I can hear their voices and traverse corpseways—"

"I can do all that," Juliet reminded him. "Plus, I'm actually dead, so…maybe I outrank you?"

Something in Juliet's voice bothered Romeo. There was a smirk to her tone that was too comfortable with the prince. She spoke the way she had spoken to Romeo that night at her father's party.

"His highness doesn't like that," Romeo said, trying to joke with them, but it came out tinged with bitterness that shamed him.

"Romeo…" Juliet began, weary disappointment in her tone.

"It's all right." Hamlet's smile was tight as he took the key and tucked it away in his doublet. "We can't stand around here. Wherever those hollow souls are, we don't want to run into them again."

Hamlet held his torch out and took a step across the corridor. The flame displayed a tapestry of two men roasting on a spit while the slavering hollow souls surrounded the glowing coals.

"Point made." Romeo considered the door. "So, how do we get in?"

"I don't know, the key doesn't work," Hamlet slapped his palm flat against the wood.

"What if we tried…" Juliet reached out daintily, took

hold of the handle, and pulled. The door creaked open. She looked from Romeo to Hamlet and back again. "Didn't you think to try that?"

Hamlet muttered sheepishly, "I thought since there was a keyhole, it would be locked."

"Before we go through," Romeo began cautiously, "How do we know this isn't a trap? That the tapestries aren't misleading us?"

"Would you prefer we stay here?" Hamlet asked, indicating the roasting men embroidered into the cloth.

"Right." How was it that Romeo was consistently finding himself the fool in their situation? Everything he said seemed to come out wrong. Every word from his mouth sounded contemptuous or worse, stupid.

If there was one emotion Romeo could not stand, it was jealousy. He'd rarely suffered from envy over a woman before he'd met Juliet. If the girl who'd caught his fancy did not return his favor, he would wander, melancholy, for a bit, but then move on to the next young lady with nary a thought to what happened to the last one. It had been the same the night he'd met Juliet; only hours before, he'd been pining miserably for Rosaline. It had taken only some strong drink and a merry party to put her from his mind.

Then he'd met Juliet. Who'd changed everything.

Perhaps Juliet had cured him, for the moment he'd seen her, he'd known he would never love another. And he'd known it with a certainty that had made all his past "loves" seem silly.

His disinclination toward jealousy had changed the night he'd seen Paris guarding Juliet's tomb. Her odious fiancé had been standing outside, keeping vigil seemingly out of grief. More likely he had been placed there by Capulet, as a lookout should Romeo venture into the city walls.

The thought of that man mourning her, when he'd never had any claim over her, had created a beast in Romeo, a murdering one, at that.

To feel even a fraction of that anger now would not help him. It would not be fair to Hamlet. He had certainly not come to the Afterjord to seduce Juliet away. He hadn't wanted to come in the first place. It had been Romeo who'd done this to him; to make an enemy of him would be the final insult. But the prince was, well, a prince. He was intelligent and level-headed, and as handsome as Romeo had been before the poison had marked him. He couldn't believe Juliet had not noticed these differences as well, no matter how he wished to convince himself that his jealousy was unwarranted.

"Romeo?" Juliet stood with a hand on the door, looking at him with a strange expression, as though she could read his dark thoughts.

Guiltily, he said, "Let's go. Open it."

She pushed on the door, and warm light spilled through, growing brighter.

"Can't be any worse than the last place, right?" Hamlet offered as encouragement.

Romeo took Juliet's hand, and together they stepped into the light.

CHAPTER ELEVEN

The warm, calm feeling of peace that enveloped Juliet the moment she crossed the threshold brought tears to her eyes. It was exactly the way she'd imagined mortal life would end, though she'd accepted, with her lifeblood flowing from her and onto Romeo's unmoving form, that the loving embrace of paradise would not be hers.

This was what it should have been like, she reasoned. No fear. No agony or doubt. The welcoming arms of eternal peace, instead of the blank, emotionless void she'd woken to.

"What is this place?" Romeo asked behind her. His suspicion was an affront; how could he not see what a perfect place they had entered?

The sun shone down from a blue sky, and though cheerful white clouds drifted above, they never cast a cold shadow upon the ground. The grass beneath Juliet's feet was the greenest she'd ever laid eyes upon, and it lay in a long, rectangular field surrounded on all sides by a stately colonnade. Souls draped in softly colored fabrics moved from the shade of the columns to a large central fountain. The water sparkled pure gold, and just the sight of it made Juliet's mouth water.

"I'm so thirsty," she murmured, shaking free of Romeo's grip on her hand. A few of the pastel-clad souls looked up, their faces serene and radiant, the way Juliet imagined angels must look.

"Hail friend, you are most welcome here," one of them, a woman with golden hair in ringlets piled atop her head, said as Juliet approached the fountain.

"What is this place?" Hamlet was behind Juliet, and his voice startled her. She had forgotten all about his presence. Everything felt so right in this place, not at all like the bleak emptiness of Sheol.

In fact, it felt so right to Juliet that Romeo and Hamlet seemed...wrong. She wanted them to leave, so she could experience this place on her own, as a soul in communion with the others. The glittering fountain beckoned. A few of the people lounging on the grass or strolling the colonnade held crystal goblets, and they sipped the golden liquid from them.

If the beautiful blond woman was disturbed by the presence of the two living men in her realm, she did not show it. She smiled kindly at Hamlet and told him, "You

have come to Elysia, traveler. Rest your weary heart here
and be healed."

"Elysia?" Hamlet sounded as though he didn't believe
the woman. "The plane reserved for mortal relations of the
gods?"

If Juliet had a corporeal face, it would have flamed with
embarrassment. To think that he would question someone
who spoke with such authority, a denizen of this holy place,
it was… well, it was arrogant and absurd. Hamlet may have
been a prince in Midgard, but here, in the Afterjord, he was
no better than anyone else.

"Becalm yourself," the golden-haired woman urged
Juliet with a knowing smile. "The secrets revealed to you in
death have yet to enlighten him. I can tell you're one of us."

"Mm?" Hamlet chewed his thumbnail. "Is that what you
tell everyone here? Drink the magic water, we know you're
one of us?"

"Excuse us," Juliet begged the woman. With another
panicked apology, Juliet grabbed Hamlet's sleeve and pulled
him aside.

"What are you doing?" he asked, sounding beyond
shocked. "Unhand me at once!"

"You…unhand yourself!" Juliet fumed. It was a
particularly cruel aspect of her personality that, should she
ever find herself angry enough to raise her voice, what came
out was usually nonsense. She forced herself to stay calm. Not
that anyone should be able to have a flare of temper in this
beautiful place. "You're being rude! Would you rather have

found ourselves among those horrible hollow souls again? Another berserker? Isn't this the much better alternative?"

"Do you really think there's nothing dangerous about a person you've only just met being exceedingly nice to you?" Hamlet arched one blond brow.

"No!" Juliet gestured toward Romeo, who had walked round to the other side of the huge fountain. A ring of beautiful, toga-draped girls had him surrounded, and their girlish titters were like the tinkling of bells. Juliet's mouth compressed in a tight line. "It was how I met him. I trusted him from the very start."

"You trusted him?" Hamlet grinned at her. "And now he's over there, with them…You don't feel the slightest bit of jealousy?"

"None at all," she declared. She would not let the haughty prince ruin this lovely place for her. "In fact, here."

She took out her dagger and, reaching up, very carefully cut one ringlet from her mussed tumble of fluffy black curls.

"Keep this safe, *your highness*," Juliet instructed, holding the lock of hair out to him between her thumb and forefinger. "In case we become separated, or you can't get me back to Midgard, give this to him. As a token of my ever undying love."

"Can we…" Hamlet took the hair and tucked it into a pouch hanging from his belt. "I mean, we can't really call it 'undying,' can we? You both died. A bit."

"He didn't die." She couldn't help another glance at Romeo, though now he was fairly invisible for the girls crowding around him. He hadn't died, and he seemed to be having a remarkably good time flirting with the girls beside the fountain. He laughed and smiled, looking for all the world like the Romeo she had fallen in love with, instead of the broken creature who'd sprung her from Sheol.

He looked so different. That was what still took her breath away. Escaping death had hardened something in his soul, and losing her had made him desperate. What kind of creature would he become if he lost her again?

How long had he waited to come for her, after he'd recovered? It couldn't have been an easy thing, to have found someone—a prince, no less—who could accompany him into the Afterjord. Had he waited for her the entire time? Or had there been others like the girls who surrounded him now? Pretty girls, who were not dead, who were pleasingly alive and who did not trouble him with the concerns of ghosts and supernatural woes?

Juliet's heart was so preoccupied with her sadness that she forgot for a moment why she'd scolded Hamlet. She sighed in resignation. "Please, just…be more polite. For my sake. I may have to stay here once you and he are finished traipsing about the place. I would rather be welcome here than eaten by something horrible elsewhere."

At least the prince looked properly chastened. She left him to return to Romeo. It seemed a bit silly to stake her claim when he had already proven his love by coming to the Afterjord to find her, but the women surrounding him touched his shoulder, his ear, stroked his cheek and played their fingers over his shorn head. That was not an insult Juliet would bear. Dead or not, she was still a Capulet. She still had honor.

But as she moved toward him, the woman with the golden hair glided smoothly into her path. "Is something troubling you, Juliet?"

"How did you know my name?" she asked with an uncertain smile.

"I know many things. I know that your heart is uneasy." The woman frowned as though she cared deeply for the troubles of the stranger before her. "Is he the one who has caused you pain?"

"I'm not in pain. I'm just..." Juliet paused to collect her thoughts. It had become more difficult to think, it seemed, ever since they had passed into this place. "I don't like the way they're behaving toward him. He is my husband, even though one of us is dead."

"The union of two mortal hearts isn't always as permanent as it may seem," the woman observed sadly. "But do not blame him. It isn't his fault. They're merely responding to the newness of him. Come, drink with me. It will cool your temper."

The woman took Juliet by the arm and steered her toward the fountain. Juliet threw a look over her shoulder at Hamlet, who watched, but did not follow. Instead, he walked along the colonnade, his gaze leaving Juliet for only a moment now and then. He didn't want to be seen spying, Juliet realized.

The woman sat on the marble lip of the fountain. With a flick of her wrist, a crystal goblet materialized from the air, and she scooped the golden liquid into it. "Here. This will soothe you. Drink up."

Juliet took the cup, but she did not drink. She'd had quite enough of drinking magic potions. "What is this?"

For the blink of an eye, the woman appeared annoyed, but then the expression was gone as quickly as it had appeared. "Ambrosia. The nectar of the gods. You will drink it and feel eternal peace."

"Now, take this vial, being then in bed, and this distilled liquor drink thou off…"

Friar Laurence's voice haunted her so keenly that her fingers tightened around the goblet, as though that fearful phial were still in her hand. The woman was still gazing up at her expectantly.

"I'm not really thirsty," Juliet said with a smile that likely looked as forced as it felt.

"Oh, but you are," the woman cooed, refusing to accept the goblet Juliet held out to her. "You need rest after your long journey. I can see your soul, Juliet. It is heavy with sorrow. Just a taste, and it could all be over."

"What do you mean?" Juliet viewed the contents of the glass as poison now, for such ambiguous wording must certainly hide nefarious intent. "It could be over? I'll drink this and I'll forget Romeo?"

"You want to stay here, among us, don't you?" The woman asked kindly. When she reached out and put a hand on Juliet's arm, Juliet felt nothing. There was no substance to this soul.

Juliet could not remember what it felt to be fully alive, but she remembered the chill of fear. Still, she nodded and whispered, "Of course I do."

"Then drink it." The smile frozen on the woman's face was chilling.

Juliet lifted the cup to her lips, then tilted it slowly. Just as the liquid should have touched her tongue, she dashed the goblet on the side of the fountain, scattering shards of crystal.

The souls in the field all gasped and turned as one at the sound of the shattering cup.

At once, Hamlet was at Juliet's side, gripping her arm and tugging her toward the arches of the colonnade. "We should leave. We should leave now."

"Where's Romeo?" Panic rose in Juliet's chest. If she'd needed to breath, she wouldn't have been able to.

The kindly souls were drifting toward them both, their unkind intentions plain. Their beautiful features exaggerated, slender brows becoming pointed horns, straight white teeth growing sharp behind smiles that resembled hungry leers.

"Have you ever read the classics, Juliet?" Hamlet asked, never taking his gaze away from the slowly advancing souls. "Anything Greek?"

She couldn't read, but she didn't need to tell him that. His question proved rhetorical as he continued. "There are creatures, sirens, who draw the unwitting sailors their deaths on the rocks. They look very beautiful. And their song drives mortals mad with lust."

Beneath the blond woman's toga, her dainty feet had become scaly tendrils that whipped the grass as they propelled her forward.

"You resisted this one," Hamlet went on, still grasping her wrist and pulling her back with him. "Because you aren't mortal anymore."

"Romeo!" Juliet shouted, scanning the place that had seemed like an oasis, but was now a horror. He was nowhere to be found.

"We can't stay here," Hamlet told her, grasping her hand and forcing it to clasp around his wrist. "Whatever they say, whatever they do, don't let me go with them!"

One by one, the creatures opened their mouths. First one, then another, began to sing, a mournful, wordless cry, beautiful and sad and strange all at once.

Just as Hamlet had warned, he became affected by the song, swaying on his feet. Juliet tightened her hold and pulled him between two columns. She didn't know where she was going, but away from the sirens would serve.

"What are you doing?" Hamlet shouted. "Let me go!"

"We need to find Romeo!" she insisted, picking up speed as they rushed down the colonnade. The sirens pursued, drifting behind them leisurely, their reptilian tails lashing the stone.

At the end of the colonnade, a beautiful countryside awaited them. Could the sirens pursue them there? How long could she force Hamlet to hold out against them?

Whatever they called it, the Afterjord was certainly hell. For no paradise could ever be so cruel and frightening.

They reached the end of the colonnade. Long grass swayed on the hillside leading down to a grove of olive trees. With one last look over her shoulder, Juliet pushed the prince down, watched him tumble head over heels down the slope.

"Romeo!" she called desperately, but he did not come, and the sirens drew ever closer.

They had already taken him, she realized, her stomach knotting in sickness and despair. She could not have lost him, not again. The same desperate feeling that had come over her when she'd heard of his banishment from Verona's walls coursed through her soul now. She loved him, perhaps more than she had realized when her reckless affection had led to reckless actions and sealed her fate for all eternity.

She had made a choice not to leave Romeo that night, in that tomb, but she'd unwittingly left him behind. Now she had to choose to leave him behind, or risk being separated from him forever.

He had come into the Afterjord to find her. She could choose to be brave for him.

With a last, fleeting glance about her, she jumped.

• • •

One moment, Romeo had been standing beneath a clear blue sky, surrounded by beautiful women who'd seemed keenly interested in him, despite his numerous protestations. Then came a shattering echo, and the sky turned black. Purple lighting streaked the boiling gray clouds.

"Juliet!" he called, but when he looked past the women, he saw the rest of the courtyard was empty, the stone columns crumbling.

"Where is she?" he demanded of the women, whose fingers still tugged at his doublet and raked over his hair. Their touches were not so gentle and cloying now, but possessive and painful; their fingers seemed bony and sharp when they had not only a moment ago.

Their faces, too, had taken on a pinched severity, as though they were starving. He pushed one of them, then another, but still they came at him, slashing now with their claws, barring their teeth and hissing.

He drew his sword, and that forced them back. "Where is Juliet?"

"Gone from you, mortal man," a lady in pink spat contemptuously. "Are you fool enough to reject us?"

"I would be a fool not to." A ghostly white hand, covered in scales, reached out for him, and he lopped it off without hesitation. The woman—the creature—it had belonged to recoiled in agony, shrieking in some foul language. The hand itself rose up on its fingers and skittered away, a bleeding, five-legged beast.

"What are you?" he demanded, bringing the point of his

sword to the pink lady's chest. The others fell back at that, and he was emboldened. "If any of you touches me, I'll kill her."

She must have been the leader, then, for the rest of them slunk back a step or two. Looking closer now, Romeo saw that beneath their togas, their bodies were painfully thin, their skin a mass of serpentine scales. In place of legs, snake-like tails pushed them along the dusty dry ground.

The grass, the sky, the peace, had all been an illusion. They'd been tricked again.

The pink lady raised her head, and a long, forked black tongue flitted from her mouth as she spoke. "They teach nothing to young men of adventure these days. You were bound to encounter us at sea. Salt water brine seasons your kind so nicely…"

"Shut up!" Every instinct in him recoiled from these disgusting creatures, and he knew he should run. But he couldn't run, not without Juliet. "Where is Juliet? What have you done with her?"

"The same we'll do to you, dear one," the woman in pink promised. Her eyes glowed golden, black slits for the pupils. "Sisters, you may feast!"

The snake women fell on him, but Romeo had never been in a fair fight in his life. He kicked one away, shoved another as he speared a third with his blade. The metal slashed up and up before he could free it from the demon's body, green blood spraying him.

He could fight, but not forever, and there were so many of

them. With his sword, he cleared a path, severed arms, hands, heads falling as he charged toward the broken colonnade and the hard-packed clay slope beyond it. When he reached the edge, he had but a heartbeat to make his decision. He sheathed his sword quickly and jumped, rolling down, his body beaten by the hard ground.

Though his head swam, he bolted to his feet, ready to dispatch any of the creatures who had followed him. But they were gone, the hillside, too. Romeo found himself in a strange, barren wasteland.

He was alone.

Of course he was alone. He deserved to be. He'd forgotten about Juliet the moment a few pretty girls had surrounded him. Surely that had been a trick of the Afterjord, but why had he not resisted harder? Why had he accepted their attentions? Had his temporary jealousy of Hamlet left him witless?

Because of his foolishness, Juliet and Hamlet were both gone. Romeo had no one to blame but himself.

CHAPTER TWELVE

Above Romeo's head, dead olive trees reached their tangled branches to the black sky. Thunder rolled, purple lightning flashed.

His chest ached; his mouth was dry. He dropped to his knees, panting, dizzy from his fall. He wished he had taken the cup the sirens had offered him; he might not have been so thirsty now.

Was Juliet still trapped with them? He forced himself to his feet once more. He looked toward the place where the ruin had been, but nothing remained. Nothing but barren, seemingly endless dusty gray spread toward the black horizon. The scent of olives was gone from the air, replaced by brimstone and ash, and the strange, airy smell of lightning.

Juliet was gone. Hamlet was gone. Separated in the

undefined, ever-changing Afterjord, Romeo despaired of ever finding them again. They were lost, or he was lost, and now there seemed nothing left to him but to walk.

He set off from the trees and had gone but a few steps when he heard his name, faintly, from the grove behind him. He turned, a hand on the hilt of his sword.

"Romeo…" it came again, a voice maddeningly familiar. Was it Hamlet? Romeo supposed it could have been, but everything they'd encountered in this nightmare world had been some trap or another.

"Hamlet?" He called out, taking a cautious step toward the trees. "Juliet, are you in there?"

The branches seemed darker than they had been before, like menacing black thorns hungry to catch his clothes, his hair, his flesh. He drew his sword and hacked at one, lamenting the damage it would certainly do his blade. But the moment it made contact, the branch disintegrated into ashes and embers. They were burnt, every last tree, standing frozen in death.

"That's a comfort, isn't it?" he muttered to himself, then called again, "Hamlet?"

The voice replied again, just Romeo's name, and he held his sword at the ready as he navigated down the row of burned trees. He thought he saw a flash of red in the gaps of the trees, but when he turned his head to track it, the color was gone. Again, the mysterious voice called his name.

"Show yourself, demon!" he shouted. "I have seen too much already to fear mine own name!"

"Romeo."

The voice came from behind him this time, and he whirled to face his tormentor. What he saw made his blood run cold as ice, cold as the saltwater wind that had blown about the sirens.

Tybalt stood before him, hale and healthy as the day he'd died. His doublet and breeches were red, like the blood that had spilled from him when Romeo had avenged Mercutio's death.

"You're dead," Romeo said. The fear that gripped his throat almost cut off his denial. "I killed you myself."

"I remember." Tybalt's dark eyes were frozen with hate. Romeo saw the reflection of purple lightning in them.

"You're not real." Though Romeo believed it to his bones, he still took a step back as Tybalt came forward. So many things in this place had been unreal, he could not accept that this was truly Tybalt. But the man had a sword strapped to his belt, a glittering gold version of the simple, efficient weapon he'd used to dispatch Mercutio and so many other friends Romeo had lost. Too many, for his young years.

"You killed me, Romeo," Tybalt said, pushing back the hood of the short cloak he wore. "You took me from my family, my sweet cousin. You harmed her with my death. No wonder she cannot love you."

"I gave up my life for her." Romeo couldn't stop himself arguing with the phantom before him.

"You tried, and you failed. You could no sooner end yourself than you could protect Mercutio." Tybalt drew his blade and slashed at the air.

Romeo hated that he flinched. If any of his fellows in Verona had accused him of fearing this Capulet scum, he would have demanded satisfaction. The Prince of Cats was nothing but a kitten, he would scoff to them, but he'd often feared that tensions between their families would eventually force a serious confrontation. Romeo had seen Tybalt duel before, knew he was skilled and brutal. The night Romeo had slain him, it hadn't been luck or skill that had allowed Romeo to gain the upper hand, but rage. Pure rage at the death of his best friend.

He had rage in him again.

"I don't know who you are," Romeo began, dropping his hand from his blade. "But you have made a grievous error."

Tybalt stopped in his slow, stalking pursuit.

"You took the one thing from me that made me want to go on living." Romeo held up his hands. "There is nothing else for me to lose. I don't care if you slay me."

Tybalt threw his head back and laughed. "I never took her from you. You ruined everything on your own. You killed your wife's kinsman. You left the city without her. She drank the potion because you abandoned her."

"I am not solely responsible for the foul deeds that took place in Verona," Romeo said calmly. "There was more at work than simple murder."

"If your conscience is so clear, you will kill me again." Tybalt took another step, his blade at the ready.

"I won't. You aren't Tybalt. You're some shade sent to

torment me, to test me for your own sick amusement. I won't be tested. I refuse. The game is over. You have won, now take your revenge if you must. For if I cannot be with Juliet, if I am condemned to walk this bleak and horrible place alone for eternity, I would rather you slay me and send me to Sheol, where I can sleep without dreaming or remembering her face."

Tybalt roared, raised his sword, and rushed at Romeo.

He didn't know what would happen to him if the false Tybalt killed him. He would likely die, and find himself in some other hellish part of the Afterjord. But he held out hope, slim though it was, that it could be different. That he might wake in a true paradise, free from the pain and fatigue of his long journey on earth and the long journey that followed.

The blow never came. As the point of Tybalt's sword touched Romeo's doublet, the vision crumbled. In the space the false Tybalt had stood in, three wrinkled and weathered faces peered at Romeo.

It took him a moment to discern that they were three different old women standing close together, and not one terrifying shapeless blob with three heads. That he had guessed the latter first seemed only natural, after all he had seen.

"You wouldn't fight," the crone in the middle snapped, her sour expression folding her toothless mouth comically inward.

"I knew it wasn't Tybalt." Romeo could not help but

imagine their faces as rotting fruit. On the left, a long, unfortunate grape withered by the sun. To the right, a mushy plum. In the center, a decaying apple with wormholes for eyes and speckles from orchard parasites.

It was that one who raised her hand and pointed accusingly at him now. "Would happier not it make Romeo to see cruel Tybalt again laid low?"

"It would have made me dead. I am not the man who killed Tybalt. Not anymore." He looked them over calmly. "Your manner of speaking is strange."

"Stranger than thy manner and dress?" the one resembling a raisin snapped.

"Respect the sisters of the Wyrd, thou foolish mortal," plum face added. "For thou knowest us beyond thy recognition of our countenance."

"If I had met three terrifying crones before, I would surely have remembered, regardless of what disguises you might have worn." He cocked his head. "How do I know you're not just a vision, like Tybalt was, sent here to terrify me?"

"The fearsome power spun into our thread sews together souls both living and dead." the middle one warned. "From no vision born of earthly doubt could spring so true a hold upon man's mortality."

One of them held up a skein of rather plain looking thread, and turned it this way and that before her.

"What are you going to do, sew me to death?" He shook his head. "I have seen far too much in the last few hours to fear a spool of thread."

"I told you he'd be too ignorant to think in verse. Don't waste them on him," plum-face harrumphed.

"This is the thread of mortal life, the thread of the universe. All that is and ever will be," the raisin said, in a voice dry as old bones on the floor of a tomb.

"You're the Fortunes, then?" That piqued Romeo's interest. "You can see what will happen? Undo what has already taken place?"

"No one can change the past," the one the in the center said. "My sisters and I are in charge of maintaining the balance of the universe. Not destroying it."

"Who are you?"

"Veroandi," snapped raisin face.

"Skuld," replied the plum.

In the center, the middle one drew herself up. Her saggy face was full of mean pride. "Wyrd. We are the Norns, boy. We hold your fate in our hands. So you'd better start treating us with some respect."

. . .

Juliet woke beneath a black sky.

No, not a sky. A ceiling.

She sat up, wincing at a pain in her head. *Pain.* She half-laughed, reaching cautiously to touch. She hadn't felt pain in such a long time, she'd almost missed it.

Beneath her fingers, her hair was brushed and bound up,

sleek against her skull. Ringlets cascaded down her back. She looked at her gown, and her arm dropped to her lap. Her eyes followed the long sleeve of black velvet, from its wide, pointed wrist to where it narrowed into a sheath of fabric tight around her elbow.

Raising her gaze, she saw her reflection, a beautiful, young woman sitting in a pool of black velvet. She got to her feet, took a few staggering steps. The dress was accented with white, and she matched the chessboard floor beneath the slippers on her feet.

The walls all around were mirrored. Juliet turned in a slow circle, taking in the room around her. When she caught a glimpse of blond hair in one of the mirrors, she gasped. Dressed in black and white as well, Hamlet blended into the floor. She was grateful she hadn't trod upon him.

Careful of the slippery marble beneath her delicate heels, she went quickly to his side. She sank down beside him in a rustle of velvet, leaned over and slapped his cheek. "Wake up. Wake up, your highness!"

She wondered if slapping him would rouse him. Probably not, so it wasn't worth the attempt. Romeo might have taken some pleasure out of it, though.

The prince's eyes slowly opened—thank goodness!— and he blinked as he took in his surroundings.

"Where are we?" He raised an arm to examine the white and black doublet he inexplicably wore. "Who changed our clothes?"

"The last thing I remember, I was rolling down a hill,

hoping you hadn't been killed in the fall." She shook her head. "What was wrong with you? We needed to find Romeo. But I couldn't stop you from volunteering to get eaten!"

"You're welcome." When she only stared at him in disbelief, his eyes widened. "What? You're never going to get the chance to push royalty down a hill again. You're just some noblewoman. Do you people even have princes in Italy?"

"We do. The prince of Verona banished Romeo, and that's how we got into this mess." She got to her feet, suddenly not feeling very nurturing. "You knew the sirens would use their influence on you. You warned me. So why couldn't you resist, just for a moment?"

"I tried," he argued. "I wanted to help you look for Romeo, but the draw of the sirens' power was too great. You can resist it, you're not mortal. Perhaps if you'd drunk from their cup, you would have been just as powerless as I was. But you were smarter than that. Smarter than Romeo, clearly."

Juliet shook her head, hating the tears that rose to her eyes. She'd spent the last days of her mortal life weeping and powerless, and she did not wish to be in such a state ever again.

"We'll find him," Hamlet said quietly, looking up at her from his place on the floor. The effect of the alternating tiles behind his form made her dizzy, and she swayed on her feet.

She wouldn't let him see her weak. She was through with weakness. "I know I will. Death couldn't keep us apart. I doubt this place can."

"Wherever this place might be." Hamlet rose and took a few cautious steps. Juliet noticed a distinct pattern to where his feet landed; at first, only on the white blocks, then, timidly, on the black.

"What are you doing?" She raised an eyebrow at him.

"Checking for traps." He shrugged. "The Afterjord hasn't been particularly friendly so far, has it? Even the most benign settings have proved to be full of monsters. It's only fair to assume the same is true of this place, even if it is entirely empty."

"I've walked on the floor. It's fine." She did consider his reasoning though. By all accounts, it really could be a terrible place waiting to trap them. They seemed fairly trapped as it was, since there weren't any doors. But the hall stretched on, out of sight, with seemingly no sign of changing or ending. "What if we go that way?"

Hamlet looked in the direction she pointed. "Why that way?"

"Because it's as good as the other." She folded her arms over her chest. "Look at us. The Afterjord took great pains to fit us in here. We've been transported, costumed, and deposited. I doubt whatever force did this to us did it because we were meant to sit quietly and wait for something else to happen."

Grim admiration showed in Hamlet's expression, though he quickly dismissed it. "Fine. I would suggest one of us travel in one direction, et cetera, but I think it would be unwise to separate our group further."

As they walked, Juliet scanned the walls, looking for some means of egress. The mirrors reflected them on both sides, copies of Juliet and Hamlet going on and on, into eternity, until she grew dizzier with every step. "I'll go mad in here."

"Why?" Hamlet examined the ceiling as they went along.

"The mirrors. I've never liked them; they make me nervous." As a child, she'd been so frightened of the polished silver mirror in her room that she'd begged her nurse to cover it with a cloth at night. These were worse, their reflections supernaturally flawless compared with the murky images in the silver one at home. She felt as though Juliet in the mirror could reach out and grab her.

"Someone who looks like you should have no fear of mirrors," Hamlet said, but it wasn't a compliment. It was a simple statement of fact, and Juliet wasn't sure if she should take pride or offense at that. "Besides, I've always found mirrors a comfort. Father had a terribly expensive one in his chambers, angled so he could see the door from anywhere in the room. 'If you can't have eyes in the back of your head, a mirror is the next best thing,' he'd always tell me."

"And you found this a comfort?" She couldn't imagine a life of constantly looking over her shoulder, waiting for someone to kill her. As a child, she'd so envied the daughter of Verona's prince, the fine gowns she wore and the servants trailing after her. She'd attended mass in a sedan chair carried by four young men, and she'd knelt on a satin cushion while everyone else suffered on the stone floor.

But if, in trade, one had to constantly guard against assassins, perhaps it was better to be the daughter of a decidedly minor noble. No one had ever tried to murder her but her.

"There's a comfort in security," Hamlet mused. "For example here. You might look about this place, with no doors or windows, and say that we are trapped. Or you might look about and think to yourself, 'ah, there are no windows or doors. So nothing can get in, except me.'"

It was a good theory, but for one foolish part of it. "You're assuming that the Afterjord plays by the rules of the real world—"

"Midgard," he corrected her.

She rolled her eyes. "You're assuming that things here are as they are in Midgard. But we already know that they aren't. We don't know if we're alone. There could be all sorts of things in here with us that we just haven't seen yet. For all we know, the floor could melt and become a throng of hungry ghosts with knives for eyes."

"That's horrible," Hamlet said with a grin, finally giving her the courtesy of looking at her while he spoke to her. "You're getting the hang of this quite well."

The floor did not turn to hungry ghosts, but after a while of walking in strained silence with a person she had absolutely nothing in common with and no clue what to talk about, Juliet hoped that it might. They walked for what had seemed like hours, with the prince attempting uncomfortable small talk all the while. He asked about the weather in Italy, the food, whether or not Italians bathed.

She had just snapped, "Of course we do!" when a movement ahead broke the pattern of the floor. She gasped.

It was Romeo.

Ignoring Hamlet's warning, she raced ahead. "There you are! I knew we would find you. Or you would find us."

His arms surrounded her in a familiar embrace, and she held onto him tight. Being separated from him seemed to hurt more now that he was back. The uncertainty was over, the answer to a much larger question decided. She did want to be with him. She *was* glad he'd woken her from her slumber in Sheol.

She loved him. In his arms, she could remember her mortal life; she could remember what it was to *be* alive. It was where she belonged.

"Juliet," Hamlet said, low and cautious. "Step away from him."

No! This couldn't be a trick. Not when it felt so real. It couldn't be.

"Juliet, please," Hamlet urged softly. "Look around you."

Reluctantly, Juliet raised her head. In the mirrors around them, she did not see herself. She saw only Romeo, standing exactly as he was before her now. But the reflections turned as one and came to stand so close to the mirrors that they seemed to touch them.

Then they did touch them, their fingertips pushing through the glass as though it were quicksilver. As Juliet backed up from the Romeo before her, the other Romeos escaped their prisons.

Surrounded on all sides, Juliet couldn't breathe. It was all her childhood nightmares coming true, people climbing out of the mirror to attack her. But now, the nightmare creature was her only love, and he pulled a dagger from his belt.

"Juliet, come away," Hamlet urged her.

She couldn't move, and Romeo came toward her, the knife in his outstretched hand. Juliet saw the flash of the blade, remembered the bite of the steel in the tomb, and screamed.

CHAPTER THIRTEEN

"Stay back!" Hamlet put himself between Juliet and the first Romeo.

Shame burned hot in Juliet's cheeks. She'd wanted so badly to believe they had found Romeo, she'd ignored the danger that now seemed obvious. Of course he wasn't what he appeared to be.

"Enough!" She shouted, pushing past Hamlet again. "I'm tired of this place. Everything and everyone is a monster hiding behind some more pleasing countenance! I understand that now. You've made your point quite clear."

Her gaze dropped to the dagger in Romeo's hand. Intricately carved from blackest obsidian, its thin blade looked sharp enough to kill her quickly. Not like last time.

"You've had worse," Romeo said with a twist of his lips.

He held the dagger out to her handle-first. "I would never kill you. Obviously, this is a trick of the Afterjord. As is our supposed friend here."

Her chest loosened a bit, and she was about to take a relieved breath when another of the Romeos shouted, "It is a trick, but he's the one playing you false! It's me, Juliet. Don't trust him."

"So, the trick is to tell which of you is my Romeo, and which of you is just an apparition pretending to be Romeo?" She hefted the knife in her palm. "Is that the game? Is this the prize?"

"They're both lying," another insisted, his jaw set hard, dark eyes glittering with anger. "You know they're false."

Two others began shoving each other, shouting, and soon, all around them, the Romeos battled each other, punching, shoving, denying that they were the pretenders.

"I don't think any of them are pretending," Hamlet called to her over the chaos. "Each seem to really believe that they're him."

The sound of steel being drawn rippled all around her, blade after blade being unsheathed, and Juliet held her hands up. "Put away your weapons at once!"

They did as she commanded, looking hurt and suspicious as they did.

She addressed the first Romeo. "What is the trick, then?"

Hamlet put his hand on her arm. Juliet saw annoyance on all the faces around her. It was so absurd, she almost laughed.

"This reminds me of a tale my mother told me when I was a child. A test of courage." Hamlet took a deep breath. "A wood cutter banished his two children to the forest at the request of his evil new wife. But she was a witch, and she'd put him under a spell. When the wood cutter realized what he'd done, he went looking for his children in the forest, only to find they had been turned into trees. To free them, he had to cut down two trees of his choosing. But if he cut down the trees containing the souls of his children, they would die."

"What does a silly story like that matter?" the first Romeo asked impatiently. He sounded so like her Romeo that Juliet thought for certain it was him. "Juliet, you aren't really going to fall for this, are you? Like you did with the sirens?"

"It means she has to kill one of you," another Romeo suggested. Juliet did not see which.

"You mean, to end the spell, she has to kill one of us?" another Romeo asked.

"Juliet, be very careful," Hamlet warned her.

Each one of the Romeos gave her such earnest, sad looks. She stared back at them in despair. "I don't want to kill anyone."

"I don't think we'll ever leave until you do." Hamlet pointed at the one who'd given her the knife.

"What do you mean?" another asked. "That he's the false Romeo?"

"You might all be false," Juliet accused, pointing with the dagger at each of them. "Any of you."

"They are," another Romeo said. "Juliet, this is madness. Kill one of them, so we can escape."

"The others came through the mirrors," Juliet told Hamlet. "But they're still thinking and speaking on their own. Look at them, they're all clearly terrified."

"I am not terrified," another insisted.

"How many of them are there?" Hamlet turned around, his finger wagging as though he were counting them, but the hall was packed shoulder to shoulder with copy after copy of Romeo. It seemed impossible to count them all.

"There must be something I'm missing." Juliet pressed her fingertips to her temples, cautious with the dagger in her hand. "I can't kill anyone."

"Don't you see?" The first Romeo asked. "The Afterjord put you here with Hamlet, but he is not Hamlet. That is the test, Juliet. You know who you must kill."

"This is madness, he speaks the truth there," Hamlet agreed. "But I am no impostor."

"Don't listen to him, Juliet!" one Romeo shouted.

"I'm the real Romeo!" One cried out, and then another, "He's not me, I am!"

"Oh, all of you just shut up, for one moment!" Juliet shrieked, clutching at her hair.

One of them, perhaps it was the very first Romeo she'd encountered—she couldn't tell anymore—came forward, raising his hand to touch her face. He trailed the backs of his fingers down her cheek, brushing aside a tear.

"All you have to do is rid us of the imposter. Juliet, you

know me, and I know all you have been through," he said softly, as though they were the only two in the room. His touch calmed her like the warmth of the sun on her face. "I wish there were another way."

She looked into his eyes, those darkly glittering eyes that had seemed so full of dangerous promise the night he'd scaled the wall of her father's garden. She had no doubt that the others truly believed themselves to be Romeo. As she gazed up into Romeo's face, she thought, *what a fearful thing that must be, to be certain of your identity, and to be wrong.* Because this Romeo before her was real. He was different from the others. He was flesh and blood and bone.

Which made it shockingly difficult when she pushed the knife into his throat. She had imagined such soft flesh would easily yield, but beneath his skin lay a network of veins and sinews that resisted the knife. Though he grabbed her wrists, she pushed on, his blood spraying her lovely gown until she stood before him dressed not in black and white, but black and red.

He staggered backward and fell, gurgling red from his throat.

"He wasn't Romeo." She wiped her face with her sleeve as she stepped back to join Hamlet.

"How do you—how did you know?" Hamlet stood between the two of them, hands open helplessly at his sides as though he wanted to run to Romeo's aid, but doubted the impulse. "Juliet, were you certain? Tell me you were certain!"

The Romeo on the floor gave a last dying gurgle, and

they all faded away, like sand being blown about in a storm. Not one of them remained.

"Romeo would never have asked me to kill you. Not after the way he left you with the grave worm. I know him." There should have been no further explanation needed, but as she did not know if she would ever see him again, she added, "He knows how valuable you are. And he knows that he did you wrong. He is a good man. If you give him a chance, he will make it up to you, I know he will."

"Will he?" Hamlet's half-hearted scoff proved to Juliet that he was not so hardened against Romeo as he pretended to be.

She opened her mouth to tease him, but a sudden shift in the room caught all the sound before it could come out. Hamlet screamed a warning and leapt toward her, pushing her down and covering her body with his as all around them, the mirrors exploded in a rain of razor-sharp glass.

• • •

"So, you hold the fate of all mortals in your hands," Romeo began slowly. He wanted to make sure he really, truly understood what the mad witches had told him. "But you can't help me get back to Midgard, or help me find Juliet?"

"Juliet is dead, and the dead belong to this realm. We have no power over them," Wyrd answered, her toothless mouth working hard around the words.

"What about Hamlet? He's not dead. He's alive. You can

do something to help me find him, couldn't you?" The three were maddening. How could they possibly be all seeing and all powerful if they were so damned incompetent in their own realm? Unless the spiteful witches were lying to him, toying with him for their own perverse amusement.

Veroandi waved a hand. "We don't treat with seers, that's a fool's game."

"They always want to know about the future for their own gain," Skuld interrupted. "They want to know who is going to die, who is going to come into money. Because they want that money for themselves. *Pff.* Mortals and their money."

"What's a seer?" Romeo was perfectly capable of deducing that a seer "saw" something, but he didn't know it applied to Hamlet. "You mean because he can talk to the dead?"

"No mortal has ever talked to the dead and learned anything of value," Wyrd pronounced. "We won't bring him here, but he's coming."

"He is? Does he bring Juliet?"

"We can't see her!" Skuld snapped. "Get it through your ugly head."

I *have an ugly head?* He pushed the thought away. He didn't know what powers the Norn commanded. If they could read his mind, he didn't want them to find anything insulting there.

"What was the purpose of testing me with an apparition of Tybalt if you have no power here, you don't necessarily care what happens to me, and you don't have the power to help me get home?"

"We were bored," Veroandi said with a shrug of her hunched shoulders. "It's rare to find a mortal wandering here. Alive, anyway."

"The least you could do is tell me where I am." Greece after a wildfire was his nearest guess.

"This the Waste. A place where souls wander in eternal torment, their souls preyed upon by fire, but never purified. It is a realm of the damned." Wyrd opened her palms, and a terrible river of flame flowed between them. She doused the flames by slapping her palms together. "Once you enter, you may never leave. Unless…"

"Unless what?" Wandering in eternal torment had never been a part of Romeo's plan, though he supposed he should have at least considered the possibility. If there was a way to avoid it, however, he was keen to know it.

But instead of answering him, Wyrd looked to the sky and pronounced, "Ha. Right on time."

An unbelievable amount of glass rained all around Romeo, and he whipped the hood of his cloak up to protect his head. Still, shards slipped into his collar, glass dust stung his nostrils. The violent breaking noises ceased, he pulled back his hood and shouted, "You couldn't have warned me?"

Between him and the Norn, Hamlet and Juliet lay in a heap, Hamlet covering her body with his own. The back of his doublet was torn, and beneath the black velvet, his ripped shirt was spattered with blood.

Romeo ran to them, rolling Hamlet to his back. Every movement resulted in a sickening crunch of broken glass. Staring down into the prince's face, Romeo felt the most unexpected pang of sadness. If he'd been killed protecting Juliet, Romeo would never forgive himself. It should have been him trapped with her in whatever horrible hell dimension they been banished to, not Hamlet.

"No, no, no," he repeated to himself, gripping the front of his doublet. "You can't be dead. You saved her!"

To Romeo's great relief, Hamlet's lips began to move. "No. She saved me."

"I don't want to do that ever again. It was awful," Juliet groaned, sitting up beside him and carefully brushing broken glass from her hair.

"Juliet!" Romeo threw his arms around her, then remembered the glass, so he eased his hold. "I thought I would never find you. I thought you were…where did you get those clothes?"

Getting to her feet with some difficulty, Juliet explained, "We fell down the hill escaping the sirens, and we woke up like this. In the hall of mirrors." She frowned as she examined him. "You weren't there as well? We looked for you, but we never found you."

"You found him," Wyrd spoke up. Juliet gasped when she saw them, and Hamlet scrambled to his feet. "You saw him."

"I saw false impressions of him." Juliet's chin raised defiantly. She grasped Romeo's hand, lacing her fingers with his.

"You saw him," Wyrd continued mildly. There was an air of something like admiration in the way she spoke to Juliet. "You saw many facets of him, and you removed the one that did not belong."

"That's right!" Hamlet said triumphantly. "The woodcutter had to cut down the one tree in the forest that was not his child. That was how the story went. I remember now."

"Are you insane?" Juliet rounded on him, dropping Romeo's hand. "You used a story you only half-remembered to convince me to kill Romeo?"

Romeo startled. "What are you talking about?"

"It was a test," Juliet began, and though he listened to her every word, they became difficult to hear over the roar of his pulse. She'd killed him? At least, someone she thought could have been him. She'd done it so callously that she could have been at home with Romeo's gang of fellows.

How could she have risked such a thing, when she knew all he'd been through to find her?

"Might I remind both of you, in the hopes of stemming what I fear is an inevitable tide of outrage, that I've never once put my life at stake, but he—" Hamlet pointed to Romeo. "—has done so twice already today? Perhaps endangering Romeo's life just this once makes us even?"

"Enough!" Wyrd shouted, and all three of them turned to face the wizened crones before them. "If you are to have any hope of escaping the Afterjord, you will listen and heed us."

"I thought you didn't know how we could escape. That's what you told me," Romeo accused.

"We knew, we just didn't want to explain it three times," Skuld said with a shrug.

"But how did you know they were going to find me here?" Romeo pressed. He didn't trust witches. Not that the only one he'd ever met, the one in Verona, had given him reason not to trust. She'd sent him exactly where he'd needed to go to find Juliet. But he didn't appreciate anyone who traded in riddles and obfuscation.

"We knew you would find them again, and that you would leave Midgard," Veroandi said. "We can see what will happen to you. It's them we're not concerned with."

"We can hear you," Juliet snapped.

"Tell them, sister," Skuld urged. "About the keys."

"Keys? Like this one?" Hamlet pulled the white feather from his doublet.

"Ooh, well if you have it all sorted, maybe you can tell *us* about them," Skuld scolded.

"Hush!" Wyrd opened her hands, revealing a pale, whirling light. It danced above her palm, until it took the shape of a small, sylph-like body with tall wings.

When Wyrd spoke again, her sisters joined her in a terrifying unison. "In the time before the false king, before the gods of men were formed and fashioned, the guardians of human souls were great in number and vast in power."

Juliet moved closer to Romeo's side as the light split once, twice, again and again, until a legion of the winged bodies filled the air between them and the witches.

"As the greed and hatred of mankind grew, so did the sorrow of the guardians. One by one they withered, and their ethereal bodies fell."

The light darkened into black wisps of smoke.

"Shades," Hamlet breathed.

Indeed, they looked exactly the same as the blackened ghosts that had chased them into Sheol.

The Norns continued, their voices growing louder. "From their discarded bodies, three keys were crafted, to open the gates between Midgard and Afterjord. One, for a fierce warrior—"

Hamlet held the key up and whistled. Juliet shushed him.

If the Norns cared about the interruption, Romeo could not tell. They went on, oblivious, "The second in the jaws of a ravening beast. The third, to those who decide in matters of life and death."

"That's you!" Romeo took a step forward, destroying the oddly hypnotic dance in the smoke between them. "You decide in matters of life and death."

Skuld sighed and rolled her eyes. "We should have continued in verse. He could barely understand that. He wouldn't have been able to interrupt."

"You told me you control fate. You decide. So you must have the third key." Romeo turned to Hamlet, who for the very first time looked as though he believed Romeo was not an utter fool.

Veroandi did not feel the same way, apparently. She

snapped, "We control mortal fate, that is true, but there are others who can intervene. Those who can restore the dead to life, who can raise mortal bones turned to ash and create a whole living form from them. Who can turn back time in the course of a single mortal life, who—"

"Yes, yes, the Valkyrie," Hamlet interrupted. "We've already met them. We came in that way."

"Through Valhalla?" Skuld asked, one eyebrow—that looked very much like a fluffy white caterpillar—hitching up over a milky blue eye. "And they didn't tear you to pieces?"

"Do we stand before you in pieces?" Romeo asked, and Hamlet held up a hand for silence.

Romeo burned with anger. Hamlet had urged Juliet to kill him. The fact that it was, fortunately, not him after all didn't make it more acceptable. Would Hamlet have rescued Juliet from the Afterjord, if Romeo had died? Or would he have left her here, alone and frightened, searching for him in Sheol?

"How do we find the other keys?" Juliet asked the Norns. "I assume you need all three to leave the Afterjord, or you wouldn't have told us about them."

"If you'd listened to the whole thing, maybe your questions would have been answered," Veroandi snapped.

Wyrd shook her head. "I don't think we've ever gotten to the end of it."

"Ever? There have been others?" Hamlet asked. "Others have walked here?"

"None have fared half so well as they would have if

they'd listened, rather than speaking," Skuld muttered.

"Others have sought the keys, and none have found them. For you to pass from this realm to the next, you must seek the three keys." Wyrd's shrewd eyes, which looked so clouded with cataracts as to be useless, fixed them each in turn with an acid gaze.

"So, the others...they're still here?" Hamlet begged. "Please, I have to know. Are there more people like me out there?"

"They no longer remain here, unless death has returned them," Veroandi intoned gravely.

"So there is a way out, without using the keys?" Juliet was so smart, at times Romeo felt very strange to think she was his wife. He'd never imagined he would marry a woman more intelligent than him. It wouldn't have been on his list of priorities in choosing a mate, but now he was very glad and a bit ashamed that he'd ever wanted a girl who couldn't think quickly and act rationally.

"There is a way out, but not for this one." Skuld raised her finger and pointed at Juliet. "For once a soul leaves its body to venture here, it cannot regain the mortal world."

Romeo's heart went still, as still as if the poison had finished its work after all.

"What?" Juliet's eyes went wide and filled with a shine of tears.

"You have no mortal shell to return to," Veroandi said, without pity, but also without scorn. She merely stated the fact, as much as Romeo did not wish to hear it.

He knew Juliet did not wish to hear it either. It seemed a confirmation of the fear she had expressed in Sheol, that she had woken from death into a nightmare she would not escape.

"There is some other way for her to escape then, surely?" he pleaded, but the crones' expressions did not offer him any comfort.

"I did warn you," Hamlet reminded Romeo quietly.

Still, he had not been with him for the entirety of his interaction with the Norns. He could not trust them to give a second way out. "If they want us to find the three keys, it's for a reason. They can see my fate, but not yours, and not Hamlet's."

"Why not mine?" Hamlet sounded alarmed.

"Because you're a seer," Romeo explained. "They're only interested in mortals, who abide by mortal rules. At least, that's what they said before."

"He's smarter than you give him credit for, your highness," Veroandi told Hamlet with a nasty sneer.

"So how do we find the location of these keys?" Juliet asked.

"We just told you their locations!" scolded Wyrd. "If you didn't listen, that's not our fault."

Skuld lifted her ancient head and sniffed the wind. "Two will call to their missing sister, but on their own they are powerless. Join them, and you will command the veil between worlds."

"But know this!" The three spoke as one again. "Many

have tried and many have failed. The guardians of the veil are fierce."

Romeo blinked, certain his eyes were fooling him, but the three women changed to wisps of smoke, each curl taking a shape. One a curvaceous female warrior holding a spear aloft. The other a snarling, snapping beast. The third, the raging berserker. When the visions had all but faded, the voices of the Norns drifted to them from far away. "They will show you no mercy."

Juliet's grip tightened on his hand. The guardians would show them no mercy? Nothing in the Afterjord had been particularly merciful so far. How much worse would their future trials be?

CHAPTER FOURTEEN

There were others like him. Hamlet's head practically swam with the thought. There were other poor bastards out there who were just like him, cursed to see and hear and speak with the dead. Some of them had been in the Afterjord and lived to tell the tale.

Romeo and Juliet walked beside him in silence. Between them, their conjoined hands swung merrily. It was all well and good that they'd found each other, really, but Hamlet was a bit more concerned with the news that he wasn't alone, in this world or the next. He'd often wondered if others like him existed, but he'd never sought them out. How did one begin such a conversation? The magicians who'd come to court to dazzle with their trickery were eager enough to have people believe them capable of commanding dark forces, but Hamlet knew that anyone cursed as he was would not advertise their affliction. Such exposure ran the risk of excommunication, accusations, and the flames. He'd given up on ever finding another soul like him. Now, he walked in their footsteps.

How odd that it had been Romeo, of all people, to have discovered such an astonishing fact for him.

Hamlet stared at his boots as they kicked up dust with each step. His kind had walked this way before, and they…

Well, at the moment it appeared they had all been reduced to piles of screaming skulls that littered the gray, baked clay ground.

But that wasn't the point. There were others, and when he returned to Midgard, he would seek them out and find them.

"So the keys will travel to each other, but only if just one is missing," Juliet repeated, holding their single key up and twisted it this way and that. "Is that what they meant?"

"It seems so," Hamlet answered, more interested in his thoughts of the travelers who'd gone before him.

I am not a prince. I am a seer. There is a word for what I am.

"What I don't understand," he thought aloud, though he knew one of the others would answer him, "is why they came to you. If I'm the seer, why did they come to you, who has done nothing of note?"

"I did travel the world in search of an egress to the realm of the dead and found it." Romeo reminded him. The sarcasm in the declaration was a strange comfort to Hamlet. "So you must recognize I have some merit, perhaps as much or more than you. All you've been able to do so far is speak to the dead, and only because you were born cursed. Juliet just died—"

"Excuse me!" Juliet stopped abruptly. "I didn't 'just' die. I faked my own death, then woke up in a tomb with my beloved's dead body, at which point I took the last shred of courage and sanity remaining to me and gutted myself on my bier. Maybe it's not traveling the world and making friends with princes, but I did do *something*."

"Yes, we're all very impressed at your suicide." Hamlet hoped he had not overstepped the bounds of good humor, yet a part of him wanted to have caused offense. It was unkind and childish to mock her death, and he saw it for the destruction it would cause. They needed to be united now more than ever, but a sick urge in him wanted to destroy any possibility of working together. He wanted to push to see how far they could go, though he despaired of the results. There was a strangely certain doubt in him, an entrenched belief that no matter how loyal a friend someone was, they would eventually see the broken, twisted parts of him, and their rejection was inevitable.

His words had changed the mood, no matter how he might have wanted it to be otherwise. Romeo's smile faded into something unsettling and stern. "You let her kill me, in the hall of mirrors you found yourself in. Why?"

"Because I saw through the illusion for the test it was."

Hamlet hoped he would understand. "It wasn't personal. I didn't want you to die. I wanted to find you again, or find out what had happened to you."

"He couldn't have known," Juliet said quietly. "You weren't there to see it."

"I must have been," Romeo said with a hollow laugh. "You killed me there."

"It wasn't you. It was a false you," she reminded him gently. "I thought it was the only way to pass the test."

"She didn't have an easy time of it." Hamlet wished Romeo could have seen Juliet's struggle. Though she'd tried to hide her terror, her hands had trembled as she'd held the dagger.

"I can't imagine that she did." Romeo's small, sad smile was unconvincing, but it was clear from his tone that they weren't meant to notice.

Hamlet considered what Ophelia's opinion might have been, if she'd known that he'd stood by passively while Juliet had drowned her. Perhaps he could understand Romeo's discomfort, no matter how illogical it was.

"Have the two of you noticed there are more skulls than before?" Juliet asked, a hint of nervousness in her voice. "I only mention it because any amount of disembodied head lying around gives me a bit of a fright."

Whatever discussion they'd been having dissolved in the face of what appeared around them. There *were* more skulls. Hamlet hadn't been paying enough attention, or he would have seen them. There were scads of them now, not just lying in heaps, but lining a very definite path across the waste.

A path that Hamlet realized they had begun to follow mindlessly.

"Are we going the same direction we were when we set out from the Norns?" he asked, giving one rotted bone sphere a nudge with the toe of his boot. "Or have we changed?"

"Do you think it's another trick?" Romeo asked, not so quick to hold a grudge as he was at the beginning of the journey. He was learning, then.

"It's the same, because look, those mountains in the distance." Juliet pointed ahead, to the hulking shape of the mountains belching sulfur and fire into the sky.

"I suppose that's meant to terrify us?" Hamlet said, to cover his fear. He had heard of such mountains, the fire in them. They existed off the coast of his father's kingdom, on tiny islands full of monsters, surrounded by sea serpents. They had been drawn on every map in the king's study.

"These must be the bones of those who tried to make the journey before and perished." Hamlet scooped up one skull, tilted it this way and that, holding it at arms' length to examine it.

"It would make sense," Romeo began solemnly. "If these were all mortals seeking to find the keys for their own gain, and they died crossing the waste, I suppose their bones would just rest here."

"But there aren't bones." Hamlet wasn't counting the numerous detached jaws lying about. "Only skulls. Which means someone or something took the rest of the bodies."

"That is almost too horrible." Juliet pressed her hand to her chest as though she might be sick.

"After all we've seen, this is what bothers you?" Hamlet dropped the skull to the hard packed ground. "But where are the ghosts. If these were seers—and mortals—they should be haunting the area where their remains are buried. It's one of the favorite pastimes of the dead."

"Unless some force is preventing them from returning," Romeo mused, crouching to inspect the other side of the path. "Maybe the skulls were chosen for their aesthetic."

"Nothing quite perks up a dull and barren waste like a few heads tossed about like decorative cushions." Hamlet dropped the skull and straightened, wiping his hands. For a moment, he thought he might have grown faint, for his body seemed to tremble all over. Then he saw the skulls jumping against the ground, and he realized that the very dirt beneath their feet moved. There was a distant roar, and Romeo predictably reached for his sword.

"Earthquake?" he asked.

A distant roar raised the hairs on the back of Hamlet's neck.

"A ravening beast," Juliet suggested, raising an eyebrow.

"She's right, let's move." Hamlet was glad he'd suggested it, for almost as soon as they'd sprinted in the direction of the monstrous bellow, the clay they'd stood upon cracked and separated, and steaming hot gas erupted from the fissure. He measured his pace; it would do them no good if he raced ahead of them, for if he was too far from them he couldn't help if one or both tumbled into one of the steaming cracks.

The fissures spread beneath their feet as they ran, putrid vapors filling the air all around them. They ran without direction, unable to change the course they had started upon until the ground opened before them in a wide arc. Boiling water sloshed in a river that surrounded them, cutting them off from escape.

"What in the seven circles of hell is that?" Romeo asked, and Hamlet was about to point out that Dante's interpretation of hell seemed rather lacking in the face of all they had already seen, but he never got the chance to speak.

Towering over them, stepping easily over the river, came a creature that was vaguely man-shaped, with square arms and legs and head. Made of roaring flame and dripping lava, the monster left great, scorched imprints in the clay where he walked.

"I think I preferred the Frost Giant to this one," Romeo said, putting himself before Hamlet and Juliet, arms outstretched as they slowly backed away.

"Mind the water!" Hamlet advised, looking over his shoulder.

Water. Good heavens, it was that easy. "Romeo! Hold him back if you can! I'll find something to carry the water!"

"If I can?" he called, outraged.

"He's a Fire Giant. What stops fire?" Hamlet snapped. "You hold him, we'll water him."

Juliet sprinted beside him to the edge of the river. "It's boiling."

"Try scooping it up with your hands," he told her, and when she balked, he rolled his eyes. "You're already dead. It might cause you a moment of pain, but it won't hurt you permanently."

She screwed up her face and plunged her hands in, and immediately jerked them out. Then, with a deep breath and determination, she scooped up two handfuls of the water. By the time she had turned to run, all of it had trickled from her hands and onto her gown.

The Fire Giant took a swipe at Romeo, knocking him back. A tendril of smoke rose from the scorched cloth the giant had grazed with his massive fist.

"Hurry!" Romeo called, scrabbling backward as a burning glob of magma splashed beside him.

The air grew unbearably hot, the choking stench of brimstone everywhere. They didn't have much time, Hamlet realized, his mind working feverishly. Soon, they would be cooked alive or strangled by the vapors.

When working over a particularly difficult mental puzzle, sometimes Hamlet saw clues, histories and solutions that he could not form in words. A flash of some long ago passage in a dusty book would spring to his mind with an answer, or the incidental words of a companion would float to the front of his brain. They came as a constant onslaught of repeated images that froze his body and seized his thoughts completely. Now he saw the skulls, the thousands of them stretching across the waste. He remembered the words of the Norns, and his own words only moments before. *You're already dead.*

"No!" he shouted to Juliet as she plunged her hands desperately into the boiling river. He grabbed her wrist, cursing at the splash of hot water that fell on his hand. "I need you. I need you to trust me!"

"What?" she stammered as he propelled her into the river. Her gown was heavy. It dragged her down.

He saw Ophelia.

He pushed Juliet under.

"What are you doing?" Romeo bellowed as he swung at the Fire Giant's descending arm with a wild swipe of his blade.

Hamlet paid him no mind, and cursed at the water that burned his hands as he hauled Juliet out. She was unburned, unharmed, but sputtering in mortal reflex, and dripping. Her hair and gown were completely sodden.

Hamlet steered her straight toward the giant. His fiery left foot descended as if to crush them, and Hamlet pulled Juliet out of the way just in time.

Then she understood, and she embraced the molten monster, shouting in surprise and pain. Steam hissed up from her clothing, and the giant bellowed.

"No!" Romeo ran at Hamlet, sword poised to cleave his head off. There was no time to explain. In Juliet's watery embrace, the giant's limb cooled to stone. Juliet staggered back and fell, steam rising from her limp body.

"Wait!" Hamlet shouted, drawing his own sword. "Look!"

He deflected Romeo's first swing easily. A man in the

grips of madness and mourning could not fight half so well against an opponent trained to be dispassionate and cunning in battle. Still, Romeo had killed before and Hamlet had not, and he remained cautiously aware of this as they circled each other.

"Why?" Romeo screamed, his face drawn in anguish. He slashed erratically with his blade, and Hamlet jerked back. The point of the blade narrowly missed his eyes.

Beside them, the Fire Giant roared in fury, both feet stuck to the ground, turning to stone all the way to its waist. It twisted, swiping at the air, a rain of brimstone falling around Hamlet and Romeo.

Romeo lunged, catching Hamlet's sleeve. "I trusted you!"

Pain exploded through Hamlet's arm. The blade had bit him, not deeply, but in a long gouge that mimicked the tear in his tunic. "Calm down! I didn't hurt her!"

"Romeo, please listen to him!"

Juliet's voice brought Romeo up short. He turned, disbelieving.

Her gown still smoldered, burned through in some places, but she was unharmed., Juliet staggered toward Romeo. "He couldn't kill me. I'm already dead."

Romeo's sword dropped to the scorched dirt, and he caught her up in his arms.

"My love, my wife," he murmured as he frantically kissed every inch of her face, her head held between his hands.

"It was the only way to stop it." Hamlet leaned over,

his hands braced on his thighs as he panted from exertion. "That's why the others failed. They were alone. This place…I can't escape it alone. I need you. Both of you."

Romeo stumbled and tried to lean on Juliet for support. She sagged beneath his weight, for withered though he was, Romeo was still taller and far broader than she. "Hamlet, help me hold him up!"

Ignoring the pain of his own wound, Hamlet hurried to them and slipped Romeo's arm over his shoulder. "Come on. He's fading. We need to find the other keys and get him back to Midgard."

"A fine trick that will be," a voice called in a peculiar squawk.

"Did you say that?" Juliet looked to Hamlet and Romeo. "Did one of you speak?"

"Maybe it was him," Hamlet suggested, looking up at the Fire Giant, who still raged impotently beside them.

A lump of magma had landed in the boiling river and turned to steaming rock. It was tricky work, but they managed to navigate it and cross to the other side, leaving the giant alone and howling.

"I need to rest," Romeo said, sounding embarrassed to admit it.

Hamlet scanned the horizon. A single, sickly black tree rose from the dead ground. "Let's take him there."

"Ooh, look at them, just lying down where ever they please." Another voice clucked disapprovingly. "It's not even their tree."

"Who is saying that?" If Juliet hadn't heard it as well, Hamlet would have thought he'd gone mad. He looked up, to the two giant black birds perched in the gnarled branches above them.

One of the ravens twisted its head and clucked in disapproval. "Who else could have said it? We're the only ones here."

• • •

"Excuse me, but did you just speak?" Juliet asked the bird, who tilted his head so far to one side it seemed it would fall off.

"As well as you can. Don't look so surprised." He nudged the raven beside him with one wing. "Did you hear the cheek of this one?"

"That's the trouble with humans, ain't it really?" The second raven clucked deep in his chest. "They're always on some quest for deeper understanding, without ever taking the first step of simply assuming other creatures could be on the same level as them. From a metaphysical, purely mental and logical sense, that is."

"I don't think you two could be considered the average raven," Hamlet observed. The only one of them, Juliet realized, who could handily ignore the fact that he was talking to a bird long enough to carry on a conversation.

"Ignore him." The raven with the missing eye pecked at his companion. "He gets carried away. Human beings excite him."

"Only because they're fascinating," the other raven put in. "It isn't as though I have some bizarre obsession with spoons or bits of string, is it? I'm interested in these creatures that can think and feel and empathize with each other on a very primal, animal level, and who have shut that bit off so they can indulge their depraved lusts for flesh, murder, and greed. It's brilliant!"

"Who are you?" Juliet couldn't help her disbelieving laugh.

"Just a pair of birds," said the other, imitating a perfect nonchalant whistle. "You know how birds are."

"We know how the Afterjord is," Hamlet said cautiously, still panting from the fight. "You're either here as a test, or to tell us something, or to spy on us."

"Or kill us," Romeo suggested weakly.

"A big, strong thing like you?" the raven replied.

"Who are you?" Juliet asked again. "I don't believe for a moment that you're just a pair of birds who can coincidentally speak."

"I can't believe you don't know who we are," the first raven said, pointing his sharp beak in Hamlet's direction. "You've got Viking blood in you. Doesn't anyone teach you children history these days?"

"I'm not a child," Hamlet responded evenly. "Am I to assume that you're Odin's ravens, then?"

"We have names! He doesn't *own* us," the second bird snapped. "I'm Munin. My less verbose but equally lovely friend here is Hugin."

"I know your names." Hamlet narrowed his eyes at them. "What are you doing *here*?"

"Oh, you know, just hanging about. Taking in the scenery," Hugin offered unconvincingly.

Juliet's patience had run out, but she held her tongue. Everywhere they turned in this place, they found unhelpful, horrible entities who wanted only to trick them or harm them.

"You don't just take in the scenery. You're spies," Hamlet accused. "Who sent you to spy on us, if not Odin?"

"Why would Odin care about you?" Munin asked, tilting his head. "Your people don't even follow the old ways anymore. Odin has moved on, he doesn't need you. He's not obsessed with you or anything."

"Sounds a bit defensive, doesn't he?" Romeo tried to laugh, but it came out a pained, dry chuckle.

"Please." Juliet could take no more. "If you're not here to help us, at the very least, do us no harm. We have come a long way, and we have even further to go."

"We never said we weren't here to help you," Hugin pointed out. "We have an invitation. For you."

The raven's gaze fixed on Hamlet.

"Why me?" He walked closer to the branch the birds perched upon. "Why not all of us?"

"Because that one's on death's door, isn't he?" Munin cawed, nodding in Romeo's direction.

Juliet looked down at her beloved. He wasn't on death's

door exactly, just a bit tired. Wasn't he?

She knelt at his side. "Are you all right?"

"Well enough that two lice-ridden bags of feathers shouldn't be pronouncing me dead already." He was, Juliet realized, trying to be brave, but she saw the same fear in his eyes she'd seen the morning of his banishment from Verona.

Methinks I see thee now, thou art so low, as one dead in the bottom of a tomb.

A shiver raced down her spine.

"What's the invitation?" Hamlet asked the ravens.

"Well, we can't tell you, exactly," Hugin replied. "We're to bring you to a specific place, quick as we can. And you're meant to come alone."

"Where is this place?" Hamlet asked.

He couldn't seriously be considering leaving them behind? After all they had been through? She'd thought for certain that the bitter argument between Romeo and Hamlet had ended with their defeat of the fiery monster. The prince had said he needed them…

He wouldn't just run off now.

Juliet's blood boiled at the very thought. When they'd been stranded together in the hall of mirrors, he'd seemed set on finding Romeo, as though Romeo meant something to him. She'd thought she'd begun to mean something to the prince, as well. Not in a romantic sense; her heart belonged to Romeo. But she'd thought she could count Hamlet as a friend, at least.

Hugin's voice took on an ominous quality. A warning

that Juliet feared Hamlet would not heed. "Can't tell you that, either. Or who sent us. But he's important, or was. And he wants to see you."

Munin whistled and chirped, imitating a songbird. "Something about a key…"

"The second key?" Romeo's gaze jerked up.

"Technically the third, if you're going by order of distribution," Hugin corrected him.

"If you want to return to the land of the living, you'll come with us." Munin's tone left no room for argument.

"All right." Hamlet squared his shoulders. "I'll go."

CHAPTER FIFTEEN

"What did he say?" Romeo gasped, staggering forward. His eyes widened, then pinched shut.

"Romeo!" Juliet caught him.

"I'm all right. I can make it." He fell more than sat on the hard ground and pulled his legs beneath him. "I just need a rest."

"Good idea. You two rest, while we take this other one." Hugin squawked, exasperated. "But we have to go now."

"This place is timeless, so what's the hurry?" Juliet demanded.

"It may be timeless here, but it isn't in Midgard, is it?" Munin snapped.

"He's right." Hamlet felt the strangest chill at thought of going on without Romeo and Juliet. He'd only just admitted that he needed them, needed their help to get back to Midgard. He didn't want to leave them now, but it wasn't every day that the messengers of a legendary god summoned him.

Trying to exploit the obvious, Hamlet said, "He's too sick to continue."

"So you'll just leave him behind?" Juliet snapped, a fierce light blazing in her eyes. "You'll strand him here in the Afterjord?"

"He isn't stranding me, because I'm not leaving. At least not without you, and we've already been told that's impossible," Romeo managed through clenched teeth. "This is nothing but a spell of exhaustion. I need only rest, and then I can continue."

"It's foolish of you to try." It would hurt the Italian's pride to say so, but Hamlet couldn't let him endanger himself. "They want to take me, alone. I recognize this could be some type of trap, but we've been separated before. I'll come back for you."

"What if you can't?" Juliet demanded. "You'll just leave him here?"

"I'm staying here," Romeo reminded her tersely. "I'm not sure why you can't grasp that. If this is Hamlet's way out, we should let him go."

"I'm not leaving the Afterjord," Hamlet protested patiently. "I'm going with these two, who have clearly been sent to us for some purpose. Then I'll return."

Romeo tried to stand, managed to get to one knee. "My

only concern is for Juliet. We don't know if I'll recover here; if this place is timeless, what's to say resting my body will do any good at all, even if I sleep for hours? If you can't come back, if I die…What will happen to Juliet?"

"Objectively, nothing worse than what's already happened to her…" Munin said, his voice dying off slowly as he jerked his glance over the three of them.

Lower, so that it was clearly intended for Hamlet's ears only, Romeo said, "You saw what it was like, where she was. I don't want her to go back to being…like that."

Hamlet wanted to say that Romeo was being silly; any of them had the potential to end up in that place, or worse, after they died. It was an eventuality they couldn't escape.

But he couldn't say it. Somehow, it seemed…cruel?

It wasn't that Hamlet didn't care about other people's feelings. He just rarely had the presence of mind to act as though he did. That had gotten him into trouble, indeed. They really thought he would abandon them. And why shouldn't they? He'd given them no reason to think otherwise.

Had he not suspected the very same act from the two of them?

Now, though, they all stood to lose from Juliet's insistence that they continue on together.

He could not please both of his companions at once. Juliet wished for him to stay, Romeo wanted him to go. The lure of what might await at the end of whatever twisted path Odin's ravens would lead him on was too tantalizing to deny.

He stooped beside Romeo. "I am not going to abandon

her. You have my vow, on my father's crown, that I will return, and you will help me out of here. I have faith that you are strong enough to aid me."

Romeo was defeated. By kindness, Hamlet did not doubt. If he had condescended to Romeo, if he had shouted or tried to impress his royal status over him, the outcome would have been much different.

Hamlet looked up to Juliet. "Stay with him, give him some time to rest. I'll go on ahead with Muggins and Crumbles here—"

"Crumbles indeed!" Munin squawked.

"—and see whatever it is they want to show us. Then I'll come back and collect you, and if it's worth our time, we can go back." Hamlet was rather pleased with the solution he'd offered, though he could tell Romeo and Juliet were not. He supposed they were thinking that the limits of the Afterjord weren't set in stone, and that walking away from them now might mean walking away for the last time. Not because he would intentionally abandon them, but because the Afterjord conspired to keep them apart.

Hamlet had certainly let that thought cross *his* mind as he'd made his promise.

"And if you're killed?" Juliet demanded, still cradling Romeo's head in her lap. "If you never come back, it will be up to me to get him back to Midgard?"

"You're capable enough in a fight, Juliet. Among the three of us, you've had the most success in battle. You rescued me from the sirens and from the vision of Ophelia.

You killed the berserker and the fire giant. All Romeo and I have done is dispatch some ugly, hungry ghosts. You even killed Romeo, remember."

"*I* dispatched a giant maggot, you ill-bred pox-blossom," Romeo muttered wearily, but his heart wasn't in the insult. "But he does have a point, Juliet. Of all of us, you seem to have the most power here. It was you who killed the fire giant. Neither the prince nor I could have made that sacrifice. You've saved us more than once. I trust you with my life."

Juliet looked from Romeo to Hamlet, her eyes wide. Then something turned to steel inside her, it seemed, for she nodded, her jaw grimly set. "All right. But you must return for us, Hamlet."

"You can trust that I will," he assured her. Looking up to the ravens, he told them, "Well, lead on. I haven't got all day."

He followed the ravens toward the distant mountain, looking back once to waggle his fingers at Juliet and Romeo, who still watched him. Only when they were out of sight did Hamlet look up to the birds soaring on the air not far from his head.

"We're alone now. You can tell me what it is you really want from me." He hadn't believed for a moment that they merely wanted to "show" him something. They'd separated him from the other two for a reason. He had no illusions about that.

"It just so happens, we know what you're looking for," Hugin cawed.

"Yeah, we just don't think the other ones are going to be

much help in finding the remaining keys," Munin confessed. "We thought you might want to strike out on your own and get all the glory for yourself."

"I'm a prince. I don't need glory. I already get plenty of attention." Hamlet raised an eyebrow. "Come down here and talk to me properly."

With reluctant, muttering clucks, both birds drifted down and perched on Hamlet's outstretched arm.

"Fine, fine. You caught us," Hugin admitted. "We picked you to win the challenge, you lucky winner."

"To win the challenge…you mean, to face some horrible challenge on my own?" Hamlet shook his head. "What is this meant to teach me? Bravery? The value of friendship? Something about the strength that lies inside of me?"

"Well, when you put it like that you make it sound all trite and depressing," Munin grumbled.

"It isn't that I don't appreciate cosmic lessons, but I fear I may have learned too many already. What is this point of this place, if all of its teachings are contradictory in nature?"

"The Afterjord doesn't exist to teach living mortals the lessons they should have learned on earth," Hugin scolded. "It's here for the souls of the dead to find peace."

Hamlet looked doubtfully at the scattered bones and wrinkled his nose at the scent of brimstone. "This is the way you seek to comfort the dead? It looks more like damnation."

"Your mortal idea of comfort is a fluffy bed and a warm fire," Munin said with an eerie, birdish tilt of his head. "To a soul tormented by a life of misdeeds, the only comfort might be pain and punishment."

"Why did you even bother coming, if you don't want glory?" Hugin asked him with a disapproving quork.

"I didn't mean to come at all." He thought back to the caverns below Elsinore. They now seemed ages away. "I meant to show Romeo the way. It seemed too great a coincidence that what he sought was the very thing that I had found, a way to enter the land of the dead. I thought perchance he might actually rescue his love and return with knowledge I could use. My father charged me with protecting the secret of the corpseway, but how was I to protect something if I had no knowledge of what it did, or where it led?"

"You could have explored it yourself," Munin said with a snap of his shiny black beak. "Your father told you to keep the corpseway safe, and you showed it to someone who sought to breach the veil and meddle with matters of life and death?"

Though Hamlet hadn't given that irony a thought, a bitter guilt in him thundered to a sudden boil, an emotion that had been held back by some unconscious force. He'd waited no longer than a day before betraying his father's secret.

"Seems to me that if you wanted to find something like that out, you should have done it on your own," Hugin suggested.

Hamlet would not admit that the bird was right. At least, not aloud. It was too cruel, to be shown for the first time something that had always been before his eyes.

I should have ventured into the Afterjord myself. But I

was too cowardly, too uncertain. My father would not have been.

He had harbored a secret hope of seeing King Hamlet again in the Afterjord, but now he didn't know if he could face him. The ravens were right; he'd let his father down.

Hamlet had dreaded that one day he would be King of Denmark. With the glory came servitude, to his people and their well-being. As he would be king, he would also be slave. All his life, he'd complained of his noble fate. An insidious doubt now crept over him, and he considered the possibility that the throne was not an obligation to be dreaded, but a vocation he should have dedicated himself to fulfilling.

Had that been why Claudius had assumed the role of king so easily? His treachery alone wouldn't have been enough to secure him the throne. If Hamlet had applied himself, if he'd been as keen to learn the workings of the kingdom as he'd been to explore foreign myths and dead languages, would his subjects have rejected Claudius's usurpation outright?

Hamlet's thoughts turned to his actions since he'd come into the Afterjord. It had taken Romeo's intervention to set Hamlet on this adventure. What kind of a leader did that make Hamlet?

He scowled at the birds. "Just take me to whatever test I'm supposed to pass or fail, and let's be done with it. If you could be clear about the instructions, that would save me a lot of time."

"You have nothing but time," Hugin cawed, flapping his wings. The two birds took off in flight again, circling, circling above Hamlet in the dark gray sky. "Until you don't, which may be soon."

. . .

"There, does that feel better?" Juliet tucked her burned skirt tighter around Romeo, huddling beside him to guard him from the rising chill in the air. She wished there were anything else she could do for him. They could certainly have used that Fire Giant now.

She snickered at the thought of the trapped demon raging as they luxuriated in the infernal heat of his blaze. Her sense of humor had never been so dark in life. *I must be going mad.*

"What's so funny?" Romeo's teeth chattered as he spoke, but his eyes somehow held humor.

When she had first met him at her father's party, Juliet had thought Romeo a very silly person. Not proper and serious like Paris, who her mother had constantly thrown into her path. Not dark and dangerous like Tybalt, who glowered fearfully and never took any joy in life. A boy so very like the stories her mother told of the early days of her marriage to Juliet's father, before the rift had widened between them and left them both so deeply unhappy. Juliet had known, with all of her soul, that it would not be so with Romeo. Perhaps that thought was driven by naiveté, and the belief that she was special, that she deserved more, simply by virtue of wanting.

But it was more than that. Romeo had been as shallowly romantic as any young man in love, professing deepest passion from the moment they had met. She'd reveled in that attention, but in his every word and gesture there had been a depth of care that had unnerved her. She had not believed him when he professed true love from the courtyard below her balcony, but she'd been content to play along with his dramatic proclamations. As he had charmed her with his passion, she'd seen the truth of him; that he loved deeply and without reservation. She'd found herself returning that love, no matter how ill advised. And now that he'd followed his love through death, she had no reason to doubt it.

"I was just thinking we should go back and set up camp by the Fire Giant. Perhaps find a talking raven to cook over his foot."

Romeo chuckled, and it looked painful.

"Hush," Juliet bade him. His hands were folded over his chest. She laid hers on top of them. "I shouldn't have said anything."

"You can't avoid making me happy," he told her, and her heart ached.

There was little they could talk about in this place to cheer themselves. Juliet feared speaking about the past and Verona. She didn't want to remind him of their despair at being separated or the drastic measures he had taken to find her again. Causing him pain would have been the worst thing, to her mind.

And yet she had to speak, because the silence between

them was too much to bear. "Romeo…"

"Don't." There was no humor in his expression now. "I know your feelings for me have changed. You don't have to pretend otherwise."

The words shocked her. What could he possibly mean?

"No, I do!" She made a tutting noise and closed her eyes, trying to unscramble her own thoughts. "That isn't what I meant. I don't have to pretend. Because my feelings haven't changed. Why would you think such a thing?"

"Because you want me to return to Midgard." He didn't level this as an accusation, but stated it as fact. "If you didn't want me to stay with you, you could have simply said so."

He thought she didn't want him. Juliet's heart ached at that. "Romeo… it is not because I wish to be rid of you that I would see you safely back in Midgard. I want you to go there because I want you to live."

He didn't respond, so she continued. "When you woke me from Sheol, it was as though we had never been apart. Well, except for your banishment. But none of that seemed real to me, anymore. You didn't seem real. Now that I've come to accept that I have been dead for some time, that days, months have passed, and that you have suffered on my behalf and with longing for me… I feel a terrible guilt.

"When I used your dagger in that tomb, it was because I couldn't bear the thought of living without you. I knew the way everyone in Verona, everyone in my family would look at me if I returned from my grave. As a miracle, a gift from God. I know that must have been how they looked at you."

He did not need to speak to confirm the truth of her statement, so she went on. "You endured it, to live. How can I rejoice in your death when you've sacrificed so much for life?"

Romeo closed his eyes. If not for the hard set of his jaw, Juliet would have worried that his mortal body had expired. He didn't move for a long time.

She bent down and gently, very gently, touched her mouth to his, as she had that horrible night in the tomb. She had hoped then that some drop of poison had remained on his mouth, enough to kill her, to take her to his side again. This time, she prayed that some spark of life would pass from her to him, though she herself was dead.

If any doubt had remained to her feelings for him, it vanished the moment their lips touched. She'd meant for the kiss to be brief, but it was like coming home. Every memory had a sharper clarity. That life had not happened to a person Juliet remembered being. It had happened to her. Every emotion flooded back, and her limbs trembled at the intensity of what she remembered.

She felt, too, the space between them, the clawing, needy separation of time that had passed for him, without her. She felt it in his mouth as it opened beneath hers. He pressed his palm and splayed fingers to her back, and she was reminded at once of how small her physical body had been, how vulnerable she had felt at his side. How safe she had felt, lying in his arms, dreading the morning that would force them apart.

"I have dreamed of you every night," he whispered when their lips parted. His nose nuzzled hers, and she giggled. She was the maiden who had fallen in love with him again. It was as though the sadness that had made them both wiser beyond their years melted away, banished by her joy.

"I was with you every night," she told him, sniffling back a tear. "Though we were parted, though I was asleep. My heart was with you."

It was not the most romantic reuniting of lovers the world had ever seen. When he lay her down, it wasn't on the soft linens of her bed, as it had been the first time. Instead, the cracked, hard-baked gray clay served as their marriage bed. But every touch brought Juliet back to herself, raising parallel memories on the surface of her mind. For a beautiful, blissful moment, she knew what it was to be alive again.

"You're not so cold anymore," she giggled, as a drop of sweat slid down his nose.

He collapsed beside her and pulled her close. "Do you remember what you said to me, that morning that I left? When we heard the call of the lark heralding the morning?"

"I said that it was the nightingale, and not the lark. I wanted you stay, though I knew it would mean your death." Her soaring spirit plummeted. "I should have gone with you."

"It would have been a far greater risk to me if I had tried. But I was thinking," he said very sternly, "that we do not have to worry about nightingale nor lark today. Our choices will be either talking raven, or talking raven."

Juliet covered her face with her hands and laughed. "I was trying to have a serious conversation with you."

"I know you were." He dropped a kiss on her bare shoulder. "But I do not want to be serious now. I've been serious for over a year, trying to find you. Things have become considerably more serious since I stepped through the corpseway. For just one moment, let us have a bit of peace."

"You're right." She reached for his hand and laced their fingers together. Perhaps she was just imagining it, but it did seem he was haler than before. There was color in his face, and his voice was not so faint or far away. "There hasn't been a day since we've known each other that has not been marred by some tragedy."

"Let us not toss the happy moments aside, few though they might have been." he said gently, stroking her hair back from her forehead.

"There will be more," she vowed. There had to be. Though the Norn had given them no hope that Juliet would ever leave the Afterjord, she had come to life in a different way, the moment she'd opened her eyes in Sheol. Whether she escaped the underworld or not, she would not waste this second chance. Knowing where she had been before would only make every step on her journey sweeter.

"Like right now," he mused with a smile. He pulled her closer beneath the singed ruin of her gown. "Granted, I might have preferred someplace a bit more comfortable."

The memory of her soft bed, in her old room, caused

a surprising ache of homesickness in her. "I feel like I'm becoming myself again, more and more. I know what the Norn said, that I cannot escape. But if I can, I want to go home, to see my mother and father and make amends. I want to feel the sun on my face and be a part of the world again."

Romeo's hand stilled on her head, and she looked up, her heart twisting at the shadows that passed over his face.

"What's wrong?" she asked, the memories of her last days pricking her mind like embers wafting off a fire. "Are you still banished?"

"No. After they learned I would live, the Prince pardoned me. But…"

She lifted her head.

"Juliet, it has been…a long time. Months. Everyone you knew believes you are dead. Our fathers called a truce for peace between our families in your name. Everyone in Verona knows you died."

As she listened, horror slowly dawned on her. Then, as she worked to bend her mind around his words, she realized how very silly they sounded. "Miracles happen all the time, they tell us so in church. St. Dennis had his head cut off and he walked for miles preaching the gospel. Surely I can be returned from the dead."

"It isn't that simple." He closed his eyes, grimacing in pain. "If I brought you back, they wouldn't see a miracle. They would see witchcraft. They would burn me, and probably you, as well."

"So my mother, my father…my nurse?" Tears rose in her

eyes. She felt them, and that was good, she knew, because she was becoming more like herself. But she did not like the pain of this loss. It was too sharp and new, in light of the fact that she'd already said her goodbyes as she lay dying on the floor of the tomb.

It was a fearful thing, to comprehend the finality of death after the deed was already done.

Now she had a chance to reverse it all, and for what?

"I'm sorry. I never thought how it might hurt you." He captured her hand and placed it over his heart. "I cannot give you back your old life. But I vow to give you a new one, one that is as happy as I can possibly make it."

For this. That was her answer, beating erratically under her palm. "I was ready to leave my family behind, to forsake everything I knew for you."

His eyes squeezed shut tightly, and when they opened, she saw shame in his mournful gaze. "I know."

Before he could apologize for failing her, before he could make himself feel any worse about a situation he could not have controlled, she said, softly, "What makes you think that's changed now?"

His arms surrounded her, catching her up tightly. The bleak emptiness around them fell away. And she was whole again, with him.

CHAPTER SIXTEEN

The ravens led Hamlet for what seemed like an eternity. They were not so friendly now that he had challenged them. It was all the better, for he preferred their silence.

They came to the foot of the volcanic mountain and started up a crumbling, rocky path marked with torches. The skulls became less numerous, though some were impaled on branches that had once grown, then died, in stone crevices.

The slope crested at the mouth of a huge plateau. The mountain rose up all around, giving the round, open space the look of an arena. The bloody bones scattered about gave the same impression. Hamlet sidestepped a pile of them and walked into the center. His legs ached. He wanted to sleep, a long, hard sleep, undisturbed by fears of his uncle's assassins or the Afterjord's ghoulish creatures. He sighed heavily, held his arms wide open, and called, "I am here now. What do you want of me?"

It moved so fast, Hamlet had no time to fear. A wolf larger than any horse he'd ever seen leapt down the jagged rocks, snarling and foaming, its eyes blazing with hellfire.

Hamlet did not bother to draw his sword. Some cold, detached part of his brain said, *Well, this is where I die, I suppose.* But there was no fear in it. There wasn't any room.

The beast skidded to a halt inches from Hamlet, its great paws raising dust into the air. The monster panted, its back arched in battle ready posture, but it did not move to slay him.

Now, the fear set in. Hamlet would have much preferred to have met his end before he'd had time to really think about it. He couldn't help but notice the length of the wolf's teeth.

"H-hello…" Hamlet put out his hand, foolishly. He wouldn't have tried to approach a stray dog in the street with an outstretched hand; it was an invitation to a bite, and this creature was like to take his whole arm off in one snap of his jaws.

"Bow, Viking," the wolf said. After the ravens, it shouldn't have surprised Hamlet to hear an animal speak.

Still, it took him a moment to recover from the shock. When he did, his mind whirled. If he were to face his destiny and become the king his father had wanted him to be, he would not bend to any creature, no matter how fearsome. "I do not bow. I am a prince."

"And I am a god-slayer," the wolf huffed, steam billowing from his black nose. "Or will be, at the end of time."

"You're Fenrir." Hamlet jerked his hand back. He recalled the stories from his childhood, and that the god Tyr had lost his hand to the fabled beast. Hamlet was certain a mortal would not fare better.

"Few still know my name." The wolf sounded sad and weary. "But knowledge of my lore beats in your blood. You have the heart of a wolf."

"In your story, the wolf is the villain," Hamlet reminded him cautiously.

"The difference between villainy and heroism lies in the way the tale is told." Fenrir moved slowly, and Hamlet backed up. "You needn't fear me, boy. When I want to kill you, you will know."

"That's very comforting." There was an intelligence to this creature that had been lacking from the stories Hamlet's mother had told him. Fenrir was a beast, a mindless monster grown so big that even the gods feared him. But as the wolf slowly circled him, Hamlet realized the falsehood in that.

Fenrir's graying black fur rippled over his lean frame. "You've come looking for the key, and you've gotten further than most."

"Have I?" Hamlet eased his toe beneath a discarded femur and lifted it, weighing it against his palm. "It looks like others have gotten at least this far."

"I said most, not all," Fenrir reminded him. "You've gotten further than all of them, because I have not killed you outright."

"I'm honored." Hamlet still held the bone, tossing it nervously from hand to hand. It was a strange sort of comfort; someone else was with him. He was not alone, even if that someone was deceased and in pieces and parts dashed about.

"What brought you to the Afterjord?" Fenrir's low growl became accusatory and hostile. "Why come here? For glory? For power?"

"I don't need glory. I already told them." But when Hamlet jerked his thumb toward the two ravens, he saw they were gone. He was alone. He swallowed and faced the wolf again. "As I was saying. I don't need glory. I'll be king one day."

"King! As if being a king were about glory!" The wolf laughed, an odd chuffing sound that sent more curls of steam from his nostrils.

"To be the king, one must be a servant," Hamlet said, repeating words he would have done well to remember the first time his father had said them. "I am here in the service of someone who needed help."

"You were forced here. You made no decision of your own." Fenrir resumed his pacing. There was an agitated energy about him; it radiated in waves like ripples on the surface of water. "You don't know what it means to command men, to rule worlds."

"No, I don't," Hamlet admitted. "But I fear I'm beginning to get a sense of it."

"You can't collect the keys without learning. You can't leave here without changing fate. You lack humility if you assume you can do this without changing yourself in the process." Fenrir snarled. "Many have tried to take the key from me. What makes you think you will succeed?"

"Because I'm not here for the glory the others sought." Hamlet knew it was a test, and that the wolf would not hesitate to end him for a wrong answer, but he could only give the beast his truth. "I need the key to return to my world. So that I can avenge my father and become the king he wanted me to be. Perhaps to become the king he wished he'd been. I cannot do that if I am trapped in the Afterjord, and while my kingdom is not suffering now, it will. If I had been brave enough to challenge Claudius none of this would have come to pass, but it has. I now need the key, so that I may right things."

"As I will slay Odin at the end of time, so you shall face your own Ragnarok in Midgard?" The answer seemed to intrigue the wolf.

Hamlet felt the corner of his mouth twitch and forced himself to refrain from a smug grin. Smugness seemed out of place here, when such a ruthless creature was showing him honesty. "I would never compare myself to so great a legendary hero."

One of Fenrir's brows lifted. It struck Hamlet suddenly how human animals could seem, even when they were not talking mythological beasts.

"You sent for me," Hamlet continued. "Why?"

Fenrir's eyes scanned the gray sky. "You were with others. I didn't want them to intervene."

"Intervene? It almost sounds as though you were afraid of taking on the three of us."

Fenrir did not appreciate the humor. "Are you calling me a coward, mortal?"

"A bad jape," Hamlet said quickly. "I would never think of applying that word to you. You're a villain of legend."

"So, our stories are not as forgotten as I imagined." Fenrir settled back on his haunches. "And what if I told you that it would please me to maul you where you stand, and suck the marrow from your mortal bones?"

"I have no doubt it would please you, but would it serve you?" Hamlet dropped the bone and spread his arms wide. "You sent for me. I can only imagine you needed me for a particular purpose."

"For the moment, yes," Fenrir conceded. "I want to help you on your quest."

"What do you gain if I do?" Hamlet asked.

"An escape from my fate. You are familiar with my story. Pray, what happens at the end?"

"You die in Ragnarok. You kill Odin, but you are slain in turn. Everything dies. So why would you care to help me?"

"Everything dies…but if a mortal wields power over death, does that still hold true?" Fenrir's slow blink displayed his nonchalance on the topic.

"So you're proposing that by changing the laws of nature, you might avert your destiny?" It was a comforting thought, one that made everything seem possible.

It was too seductive to be trusted.

"The role set aside for you brings you to your doom, and pain to those you love. There is no way for you to avoid it, and yet you plunge forward, taking everyone you love with you." Fenrir mused. "If you could change that, would you?"

The hairs on the back of Hamlet's neck rose. "What do you mean, doom?"

"You think you can save your friends? Their destiny is to be parted." Fenrir's head lowered, and he growled in his chest as he spoke. "Everyone you love dies. Unless you change that."

He thought of his father. He thought of the vision of Ophelia.

"You're wrong." He shook his head. "I don't love. I'm too arrogant and selfish to love."

He thought of Romeo, and of Juliet.

He thought of Horatio.

Fenrir snarled. "Say it often enough, and you'll probably believe it."

"How do you know I am worthy to wield the power of these keys...Is any mortal worthy? Can any mortal be trusted in matters of life and death?" His shoulders slumped. "I am not asking to be all powerful. I'm just trying to help someone who was so desperate and alone and sad that he would do anything to bring his lost love back."

"So noble of you, to risk your own life for another's lost love." The wolf sounded bored. His muscles tensed.

He would spring and kill him, Hamlet feared.

"Your father was a great king, and what did it earn him? Death. For your birth turned over the hourglass, and Claudius's time to seize the crown was short. Your birth marked the end of your father's days." Fenrir chuckled. "Mortals. Every man and woman who journeyed into this arena thought they were different. That they were the hero of a legend yet to be written. Well I tell you, they were not. But you could be."

Hamlet's mind whirled. If he collected the keys, he would be able to walk between the worlds freely. What better way to avenge his father's death than to revoke it completely? The king could return to his throne. Denmark would become more powerful than any other kingdom.

"Then give me the key."

"It is not mine to give away." The wolf sounded disappointed at that.

"Then all of this was for nothing? I'll just live on, ruining lives all around me?" The words were bile in Hamlet's mouth.

"You can take the key, but I cannot give it." Fenrir's enormous paw flexed, the black claws scratching at the dirt."

"I must fight you?" Why hadn't the wolf chosen Romeo? Was he not the better fighter?

A leader does not lead by the sword, but he may wield it in defense of his people. King Hamlet had been wise, and his son despaired of ever matching him.

"We are alike, you and I. We are harbingers of destruction." The wolf settled down, his bushy tail curled around him. "You can change the course of mortality and rescue your friends. Or you can die here."

Hamlet's mind raced. Fenrir had a destiny in the lore of the end of the world. "If I take the key and rescue a mortal from death, I will be changing all that has ever been written."

"We are old legends, wisps of memory. Bedtime stories, fables. We are no longer worshipped. When there is no one left to remember the old gods, the pantheon dies. Ragnarok *is* coming but not as we expected. And I will not fall to the blade of some unworthy god." Fenrir's eyes narrowed to glowing yellow slits. "Even if it means tearing apart the laws of this world and the next."

"So…you're committing suicide, then? You'll just let me kill you and I'll take the key and be on my way?"

"Killing takes a piece of you, every time you do it. I am but a shade of my former self, and I am living for what? For the chance to commit one last, glorious murder at Ragnarok. Fie on that, I say." The wolf rambled now. "No, boy, it won't be murder that you do, nor will I murder myself. You will fight me, and you will win, because you must."

"And if I don't?" Hamlet didn't want to think about the heaps of rotting bones and scraps of flesh all around him, the bloody stains on the rock.

"Then you will walk from this battle ground. You may take two steps. Perhaps three. But you will go no further." Fenrir pulled himself up again, swaying on his legs that did not look so powerful as before. "Come, boy. Fight me."

Hamlet drew his sword. His fingers trembled around the

hilt.

"I have one last question!" he called as the beast tensed to spring. Fenrir blinked slowly, and did not make his lunge, so Hamlet continued. "What of my friends here in the Afterjord? The Norn said Juliet couldn't return to Midgard. But if we have all of the keys—"

"Romeo and Juliet have been marked from birth to love each other across impossible barriers. Nothing you do can change that."

"But if I had all of the keys, I could change things. Couldn't I?" Hamlet shouted, his arms aching from holding his sword at the ready.

But the beast did not answer him. Jaws snapping, he charged, and Hamlet did what he knew he must.

. . .

A loud caw broke the air.

Juliet looked up. Beside her, Romeo still slept. She did not disturb him.

She'd donned her gown again, though the front of it was stiff and itchy with blood. She gathered her skirt around her as she rose, looking about for a sign of black wings against the darker sky. In the distance, she spotted the figure of Hamlet by the white of his shirtsleeves.

"He came back," she breathed, joy and terror warring in

her breast. "He came back."

She dropped to Romeo's side, shaking him gently. "He's back! Hamlet is back!"

Romeo's eyes opened slowly, and he blinked in confusion. He pushed himself up on his elbows. "What?"

Juliet pointed toward the horizon. Romeo's eyes widened. He got to his feet and found his clothes, his boots, and hastily put them on. He stopped in the middle of buckling his belt to lift his arm and wave.

It had seemed strange to her to think of Romeo as friendless; in Verona, he'd been popular with everyone. Well, everyone not named Capulet. It must have caused him much pain to leave that life behind. Though he'd traveled with Friar Laurence, it was much different to having friends of one's own age. As much as Romeo professed to annoyance at the prince, he was as close to a friend as Romeo had at the moment.

"Here, take this." Juliet helped Romeo to straighten his doublet, and they walked out to meet Hamlet.

It was the ravens reached them first, cawing and crowing as they came.

"Look who survived!" Hugin cackled. "You all must be very impressed.

"What happened?" Romeo called to Hamlet. "Where did they take you?"

"They took me to the second key."

Juliet gasped at the sight of him as he drew closer. His face was smudged with soot, the soot streaked with sweat and blood. His sleeves were ripped; blood stained them. He reached for the key, held round his neck on an impossibly slender silver chain. He held it out.

"My god, what happened?" Romeo asked, crossing himself.

Hamlet's eyes met Juliet's. There was a haunted look in them that cautioned her to silence.

"I found the second key," was all he said. Then casting his gaze to the ravens overhead, he growled, "Tell us how to call the third."

"You don't just call the third." Hugin landed on the ground and scratched his feet in the clay. "If you had three sheep, and one went missing, as the shepherd, would you merely stand and call to it?"

"Of course not, you'd go and find it," Romeo replied. "So what, we use these two like dowsing rods to track the third?"

"Don't be stupid, dowsing rods don't work." Munin landed beside his fellow and puffed out his feathers. "You put them together, the two keys, and they'll find the third."

"Be sure to hold hands," Hugin warned. "Don't want any of you to get left behind."

Hamlet put one hand out. He held up the key in the other. "Everyone put a hand in. Hold on."

"What's going to happen?" Juliet asked uncertainly. She remembered the unpleasant feeling of shattering in the hall of mirrors and reforming in the waste. If there was no way to avoid that feeling, she at least wanted to be ready for it.

"Who knows?" Munin squawked. "Nobody's done it

before."

Juliet gripped Hamlet's hand and raised the other key.

Romeo looped his arm through hers and grasped Hamlet's hand, as well. "If this doesn't work…we can't say we didn't try."

"No, that we can't," Hamlet agreed, grim.

What had he done to gain the second key? What horrible task had he been forced to endure?

There was no time to ask it. Hamlet brought the tip of his key to touch the one she held. At once, the wasteland began to spin. As it picked up speed, Hugin and Munin became two dark blurs.

"Ooh, watching that will make me sick," Hugin cawed.

"Good luck," Munin called to them. "You're going to need it."

Juliet shut her eyes. When she opened them, the light was so bright, she stumbled.

"Careful!" Romeo caught her, and she leaned against him, her chin tucked to her chest.

"What?" Hamlet's indignant cry forced her to open her eyes, and Juliet saw that beneath her feet, the only thing keeping her from plunging into a black void was gossamer light.

"We've been here before," Romeo murmured. "It takes a moment to get used to."

"I suppose it would." She lifted her head, then blinked in wonder at the ripples of rainbow light all around them.

"I don't understand." Hamlet walked in a very brave

circle, skirting the edge of the ribbon of light. "Why would it bring us back here? There is no key to be found. The Valkyrie are in Valhalla; it should have taken us there."

Juliet followed Hamlet's gaze. Far in the distance, a shimmering golden fortress stood against a similarly gilded sky. "We're going in there?"

"We were banished from there. By some very insistent warrior women." Romeo sighed wearily. "What shall we do now?"

"I haven't a clue. I suppose we could try knocking on the door and asking politely." Hamlet stroked his chin as he considered.

A breeze stirred the light, and the wisps of a curl brushed her cheek. There was a familiar sound, so maddeningly faint that Juliet worried for a moment that she had imagined it.

"Juliet?" Romeo asked. He and Hamlet had moved away from her, toward the fortress in the distance.

But her heart pulled her away from them, toward the sound. "I hear something... something from my childhood."

The tone and inflection were clear, even though they were faint. It was...·

"Juliet, this place is full of tricks," Hamlet reminded her.

But it wasn't a trick.

"It's my nurse."

CHAPTER SEVENTEEN

Juliet bolted in the direction of the sound, ignoring Hamlet's shout. Romeo was but steps behind her.

"Wait," he panted, reaching for her arm. "Wait, you don't know what you're doing."

"I hear her, Romeo." She continued on, but slowed her steps so that he could walk beside her. "I know this place is deceptive, but I've seen through its tricks before."

"Not in the hall of mirrors," Hamlet reminded her as he fell in step beside them. "You didn't see that for the illusion it was. You had to trust *my* senses."

"Then loan me your senses," Juliet demanded. "Follow me or don't, it matters not. I hear Nurse. If she is here, I will not miss the chance to speak with her again."

"If she's here, she is dead," Hamlet said, and that slowed

Juliet's steps.

Nurse had not been young. And not in the best of health, that was true, but certainly she had not been so close to death.

Surely she had not *died*.

The question only firmed Juliet's resolve. When she'd arrived in the Afterjord, she had been frightened and confused. Her heart broke to think of Nurse in such a state, dear woman that she had been.

Juliet stopped to face them both. "If this is a trick, then so be it. I will rejoice if it is, for it will mean my beloved Nurse has been spared the horrors of death. But I must know, either way, and the only way to find out is to go to the sound."

"The key—" Hamlet began.

Romeo cut him off. "The key can wait. I doubt Valhalla will fall in a span of minutes."

Juliet gave him as much of a smile as she could conjure. It wasn't much, but she hoped it showed him the depth of her gratitude.

Hamlet was not yet convinced. "We are closer than ever to the escape that will rescue you from the grave. You're willing to turn your back on that for an illusion?"

She drew herself up tall. "This woman held me to her breast and dried my tears and loved me as though I were her own babe. I would gladly turn my back on a chance at second life to comfort her."

Romeo and Hamlet looked at each other in silence,

and it was Hamlet who glanced away first, a simple defeat expressed in the briefest downward flick of his eyes.

"Fine. We'll go. But I won't venture into Sheol again, not for you, your nurse, nor anyone else."

They made their way from the light bridge to the sturdy stone of a tree-lined plaza. Juliet marveled at the mass of humanity that swarmed the area. Souls of all kinds, from all over the earth, wandered in the space. She recognized it at once.

She recognized, too, the plump woman weaving among the bodies, her gray curls askew. She held her hand to her forehead and shouted, "Juliet! Juliet, where have you gone?"

"Go to her," Romeo urged. Then, he grabbed Juliet's arm. "Wait. Hamlet, give me one of the keys."

Uncertain, Hamlet took the Berserker's key from his doublet and handed it over.

"Take this," Romeo said, folding the key into her palm. His fingers burned where they touched hers. "We will look out for the shades that guard this realm, and keep them from you. If we are separated—"

"It takes two keys to call to one," Hamlet reminded him.

"If we are separated from you," Romeo began again, ignoring the prince, "Hamlet and I will retrieve the third key and use it to find you."

Juliet squeezed his hand, took the key, and walked toward the figure that appeared to be her nurse.

"Juliet!" Nurse turned, scanning the sky that was not there. Juliet wondered if she saw the gilded Venetian blue over Verona, and not the cavernous darkness looming above them now.

"Good woman, what causes you such distress?" Juliet asked, and the moment Nurse's terrified gaze fell upon her, she knew. It was her Nurse, not some vision.

Nurse had died.

The grief in Juliet's heart surprised her; what mattered life or death when both of them were in the Afterjord together? But the mortal thread that still wound within Juliet wove an emblem of sorrow on her soul. Since the moment Juliet had learned about death, she'd feared most that it would steal away those that she loved.

It did not seem that Nurse recognized her, for her distress did not abate. "Oh, I have lost my sweet babe! I have lost my Juliet! I looked away only for a moment...the river!"

Nurse clutched her chest, and Juliet's memory gave way to a long ago tale. Nurse's calm, steady voice rolled through her mind. *When you were but a speck of a thing, barely able to walk, you got away from me at a merchant's stall. It was midday, market day, and I turned my head for but a moment...I was sure you had slipped over the bridge and into the river.*

"Good lady, you misremember," Juliet said patiently. "That was so long ago. You found your charge, hiding behind the skirts of a noble lady, enthralled by the sight of her pretty lace parasol."

"Yes...yes, I remember now..." But Nurse's features did not soften. "She had never seen one before..."

"You found her, and you caught her up and kissed her, and made her promise she would never worry you so terribly again." Juliet's tears burned her eyes.

"I did." Nurse appeared to ease a bit, but her bewilderment did not fade entirely. "How did you know that?"

"Because I am your Juliet." Her heart ached. Nurse did not remember her, and she had not been able to keep her promise. "I am so sorry."

"Juliet?" Some of the haze lifted from Nurse's eyes, only to be replaced with sadness. "But Juliet is…"

"Dead. As you are now." Juliet motioned to one of the trees rising from its huge stone urn, and led her Nurse to sit with her on the edge. "How did you come to this place?"

"I came down with a fever…" Slowly, Nurse came to understanding, horror and clarity at war in her expression. "I had no reason… I had no…"

She'd had no reason to get well, Juliet realized. The last child she would care for was dead, buried in unconsecrated ground. Nurse would consider that an abysmal failure in her duties to the Capulet family.

Nurse gripped Juliet's hands too tight. "I should have never delivered you to Friar Laurence. I should have never taken messages to the Montague."

"You had no way of knowing what would happen," Juliet soothed her. "It is I who failed you."

"My sweet child…you could never fail me."

All Juliet had longed for since the moment she'd arrived in the Afterjord had been the comforting arms of her nurse.

Those big, soft arms now enfolded her, pulled her head to rest against Nurse's round, plump shoulder.

In Nurse's embrace, Juliet felt like a child again. How she'd longed to grow up, faster than her years. Now she would give anything to be that little child again, living happily with her Nurse, hearing daily how clever she was.

She *had* failed Nurse, and Mother and Father, and even Tybalt. She'd turned her back on her family and caused them this pain.

She cried, and her tears were real tears, not some illusion in death. Her sobs hurt her chest, hurt as though she were living. At once, she was back to the night of Tybalt's death, the bleak hopelessness and cruel despair. She wished she could erase all of it; all of it but Romeo, and that one perfect night on her balcony, when everything had seemed innocent and utterly possible.

She wanted Romeo. She wanted life. She wanted to undo all the death and pain, and the knowledge that she never would twisted cruelly in her side.

"Juliet!"

It was Romeo's shout that tore her from her dark thoughts, but when she raised her head, there was nothing *but* darkness. It swirled around her, compelled her, tore her from her Nurse and swept her along.

This, she remembered. The clawing terror, the sudden realization that all she had been told of death was a lie, and yet none of it had been, too. The knowledge that her deeds in life were counted against her, and she had been found wanting. It was as if her own despair condemned her…

She'd done this all before, and she would not do it again. If she was sole judge of the destination of her soul, she would not send herself back to Sheol. The key was still clutched in her hand. She brandished it like a weapon against the darkness, and roared, "No!"

She saw the raw edges of her scream ripple through the blackness, and the shade that had held her recoiled. From her, or from the key, she could not say, but she held it before her as a weapon, put herself between Nurse and the creatures who would drag her away.

The mistakes of the past were written in stone, and Juliet was no force to wear them away. But she would no longer punish herself for them. She could not force herself to carry that guilt another step.

"Juliet, look!" Romeo was at her side, hand on the hilt of his sword as the shade faded. She followed the line of his arm, to where he pointed at Nurse.

Flowing white rippled around her, a shade made of light instead of darkness. Its arms enfolded her, urged her toward an arch with a chalice carved into the keystone.

Juliet started forward, and Romeo stopped her. "Let her go."

"But Juliet," Nurse said, turning her head to catch a last glimpse.

"I will come anon," Juliet called after her. "We will not be parted for long."

Romeo's hand closed over Juliet's shoulder. She watched

her nurse go toward the arch, and then through it.

"It is right," Juliet said, wiping at her eyes. "No better mother has ever lived."

"Certainly not mine," Hamlet put in sadly, stepping up to join them. "Your Nurse would have gone into Sheol, carrying with her all the guilt she felt for failing you."

"How do you know that?" Romeo asked, a note of skepticism in his voice.

"The ravens told me, on our walk to the mountain. They said the Afterjord exists to comfort mortals in death." Hamlet shrugged. "Perhaps for some, eternal torment is kinder than giving up their guilt or facing the shame of their deeds. Not that your nurse had anything to be ashamed off—"

"She thought she had failed me." Juliet closed her eyes. "That she had failed *me.*"

"Don't talk like that." Romeo lifted his eyes to the sky, and Juliet realized he was not simply offering her a platitude. He feared what would happen if she continued with her guilt.

"You needn't worry," she reassured him. "I kept them at bay with this."

Hamlet took the key from her and held it up, turning it this way and that as he examined it. But it remained inert, as it had before. He handed it back to Juliet with a shrug.

"Well, if we're finished here," he began, sounding a bit put out at the delay, "We should move on."

They returned to the bridge, easily warding off a shade that attempted to block their path. The key, it seemed, was more than a key to the gates between the Afterjord and

Midgard, but a symbol allowing them entrance wherever they might seek it.

"If I had known how well it worked, I would have used it against the sirens," Juliet lamented. "It would have saved us a fair amount of trouble."

"It may have worked against the sirens," a voice spoke from above them, "but it won't work against us."

There was a rush of wings and a flash of arms, and before Juliet could understand what had happened, she was jerked from her feet and soaring through the air, away from Hamlet, Romeo, and the stone plaza entirely.

• • •

"After her!" Hamlet shouted, grabbing the front of Romeo's doublet.

It had all happened so suddenly, Romeo hadn't had a chance to move to grab Juliet from the Valkyries' arms, and now two of them bore her away, twisting and shrieking through the sky over Bifröst. His slow reaction shamed him, but he could worry about that after they'd rescued Juliet.

Hamlet's feet skidded on the stone just before the light bridge began, and he tested it with one foot, quickly, saying, "Just in case." When Bifröst held him, they charged ahead.

"What do they want with her?" Romeo gasped. His lungs burned, and his limbs grew weary long before they'd covered half the journey. He concentrated on Juliet, on the thought of losing her again, and it gave him the speed and breath he'd lost.

"I don't know," Hamlet seemed vaguely surprised that Romeo could keep up with him. "But whatever it is, it's counter to our purposes. Juliet has the other key. Which leaves us with—"

Bifröst disappeared beneath their feet, replaced by blood-splattered stone. Romeo's head swam at the sudden shift. They stood in Valhalla once more, inside a wide circle of menacing warriors and their villainous counterparts. There were giants, like the fire giant they had battled in the wasteland, and others who were made from snow and ice. Rows of warriors, no less fearsome than the berserker, stood cradling axes and swords, their shields glinting in the torchlight. Above them, clad in flowing white and intricately wrought armor, winged women brandished spears.

And between two of them, Juliet.

One of them glided forward on the air, the toes of her golden boot pointed as she landed on the light bridge. "Welcome to Valhalla," she said with a malicious smile. "I assume you've drawn up your battle terms?"

CHAPTER EIGHTEEN

"Let me go!" Juliet shouted at the two Valkyrie who held her. Hamlet looked up, pleading silently. He caught her eye and only barely shook his head, and she stilled.

But she glared at them, the fiery girl.

"Why did you bring us here?" Hamlet demanded of Hildr. She smirked at him and took a few lazy steps forward.

"I brought you here because you have something that does not belong to you." She held out her palm. "I'll have it back now."

"No!" Romeo stepped forward and flung his hand out, as if to prevent Hamlet from taking a step toward the winged woman.

He needn't have worried. Hamlet would no sooner give over the last key that remained to them than he would voluntarily lay his neck below one of the Viking axes that surrounded them.

"Give us Juliet, and we'll give you the key," Romeo promised.

Hamlet felt an admonishment rising up his throat, then he paused. He wondered of the polite way to tell Romeo that there was no chance in any of the hells they had traversed that he would trade away their last hope of returning to Midgard.

"No, we won't." Hamlet gently pushed Romeo's hand aside. "We've taken these keys—" his gaze flicked to Romeo, entreating him to be quiet about which of them possessed the other key— "and we will use them to return to Midgard. It is our only chance of leaving this world, and you do not want us here. Give us the maiden, and we shall go."

Hildr lifted one golden eyebrow. There was a high flush on her porcelain cheeks. "Let me warn you, mortals, that what you are attempting is anathema. The keys are kept separate by the will of a power higher than any god, and they will remain separated."

"Then you have no notion of what we are capable of," Juliet shouted.

The Valkyrie laughed. Her legion of sisters smirked. "We are the finest warriors who ever fought and died in the mortal realm. There are eighty-thousand and more dying in wars every day. Men here have ridden tigers into battle to subdue their enemies. What have you done?"

Hamlet imagined his father and heard the steel of King

Hamlet's voice in his words. "I killed Fenrir, the beast so fierce that even you fear him. As I will kill you."

Hildr glowed with a blaze of golden fury at the insult. "I fear no one!" She motioned with her spear and called to the other Valkyrie. "Go and revive the mangy dog. And don't be gentle about it."

Hildr came so close, Hamlet swore the tips of their noses would brush. She stared him down for a long moment, and when he did not cower, she laughed, a haughty sound that rattled Hamlet to his bones, though he would never show it.

"Fine, mortal. If you wish to fight, then so be it. You will not get the third key." She raised her chin and addressed the horde behind them. "See these gallant fools out."

"I thought we were going to fight?" Romeo demanded. "What about Juliet?"

Hildr fixed her gaze on Juliet. A particularly frank gaze that Hamlet swore Romeo would not have tolerated from a man. "Juliet stays. She is one of us now."

"Time to go, mortals," a big, brutish mountain of a man chortled behind them, and two pairs of impossibly huge hands closed over both their shoulders, dragging them back.

"Make your preparations," Hildr called after them. "And we will make ours. We shall meet on Bifröst."

· · ·

"I said unhand me, you winged harpies!" Juliet screeched as she watched Hamlet and Romeo dragged, shouting, from the hall.

"As you wish," the Valkyrie to her left said, and at once they released her. Juliet plummeted to the stone floor with a resounding thud.

The tip of one golden boot nudged her in the ribs, as gently as an armored foot might nudge. "All harpies have wings, by their very nature."

Juliet scrambled to her feet, backing away from the winged woman who smirked at her. The woman raised her golden head and said, "My sisters, stay. The rest of you, leave us."

The horde of monsters and warriors noisily retreated, and the Valkyries formed a tighter circle around Juliet. She forced herself to stay still, to not flinch from them as they drew closer.

"What do you want of me?" she asked the one who appeared to be leader.

To Juliet's surprise, the fair woman did not threaten her, nor did she attempt to overly charm her. She held out her hand and clasped Juliet's forearm. "I am Hildr, daughter of Högni, wife of Hedin."

It seemed only fitting that she should respond in kind. "Juliet, daughter of Capulet and wife of Romeo."

"Your husband is very brave, entering the Afterjord to find you," Hildr mused. "But you are braver by far, and you shall have a reward."

Juliet shook her head. "You are mistaken. I am not brave. I have been gripped with terror ever since Romeo woke me in Sheol. He is brave. He deserves any reward you have to give, though I am certain the only reward he desires is to return to Midgard."

"So, you are courageous. Not brave." Hildr raised one pale brow. "This only intrigues me more."

She motioned to two of her fellow Valkyries, and they moved, clearing a path that Hildr indicated with her spear. Juliet followed, for she felt she had no other choice.

"What do you see, when you look around this place?" the Valkyrie demanded of Juliet. The other winged women walked behind them, their curiosity plain on their faces.

"I–I see…" Juliet hesitated. She had seen so much in her travels through the Afterjord, nearly all of it impossible to describe. But this place seemed clear enough. "It is a fortress."

"It is a feasting hall," Hildr corrected her. "A warrior's paradise, where Odin's chosen warriors prepare for battle at Ragnarok, the end of time itself."

"Ragnarok isn't going to happen," one of the other Valkyries reminded her. "The mortal prince killed Fenrir, the beast so fierce that even you fear him."

"I fear no one," Hildr said proudly, but her eyes flared momentarily in shock at the remark. She motioned with her spear and called to the other Valkyrie. "Go and revive the fool. And don't be gentle about it."

"What does any of this have to do with me?" Juliet demanded. "I am not a Viking. I don't believe in your strange traditions. Why hold me prisoner here?"

"Prisoner?" Hildr laughed, and her sisters followed suit. "We don't seek to imprison you. You slew the Berserker. You defeated the illusions of Sheol. You stopped a fire giant by flinging your own body at him. That alone is impressive. You have more than redeemed your mortal cowardice."

"Cowardice?" Juliet's face burned with her anger. "I was no coward!"

"You ran away from the challenge set before you in Midgard, did you not?" Hildr asked, as if daring Juliet to argue further.

How dare this stranger make such assumptions about the end of Juliet's life! Juliet's limbs trembled with the force of her rage. "I did what I had to do! Imagine, waking in your own tomb, to find your love dead beside you, and see if you choose differently!"

"I care not about your mode of death. But the potion you took to find yourself in the tomb in the first place... that was cowardice." It was clear to Juliet that Hildr meant no insult, though her words were certainly insulting. She stated them as fact she regarded with no opinion or emotion.

Somehow that made it worse, and Juliet could barely control her anger. She struggled to keep from raising her voice, conscious as ever that the women around her all bore intimidating sharp spears. "I had no choice. I couldn't have married Paris. I'd already married Romeo. My immortal soul was in danger."

"And isn't it in danger now?" Hildr asked with a smirk. "Stop your protesting. It makes you appear weak, and you most certainly are not."

Juliet didn't know how to respond to that.

"What do we want with you?" Hildr repeated Juliet's question back to her. "You are a warrior, and the best warriors reside in Valhalla. But you have done more than display courage on the battlefield; you fought against the natural order of the Afterjord. You were in Sheol. Your soul chose to forget the pain of your mortal life by sleeping eternally, and yet you're still here."

"Because Romeo woke me!" Juliet shook her head. "This is madness. You want me to become a warrior? All I want is to go home, back to Midgard, to live a mortal life with Romeo."

"The Norn have told us of you. You and your love are marked by fate to love across impossible barriers. That destiny should have been fulfilled when Romeo swallowed the poison beside your bier, but your despair got the better of you, and you altered your destiny." Hildr no longer spoke in haughty tones, as though Juliet were a child who needed education on the matter. Her voice softened, almost in pity, and Juliet realized with a shock that she would have preferred the proud, condescending warrior.

"I am offering you a chance to alter your destiny once more," Hildr continued. "Become one of us. Ride with us over the battlefields of Midgard. Wield the power of life over death, and reside here with us, in Valhalla. You will become legend, as one as brave as you are deserves to be."

Juliet's mind raced. What was this woman offering? A

chance to be legend, but Juliet had never once desired such status. But another part of her statement had pricked Juliet's mind. "I would be able to return to Midgard?"

Hildr's eyes narrowed. "You would, when you ride with us. The Valkyrie are present at all great battles, finding those warriors who fall and recruiting them into the ranks of the Einherjar, the chosen warriors of Valhalla. Do not deceive yourself into believing you can have a normal mortal life once you join us."

"But you said you have a husband," Juliet reminded her, a strangely panicked hope growing in her chest.

Hildr's smirk widened into a grin. "The stubborn man is locked in eternal war with my father. Is that the type of marriage you would have?"

Their walking had borne them to a tall, gilded door. Hildr opened it, revealing an armory of sorts. At least, that was the conclusion Juliet arrived at as soon as her eyes adjusted to the burning glare of sunlight—sunlight!—off the gleaming golden surfaces of shields, weaponry, and armor.

In the center of the room, on a wooden form, hung a golden breastplate. The metal was worked into an image of feathers, matching the armor worn by all the Valkyrie.

"It is yours, if you will have it." There was no mocking in Hildr's tone, none of the condescension she'd displayed before. "You have the choice to be brave."

• • •

As the horde bore them toward the doors of Valhalla, Romeo had the strangest, angriest feeling at having been there before. The enormous doors opened, and with very little ceremony—as last time—they were shoved out. Hamlet fell forward and sprawled on the ground, but Romeo managed to stay on his feet, skidding on the stone. He turned and attempted a run at the closing doors, but there was no hope of getting through them. Not without being ground into paste.

Every instinct urged him to pound on the doors, to scream and threaten, but what good could it possibly do him? Inside the impenetrable walls of Valhalla assembled the greatest warriors ever to die in glory. And they had Juliet. What had they to fear from a single, wailing mortal?

He went to Hamlet and helped him up. The prince's lip was split, and thick red blood dripped from it.

"Do you think you're the only person in the Afterjord who's bleeding right now?" Romeo mused. "It's entirely possible that you are."

Hamlet lifted a pale brow and dabbed at his mouth with his sleeve. "Your wife is trapped in there. You're taking this quite well."

"I have no choice but to accept the situation, or else beat my head against an immovable force." It was somehow freeing to admit it. Without the rage and howling unfairness to cloud his judgment, he was able to concentrate on the problems at hand. "What do you think they want with her?"

"I'm not sure," Hamlet admitted. "Collateral? But we

owe them nothing. Perhaps they seek to return her to Sheol? But why them? That is the job of the shades we saw before, not the Valkyrie."

"The Valkyrie do not seem like creatures who do something without reason. If they took Juliet, they have a use for her. But what?"

Hamlet's bloody mouth broke into a painful looking grin. He grimaced and dabbed his lip again, but a hint of the smile remained. "Could it be that Romeo is finally becoming a man of thought, rather than action? I'm quite impressed that you didn't draw your sword and get us killed right there in Valhalla. Well done."

Before, Romeo might have bristled at Hamlet's patronizing words, but there was no reason to purposely misinterpret his attempted humor. He'd seen Hamlet's steadfast courage and loyalty. So he let himself jest in return. "I've learned things on our journey. Would you mock me for my newfound wisdom?"

"Not at all." Hamlet's smile faded into seriousness, blood still dribbling down his chin. "Though wisdom sounds a bit haughty, doesn't it?"

At that, Romeo had to laugh. When he did, the thought struck him that had they not tumbled into the Afterjord together, they would never have addressed each other as equals. Hamlet was a prince, and Romeo, although his family was wealthy, was certainly not royalty.

He wondered if that would last, once they returned to Midgard.

It wouldn't, if he did not attempt to make amends for his behavior. "Hamlet...I'm sorry."

The prince frowned down at the blood on his hand. "It's nothing serious, just damned annoying. It will heal, in a day or so."

"Not about your lip. About..." Ah, there was the rub. Romeo had lost track of the apologies he owed the prince. He settled on, "I'm sorry that I pulled you through the corpseway. It is entirely my fault that you are trapped here."

"It is," Hamlet agreed. Then he shrugged. "I suppose I shouldn't forgive you until I know we'll return to Midgard and be free, but if we die and are trapped forever, I don't want to pass up this opportunity to thank you."

"Thank me?" Romeo tried to imagine thanking someone for pulling him into a nightmarish Hell world. He couldn't readily picture it.

A bit of a flush rose to Hamlet's cheeks, and he said, almost bashfully, "You are not the only one who has learned something here. Let us leave it at that."

It was difficult, Romeo realized, for the prince to admit any fault or gap in his knowledge. To say that he'd gained wisdom denied that he'd known all the answers before.

Romeo thought he might be beginning to understand the young man, no matter how disparate the circumstances of their births.

With a lofty sigh, Hamlet admitted, "Fine. If we're tying up all our loose ends out here... I've come to enjoy your company, Romeo. I might even—I cannot believe I am saying this—I might even like you as a person."

"Was that so difficult?" Romeo punched him in the shoulder, a sign of affection once reserved for Mercutio.

"Come," Hamlet said, gesturing toward the long staircase winding down toward the rainbow bridge. "They said we would do battle on Bifröst. Since there is no time in this place, I can only assume that the meeting time is set at whenever we're actually on Bifröst. Best to get this out of the way."

Hamlet jogged down a few steps. Romeo did not follow. "Hamlet?"

The prince turned back with a quizzical expression, and Romeo lost his courage to say what he'd meant to say; that he considered him a friend and ally, that he could never thank him for all he'd done, not just for Romeo, but for Juliet as well.

So instead, he said, "Don't trip and break your neck. I'm sure I *can* defeat that entire army of Vikings, but I don't want to."

A short chuckle burst from Hamlet, and they hurried down the steps.

. . .

Once their feet touched Bifröst, they did not have to wait long. High above them, Romeo heard the doors of Valhalla scrape open, and a trembling thunder as a mass of warriors and armor clattered down the steps. The Valkyrie flew ahead

of them, their spears held aloft, and they were the first to
touch the ground.

Romeo saw no sign of Juliet, until one Valkyrie broke
away from the rest and rushed at him.

"Romeo!" Juliet cried as she collided with him, her
arms nearly crushing the life out of him with supernatural
strength.

"Juliet?" He disentangled himself, wincing, and held
her at arm's length. She wore the golden breastplate and
white linen toga of the Valkyrie. Her black ringlets lay loose
against her cheek beneath her golden helm, and behind her,
two huge wings of snow-white feathers stirred restlessly.

"I'm sorry, did I hurt you?" she fretted, as though this
were the most immediate concern. "I didn't realize how
strong I was now."

"Juliet, you're..." Romeo's voice faltered. Was this a
blessing or a curse? "You're one of them?"

"How did this happen?" Hamlet boggled beside them.
He walked around them in an agitated circle, as though he
could find a viewing angle that would make all become clear.
"Juliet, what did they do to you?"

"They gave me a choice," she said with a shrug. "I thought
this would make me more useful."

"Mortals!" Hildr called, and when she crooked her
finger, Juliet was compelled to return to the host. Romeo's
arms ached to hold her again, after so brief a reunion, but his
mind swam. They had given her a choice? She'd chosen to
become a Valkyrie...Did that mean she wouldn't leave the

Afterjord with him?

There was no time to concentrate on that, now, for Hildr approached as Juliet faded into the ranks of the Valkyries. Hildr held up the whistle chained around her neck and called to Hamlet and Romeo over the short distance. "At my signal, all the fury of Valhalla will descend upon you. Are you prepared?"

"As prepared as any man, to die," Hamlet called back. "If we cut our way through your ranks, you will not prevent us from gaining the corpseway?"

"You have my word as a daughter of Odin," Hildr vowed. She looked over her shoulder and barked, "Juliet!"

Juliet stepped forward.

"Do you stand with them?" Hildr asked Juliet, gesturing with her spear, moving it from one hand to the other.

Juliet pulled her dagger. "I do. I may be one of you now, but I must fight for them. It is only honorable."

Appealing to Hildr's sense of honor had worked. "You'll get yourself killed with that." She tossed her spear to Juliet. "Make good use of it." Then she put a hand on Juliet's bare shoulder and leaned in close to say something Romeo could not hear.

The Valkyrie took flight, hovering just off the ground. She held out her arms, and two of her sisters flew to her side, one with a small, round shield, the other with a replacement spear. Another came to her with a helmet and fit it over her golden hair. The gleaming nasal of her helm cut a swath of light between her ice blue eyes. "Make peace with your gods, and plans for your eternity, for here you will die, and you will not have a seat at our feasting table."

Juliet looked up at Romeo, her eyes filled with tears, but fierce as well.

"What did she tell you?" Romeo asked her, his gaze lifting to the retreating form of Hildr. "When she whispered to you, what did she say?"

"Nothing of concern." Juliet wiped her eyes with the back of her hand. "I will fight with you. When you die, I will come find you as you found me. I promise."

That was why she accepted their offer. It became clear as crystal to Romeo then. She knew that he would die in this battle, and once his soul left his physical body, where would it be bound? As a Valkyrie, Juliet might seek him out, and rescue him as he had rescued her.

He thought back to the night of the ball at Capulet's house, and how he'd looked upon her and thought her a delicate flower. Now, he knew her to be stronger than oak.

"Let's just hold off on the final good-byes," Hamlet interjected. He kept his voice low, glancing over his shoulder at the retreating Valkyries. "We don't need to battle all of them. We just need to get to the doors of Valhalla. The final key is around Hildr's neck. If one of us can get it, we control the veil. I believe what the Norn told us, that Juliet cannot leave the Afterjord. But I also believe that if we control the barrier between life and death, their rules must change."

"I agree." It might have pained Romeo to admit it before. "So, which one of us should do the deed?"

"Romeo, you're more skilled at melee combat, are you not?" Hamlet asked. At Romeo's nod, he continued, "Then you keep them away from me, while I get the necklace."

"And what will I do? Stand by prettily? I'm a Valkyrie now. I'm stronger and faster than the both of you. I'll fight, the same as you, but I want to make sure I'm doing something helpful." Juliet snapped, and Romeo's heart nearly burst with pride.

"You have the spear. You can't maneuver in close combat, but you can keep enemies from reaching Romeo, on the ground and in the air. I have no doubt the Valkyrie will attack from above." Hamlet's mouth set in a grim line. "Juliet, nothing can harm you. You are quite literally unstoppable, unless someone gets their hands on you and holds you back. Do not let that happen. You may be our only hope. Are we ready?"

"Ready as I'll ever be in the face of certain death," Romeo said with a long, slow breath. When the other two gave him a strange look, he shrugged. "It isn't like I haven't done this before. Just in fewer numbers, and with fewer monsters."

"Great. I'm the only inexperienced one here." Hamlet looked back to the horde that awaited them, and grimaced.

Romeo clapped him on the shoulder. "Thank you, your highness. You did not have to sacrifice yourself for me, but you did."

"It is no less than I would do for any of my friends." He looked into Romeo's eyes, and then into Juliet's. "And you have become, in a very short time, people I cannot imagine living without."

"We're your friends, are we?" Juliet chided him.

"You can doubt the stars are fire. You can doubt that the sun moves in the sky. But you cannot doubt my friendship." Hamlet took their hands. "I have no regret. No matter what happens."

One of the Valkyrie approached. Hildr had not deigned to return to them, Romeo realized. Perhaps she knew their plan.

The Valkyrie did not touch the ground, but hovered in the air, spreading her wings, making herself more imposing. "Are you all still content to spill your blood today? Or have you changed your minds?"

Hamlet looked to Romeo. "I don't know, are we content?"

It was true that Hamlet knew more about this place. It was also true that, when pressed for civility, Romeo was not terribly good at finding it.

But Romeo knew more about anger and fear.

"No. We are not content. We're angry, and we're thirsty for the blood of heroes. I say, come. Let us show you what we can do."

The Valkyrie's lips quirked, as though she found them funny. "I will inform my commander."

Romeo felt Juliet's stare before he looked down at her. She gave him a tremulous smile. "Is this...was I really worth it?"

He caught her up and kissed her, knowing full well it could be the last time. He let that form his answer, pouring all of his passion, all of his love, all of his fears and hopes for their future, into a single kiss.

They turned as one to face the sea of enemies. They could not stem the tide, but they could be the rock that broke the wave.

Romeo prayed it would be enough.

CHAPTER NINETEEN

The battle was lost before it began. That was what made Hamlet fight.

He scanned the skies for Hildr, called out her name and demanded, "Are you too much of a coward to face me?"

There was a haughtiness to bravery that Hamlet knew well. It was easy to be brave when one had no fear of the consequences. She would come to him.

Juliet's spear seemed to amuse the first of the horde; they struck out at her with teasing blows, and she fended them off admirably. One warrior chided, "Come on, girl, you've got nothing to prove. You're just as dead as we all are."

But not all of them seemed content to amuse themselves taunting a dead girl. One brushed her spear off easily enough and charged Romeo, axe above his head. Romeo took no time at all driving his sword between the Viking's ribs. It was as smooth a motion as Hamlet had ever seen from a fencing master or trained warrior. Romeo plunged his blade and drew it back without pause, whipping a trail of blood from the Viking's chest.

Juliet swung the tip of her spear in a wide arc, and Hamlet guessed it was instinct more than fear that made the warriors fall back.

Yes, the host of undead warriors was large, and yes, they were fearsome, but Bifröst proved excellent ground in their favor. Though the bridge was wide, it was still a bridge, and there wasn't enough room for the entire opposing force to overcome them.

Then the Valkyrie came.

The winged women warriors were not held by the constraints of the bridge. One struck her spear downward, nearly cleaving Romeo's head. He dodged the blow and swung his sword, but he couldn't fight both the enemy in the air and the one on the ground, so he took to dodging the attacks of the Valkyrie while fighting off the warriors.

"Throw them off," Hamlet shouted plunging his sword into the belly of a shocked warrior. He lifted his foot and kicked the man back. He tumbled from the side of the bridge. "That way, they can't wake to fight us again!"

Hildr had that damned whistle around her neck, the tone of which would raise her army from the dead. Hamlet decided he would stomp on that, when he got the chance.

Romeo grabbed a warrior by the front of his vest,

brought their foreheads together with a sickening crunch and tossed the man over the side. If this was how he fought weakened from poison, Hamlet could see why he'd been such a dangerous man in Verona.

Equally as dangerous was Juliet. For a noble woman, she had already proven herself surprisingly skilled in battle. Now with the power of the Valkyrie, she fought with the grace of a cat, almost dancing between the blows dealt to her. The warriors no longer played with her; their patience was up. Hamlet noted, as he kicked one back and narrowly missed the blade of a short sword to his ribs, that some of the Valkyrie hung in the air, watching Juliet in amusement.

Finally, Hildr came to him, as Hamlet knew she would. The Valkyrie was too stupidly prideful to let his insults go. No doubt, she had grand visions of murdering him where he stood.

"This has been very amusing, mortal. But it is time to end it," she said with a weary sigh. "You've fought valiantly, et cetera."

"I'm not leaving without that key." He pointed to the chain around her neck. "We are not leaving without Juliet."

"And without your father?" Hildr's eyes sparkled with malice. "You came all this way to save a stranger, but you didn't think to rescue him?"

Shame burned in Hamlet's cheeks, and he hated how easily his face betrayed his emotions. "My father asked for revenge, not rescue."

"You didn't think that revenge would be sweeter if he

delivered the killing blow himself?" Hildr's lips twisted in a sneer. "You don't want your father back."

There was a scream, and Hamlet's gaze jerked to Juliet. She held her spear aloft, roaring in anger, the end of it pierced through another Valkyrie's wing. The Valkyrie struggled, like a kite in a strong wind, but could not break free, and Juliet tugged her down, down. One of the warriors drove a pole axe into Juliet's back, and she fell forward.

"This was folly," Hildr said with a laugh. "Must your friends die for you to see that?"

Juliet climbed to her feet, grimacing, but unharmed. The other Valkyrie limped away, dragging the spear, Juliet's only weapon.

Romeo kicked another warrior back, but held fast to the man's sword, so that as he tumbled backward, he was disarmed. Romeo tossed the sword to Juliet and she caught it, spinning to slash across the eyes of a Viking who moved to grab her.

At the sight of one of her sisters wounded, Hildr's manner changed. She had thought, Hamlet surmised, that this would be an amusing diversion, a break in the monotony of the eternal battle in Valhalla. She had not expected them to fight so well. They had not expected a real fight.

Hildr raised her spear, lifted the whistle to her lips and blew a shrill call. The host charged as one, driving back Juliet, driving back Hamlet and Romeo.

Hamlet's sword barely held Hildr's spear. She did not banter with him now. There was no witty insult to pad her blows. She fought to kill him.

It was to Hamlet's advantage. It helped to narrow his focus, to force his concentration. He had to live long enough to gain the key. That was all that mattered.

He was aware of only a few things, as he sparred with the Valkyrie. One was that despite the numerous warriors around them, none tried to strike him. She had marked him out, then, as her own prey, and they were expected to let her finish the job herself.

Romeo shouted, "Juliet, no!" and Hamlet's attention jerked, only for a split second, to his friend. Only long enough to see Juliet lift him off his feet and throw him over the edge, to tumble down the chasm beneath Bifröst.

Hamlet did not have time to wonder at Juliet's betrayal. Hildr had seen it as well, and in that moment she let herself become distracted. Hamlet grabbed at the chain around her neck and pulled sharply. It did not come undone.

"You mortal fool!" Hildr grabbed his wrist and wrenched it, hard. He tried to swing his sword at her, but she blocked it easily with his shield, and the impact tumbled the blade from his hand. The chain wound around his fist; though he released it, it would not release him.

"This is the same filament that bound Fenrir in legends of old. Did you really think I would leave the key in such a vulnerable position? To remove it, you would have to remove my head. That will not happen today."

"Hamlet!" Juliet screamed, running to his side.

But it was far too late. Hildr took to the sky, dragging

Hamlet with her, his legs kicking futilely. The chain cut into his wrist, and he feared it might sever his hand.

Below, Juliet was overcome. She fought, nobly, admirably, but she could not fight them all. He saw one Viking fall beneath her blade, another kicked viciously away, but they grabbed her, subdued her, and swarmed over her like ants.

"Let her go!" Hamlet shouted in Hildr's laughing, cruel face. "Let her go, she's nothing to do with you."

"Oh, I think she'll have quite a lot to do with me, once we get to know each other," Hildr snorted. "Of all of you, she is the one with the bravest heart and the fairest face. She may be of great use to me."

"Romeo will kill you!" Hamlet vowed. "Lay one finger upon his wife, and he will end you."

"Yes, and he did so well at that task before." She sneered. "It is not her flesh I desire, but her soul."

Hamlet could not see Bifröst now. They soared ever upward, and he found himself clinging to Hildr's shield arm, though he hated himself for so great a display of fear. "Where are you taking me? You won. Kill me now."

"You're right, I think this is far enough." She gripped him by the back of his doublet, as though he weighed nothing at all and shook off his grip. The chain loosened, and his arm slipped free. "Let this be a warning to you, mortal, should you ever dare to tamper with the realm of the dead again. I will be waiting for you. And I will not be so merciful next time."

With that, she released him, and he tumbled, down, down,

endlessly, the wind whipping his face like a lash, tears leaking from the corners of his eyes as he blinked against the speed of his fall. He saw Bifröst, only for a moment, as he plunged into the cavern beneath it. A spectral blue river rushed up at him, and he put his hands out to stop himself when he hit; that was the worst of it, the impact with the once intangible substance of the corpseways. It hit Hamlet all over, like a field of knives and rocks, and a shock of impact vibrated up his arm. Then everything went dark.

His first fear was that he had lost his sight when his head impacted the stone. Then he feared death, but that didn't seem right either. He had walked with the dead, they did not feel this pain.

Then he heard the screaming. The wrenching screams of a wounded man dying.

A wounded man who wants to die.

Every movement was agony. His right arm wouldn't move without spears of pain lancing his whole body. It hung at a strange angle, and he held it to his side as he went to Romeo.

The portal was stone, dark black as the walls of the cave around them, and Romeo clawed at it, beat it with his fists and howled.

Hamlet edged backward, found the cavern wall, and slid down it.

"Romeo and Juliet have been marked from birth to love each other across impossible barriers. Nothing you do can change that."

Any warmth left in his heart froze.

"No! No, no, no!" Romeo slumped, sobbing, and with a last, wrenching breath, he screamed her name.

Hamlet would hear the sound in his nightmares until the day he died, and accept the punishment gratefully. No matter his good intention, no matter the love in his heart, he had failed his friend.

In the cold of the haunted caverns below Elsinore he ignored his pain and listened to his Romeo's. He felt each ragged sob like the tail of a scourge against his unworthy heart.

It was Horatio that found them, hours later, Romeo weak and cold, Hamlet the same, blood from his broken arm slowed to a trickle down his side. It seemed ages before the guards arrived, Romeo's friar with them. As they emerged from the cavern, into the full and glaring light of the morning sun, Hamlet knew only that he had been reborn into a cruel nightmare.

CHAPTER TWENTY

Something was burning. Brimstone? No, embers, Romeo recognized, his nose twitching. And incense. To keep virulent humors at bay. He blinked his eyes.

Had it all been a dream? Had he woken beside Juliet, to the call of the lark and his banishment? Had he been forewarned by a nightmare? Or did he wake now in Friar Laurence's care, the poison in his veins still killing his flesh from the inside even as the antidote worked itself through his blood?

No, neither of those, he knew in a shattering moment. None of it, from his near death to his sojourn through the land of the dead, had been a dream. He had found Juliet. He had found her and failed her.

The moment his eyelids fluttered, Friar Laurence was

there, cradling the back of Romeo's head and pressing a goblet of water to his mouth. "Drink. Your lips are like parchment. Drink."

Romeo did not wish to drink. He considered Christ on the crucifix, begging for water, for mercy. Romeo had always wondered at that, the need for physical comfort amid the agony that would only be prolonged. He understood it even less now, for all he wished for was death.

"Where am I?" he croaked, reaching to push the cup away.

"Elisnore. We are…" Laurence grimaced. "We are prisoners, implicated in the kidnapping of Prince Hamlet."

"Kidnapping?" Romeo laughed bitterly. "A man cannot leave his home for a day voluntarily?"

"A day?" Laurence's shocked face contorted even more. "Romeo…Prince Hamlet has been missing for over a year."

A year? Romeo pushed up and took the cup he had rejected. He saw now that the curtains about the bed were tattered, that the room was a jumble of draped furniture and dusty artifacts. "Where are we?"

"A tower room, under constant guard." Laurence nodded to the door. "I enter and leave only at the King's command. Usually, to go off on one of Horatio's errands to track you down."

"Horatio knew the truth. Why didn't he just tell the King?" As he said it, Romeo answered his own question.

Laurence articulated it for him. "Tell the King that his nephew was on a quest to avenge his father's murder? That

Hamlet the Elder shows his ghostly face below the cliffs and names Claudius his murderer? And reveal the existence of the very portal Hamlet was charged to defend?"

There was no arguing with that.

"I found her." Romeo closed his eyes. "I found her, and then I lost her. Or… She lost me. She pushed me over…"

How was he to explain it to Laurence, who had not seen the terror and wonder of the Afterjord for himself?

"I lost her," Romeo repeated in defeat.

Laurence crossed himself and closed his eyes. "Then you must accept it as the will of God."

"How?" Romeo asked bitterly. The good Friar was only trying to console him. Now that he'd seen the Afterjord, Romeo wasn't certain he could believe as he had before. "Which God? For they all seem petty, vindictive and cruel."

"No. Whatever foul realm you visited, whatever horrible things you saw there…you must not blame the Holy Father for them."

Foul realm? Horrible things? "You've spoken with Hamlet."

"I have. His uncle tried to forbid it, but he has come every day to see you. He worried about you." Laurence's face fell. "But he is unsure he can persuade his uncle to release us."

"He can." Romeo nodded grimly. "Hamlet can do anything."

It was Romeo who had failed.

. . .

"Under no circumstances."

Hamlet stood before his father's throne and faced the pretender who sat upon it now.

Claudius did not wear the crown so well as his brother had. Hamlet the Elder had sat up tall and straight, the golden circle a gleaming halo of responsibility and honor. It was tarnished now, dimmed by the unworthy man who wore it. Despite being the younger brother, Claudius looked older; no doubt he had been aged prematurely by the guilt of killing his own kin. His cropped hair had gone to white, and the lines around his steely eyes had deepened.

Perhaps being king wasn't exactly as he had envisioned it, Hamlet thought meanly. If one was entirely unsuited to the role, it must have been perilously stressful.

Hamlet hoped his uncle felt the full force of his unkind thoughts. "Romeo did not kidnap me, uncle. Your concern for my safety is touching, as always, but I left Elsinore of my own accord."

It sounded like a lie, because it *was* a lie, and Hamlet cursed himself for not being better at deception. Since returning from the Afterjord, Midgard seemed surreal and unimportant, and he had no energy for intrigue, even when it would benefit his friend.

"It won't happen again," Claudius snapped. "You worried your poor mother half to death."

Alas, she could not manage the other half. "Then she will understand the depth of grief that required me to absent myself from court."

"You could have left a letter to say where you'd gone. Or at least that you were going at all."

Hamlet noted that his uncle didn't address the grief aspect. Possibly the guilt of knowing he'd caused it would keep him from concealing the truth of his treachery.

"Mourning makes one forget social niceties, I'm afraid." Hamlet looked about him. "Where is my grief-stricken mother, then?"

"Consoling poor Ophelia, I am certain." Claudius's brows lifted in mock surprise. "You've been gone for so long, I had forgotten."

"What? What's happened to Ophelia?" The vision of Ophelia drowning again and again had faded from Hamlet's thoughts as one by one the terrors had stacked against them. Now it swam to the front of Hamlet's mind, and he saw Ophelia in her watery grave as though it had truly occurred.

"Your absence…" Claudius shook his head. "I fear she took your absence as a rejection of her love. She has gone quite mad."

A cold sweat broke over Hamlet. "No."

The role set aside for you brings you to your doom, and pain to those you love. There is no way for you to avoid it, and yet you plunge forward, taking everyone you love with you.

He shook the words from his mind. "No. I don't believe you."

"I would suggest you go to her, to see for yourself, but I fear you may only upset her further." Claudius could not hide the sick pleasure he obviously took in those words.

"You hurt people, Hamlet. Now you must pay the price. Your friends must pay the price."

"Romeo is already paying the price." Hamlet glared at his uncle, his stepfather, his enemy. "Nothing you can do to him will ever compare to the hell he already endures."

Claudius was unmoved. He sat back in the throne that should have belonged to Hamlet and said, with a malicious smile, "Well. We'll have to see about that, won't we?"

. . .

As weeks passed, the restrictions on Romeo and Friar Laurence did not abate. Hamlet visited his friend daily, brought books and paper for the Friar, brought extra food to relieve them from their meager rations, but he could not earn them their freedom.

"What is left for me in Verona, anyway?" Romeo asked Hamlet, for what seemed like the hundredth time. It had been days since Romeo had last risen from his bed, and he appeared to Hamlet a skeleton, frail and sweaty, his skin as white as the bed linens. The hollows around his eyes were like bruises; he was not eating.

If it was his intent to starve himself, Hamlet knew he had no power to force his friend to change his course. But he would not let him face the darkness alone.

"Your lady mother, who no doubt grieves your absence," Friar Laurence piped up from his place at the desk. He wrote letter after letter, to the heads of as many countries as he could think of, begging for help to escape their imprisonment. The letters never left the castle, Claudius made sure of that.

Romeo had heard that before, Hamlet knew. He tried another tact. "All is not lost. If you regained your strength, we could try again."

"The corpseway is closed. You told me so yourself." Romeo coughed miserably.

"Yes, but…" Hamlet felt his doublet. He had kept a memento, one he should have given Romeo weeks ago. But some impulse had warned him to keep it, to save it for when he really needed it. "I think we might stand a chance."

He pulled the key from his shirt and laid it beside Romeo.

"We needed the third key, and now we have only one." Romeo reminded Hamlet weakly. "Take it away. There is nothing we can do now."

"But shouldn't we try?" Hamlet reached for that token of comfort, barely believing it had survived in Midgard. He pulled out the lock of hair Juliet had given him, that he had tied with a bit of string, and pressed it into Romeo's lifeless hand.

He stared at it, disbelieving, and asked, "What?"

"She gave it to me, before the sirens. She wanted you to have this, if things went wrong. And I can't help but wonder…"

Hamlet was not a romantic. No power on earth could convince him of the mystical properties of love to overcome obstacles, not even with what he had seen of Romeo and Juliet in the Afterjord.

"What if we could open the portal? This is a part of Juliet; she belongs to the Afterjord. I don't know that it will work, for certain. But if there's a chance...wouldn't you try?" Hamlet knew he pleaded for something Romeo might not be able to give. He was too weak now, weaker than he had been when they'd first set out on their journey, with the poison still ravaging his body. But Romeo was his friend, whether they'd intended to become friends or not, and Hamlet could not sit idly by and watch him die. It was a slim hope, for Hamlet had no idea if a single key and a token from the Afterjord would work to stir the portal. But it was the only hope they had.

"Romeo," Friar Laurence began, warning. "You used dark forces to your own ends before, and you are punished for it now. Do not do this."

Romeo's fist closed around the lock of hair. "I left her there. I do not know how they are torturing her for my actions. I must do what I can to free her."

"There's my friend back again." Hamlet ignored the Friar's utterance of despair and clasped Romeo's shoulder. "The king won't let you leave this room. So it will take some time, and some cunning, to return us to the portal. You need your strength. Promise me you'll eat, and drink. You'll need the good Friar's assistance. You must commit to life. You have to live."

"Will you help me, Laurence?" Romeo asked, trying to push his weakened body up on the flimsy, moth-eaten pillows.

"To keep you alive, boy, I would move heaven and

earth itself." Friar Laurence dropped his pen and went to the hiding place where he kept the extra food Hamlet had brought them.

"Thank you," Romeo told Hamlet, and for the first time, there was no shame in his reliance upon his friend. That warmed Hamlet more than he'd expected.

"Don't thank me yet," he reminded Romeo gently. "We will need help. But I know who will be willing."

. . .

Horatio held the torch aloft. "Come now, quickly."

Romeo leaned heavily on Hamlet as they negotiated the stairs. His weeks abed had atrophied his limbs; though he could walk well enough on steady ground, the steps gave him trouble.

Horatio motioned to the young man behind him. Dressed in rags and skinny from starvation, he could have easily been mistaken for Romeo but a few days ago, before he'd given up his hunger strike. "Go inside. The Friar will instruct you."

If any guards—any that Horatio had not plied with drugged wine—came to inspect the room, Laurence would make as many excuses as necessary to keep them away from "Romeo" in the bed, but the peasant would play his part if it came to it. In reward, he would receive enough gold to keep him and his family from hunger ever again.

Hamlet had to admit, Horatio was good at coming up with plans.

It seemed a dangerous thing, Hamlet reflected as they passed one of the drugged guards, to plan an escape on such a slender hope as they carried with them.

It had to be enough. It simply had to be.

Negotiating the main hall of the castle was not an issue; the winding tower steps led to a postern door they slipped out of to meet Bernardo. His round face was sweaty beneath his helm. "There's a strangeness in the air tonight, your highness," the guard warned.

"As well there should be. Lead us back to the place where you found us."

The way seemed longer this time, perhaps because Hamlet was so aware of Romeo's frailty. Horatio followed behind them, chewing his thumbnail. He didn't like this business with the portal, and, Hamlet suspected, any business to do with the Italians in the tower. He was a good friend, though, and said nothing. Hamlet had impressed upon him the importance of this errand.

When they reached the corpseway, Hamlet's heart fell. He had hoped, stupidly, that it would have opened once more. There was no reason for it to have done so, but it had been one of those vain hopes borne of desperation, a thing one believes without really wanting to, for they knew the disappointment that would come.

"What should we do now?" Romeo rasped, slumping to the stone floor of the cavern.

"I suppose we…" Hamlet pulled the key from around his neck and pressed them to the stone of the corpseway.

Nothing happened. "Come on, you bastards. Let us back in," he muttered under his breath.

The stone face of the corpseway held.

"Are there words you must say? An incantation?" Horatio asked.

Hamlet shook his head. "I don't know. I thought…"

He didn't know what he thought. He'd just blindly hoped he would be successful, because they'd deserved it. To be cruelly denied not once, but twice at the end of their quest was soul shattering.

"It's time to give up," Romeo said quietly. "Hamlet, it isn't that I don't appreciate all that you've done for me. I do. But it's over."

Hamlet pounded his fist against the stone. If Romeo had truly lost Juliet, then Hamlet had lost Romeo, and that, he could not accept. The key cut into his palm, and he cursed, dropping it. His blood smeared on the stone.

A crackle filled the air, like the feeling just after a bolt of lightning. Blue light streamed from a fissure in the stone.

"Hamlet," Romeo said in disbelief. "Hamlet, what have you done?"

He wasn't certain it was anything he had done, but there was no time to say so. The cracks spread over the stone in the corpseway, the water blue filling them, bursting the barrier apart. Through the corpseway, a golden figure emerged, bruised and bloodied, holding a sword and breathing heavily.

It was Juliet.

CHAPTER TWENTY-ONE

Romeo was certain that this time, he had truly died. For his Juliet stood before him, whole, if not entirely healthy, smiling despite the rips in her toga and the blood streaming from her temple.

"See? I told you I would find you."

The strength that had deserted him for weeks seemed to return all at once. He propelled himself to his feet, to her, pulling her into his arms. "My love, my love," he murmured, kissing her forehead, her hair, her bloodied, split lips. "What did they do to you?"

"Time moves differently in the Afterjord," Hamlet reminded him. "Juliet... You've just come from the battle. I saw you..."

"Saw me overcome, yes. But I'm immortal. They also

called me valiant, so there's something…I'm going to be rewarded." She looked up at Romeo, and her expression changed from one of happiness to sorrow. "I am sorry I had to do that to you. But it was the only way, my love."

"It matters not," Romeo began, holding her tighter, as though he could stop the powers of the Afterjord from reclaiming her. "You're here now. You're safe."

"I am only here for a short time. I wanted to tell you why I did what I had to do. I wanted to know that you weren't angry with me." The pleading in her eyes would be his undoing.

"I am…confused, not angry. But why, in God's name? Why did you throw me from the bridge?" He remembered her face, the horror, sadness, and resolve in her expression, and he felt more pain on her behalf than on his own.

"Hildr told me to, before I crossed over to fight with you."

Romeo recalled that moment, the low voiced comment that had aroused his suspicion. "You knew that by throwing me over, I would be returned here?"

"I would not have done it if I had not known," Juliet said with a wry quirk of her lips. "Hildr has a husband she is separated from, as well. She understood our plight. But our destiny is written in crossed stars, Romeo. We are fated to love each other across impossible barriers. This was the only way I could ever see you again."

"Did you get the third key?" Hamlet asked, starting forward. Horatio stopped him, and rightly. This moment was for Romeo and his Juliet. He did not want it interrupted, even by the friend who had stood beside them in the Afterjord.

Juliet nodded. "The Valkyrie share guardianship of the keys as one. I have the one that you gave me when we found my nurse, and since I murdered the berserker to claim it, it is mine by right. Just as the one you have is yours, by right of killing…of killing Fenrir, Hamlet."

"So, we have all three keys?" Romeo said with a disbelieving laugh. "Then we control the veil! You can return to Midgard."

"I cannot." Juliet smiled sadly. "I made a sacred vow in trade for your life, to save you from the Afterjord. I am bound to it now, or you will perish."

"He'll perish anyway," Hamlet said quietly. "Unless you can convince him to eat something."

"No." Romeo shook his head and held Juliet's hands tighter. "If you're staying there, I'm staying with you."

"The Valkyrie maintain the balance between life and death. I'm protecting that balance now, too. Valhalla is only for warriors who have proven their loyalty to Odin." She nodded toward Hamlet. "Or his descendants."

"Descendant?" Hamlet's surprise was evident.

"The gods weren't always so far removed from mortals. Hamlet is of Odin's line. Protect him, Romeo. Aid him, as you vowed you would, and you will earn your place in Valhalla. You can be with me."

She might as well have plunged her fatal dagger into his heart, as well, if she would condemn him to a life without her. "I can't, Juliet. I wanted to save you."

"You did," she told him, reaching up to touch his face. "In life and in death, you have saved me. There is nothing for me here in Midgard now. You told me as much. Let me have a life, then, one that is immortal. Go out, and have your own life, full of joy and love and happiness. In the end, you can return to me."

"I am too weak now," he despaired. "I cannot fight anything. I could barely walk here."

She smiled bravely at him. "Romeo, I am being given a gift. A power over life and death. I already know what it is to fear death, to die. I would not have you suffer the same. That's why I made this choice, and accepted Hildr's offer."

"I can't change your," he hiccuped, the sound shaming him. He didn't want to cry in front of her. A mean part of him thought she did not deserve his tears, if she could sentence him to a life of such aching loneliness. "I can't change your mind then?"

"No." She rose up on her tiptoes and pressed her mouth to his. "Now, let me give you the gift you have given me."

She poured into her kiss every emotion they had shared in their short time together, and each one washed through him. All of the piercing sadness, the most exquisite joy. Threads of fear and hope and loss wound together into tendrils of sparkling mist that formed around him. He felt more than saw the change that came over him, the way his limbs became hale and healthy again, the way his shorn and patchy hair curled from his scalp to brush his collar. The weariness that had plagued him fled. He felt younger, as if the weight of all of his sadness had released him.

The mist surrounded Juliet as well, healing her wounds, enveloping her in white light that was too bright to look at. Romeo raised his forearm to shield himself from the glare, and when he lowered it, Romeo barely recognized the woman who stood before him. Clad in the same armor as the other Valkyrie, with her black curls tumbling over her shoulders and arms, Juliet was no longer mortal perfection; she was immortal and perfect, her brown skin gilded by sun that had not kissed her in the tomb. She stretched her two huge white wings behind her and sighed in pleasure as they fluttered closed gain. "That's better."

"God's teeth," Horatio breathed in the silence of the cavern.

Juliet turned to Hamlet. "Keep your key. If ever I should need either of you, I will use it. So you had best stick together from now on."

Romeo noted how Hamlet trembled. He was frightened of her. No, not frightened. Awed by her.

Romeo was as well, but he felt a new sadness. His Juliet lived, but they would still be parted. She was not the maiden he had once loved.

As if she could hear his thoughts, Juliet took Romeo's hands in hers, the keys pressed between their palms. "Nothing has changed. You are still my love. My husband. We'll just be separated for a little while."

"For the rest of my life." A tear rolled down Romeo's

cheek.

"Everything ends. Even time itself," Juliet told him. She rose up to press her lips to his and murmured, "Everything except my love. I will be with you, always."

He did not want to let her go, but he knew he must. Still, he held onto her hand as she stepped through the arch, his fingertips lingering on hers until the very last moment, until the light of the corpseway closed between them.

The surface of the portal did not close again, and it took a great strength not to lunge through it, after her.

Hamlet must have known this, for he clapped his hand over Romeo's shoulder. "You look well, sir. Shall we adjourn to your prison cell?"

It spoke well for a man, Romeo thought, to know when to indulge sorrow, and when to leave well enough alone. He could not have loved his friend more at that moment.

. . .

"Remarkable," Friar Laurence said for the tenth time in as many minutes as he examined Romeo.

Hamlet lounged on the mildew-ridden bed in the tower room, watching with cautious optimism. Romeo was indeed a new man; he no longer resembled the emaciated, desperate stranger he'd met in the tavern a year before.

"I suppose being married to a Valkyrie has its perks," Hamlet observed. He would continue to joke and remind Romeo, as often as possible, so that their separation wouldn't seem so definite. For if Juliet were a Valkyrie, she would no doubt find him in the Afterjord after he passed.

And there was no doubt in Hamlet's mind that Romeo could earn a place among the exalted in Valhalla.

"Thank you," Romeo said, turning to him. He pulled his shirt back on, after doffing it to show further proof to the good Friar that he was, indeed, restored to youthful vigor and had the impressive musculature to prove it. He mussed his glossy black curls and shook out his strong arms. "Without you, Hamlet, I would never—"

"You would have," Hamlet insisted. "I've no doubt in my mind that you would have found her, eventually. With or without my help."

"I made a vow to you, that I would help you avenge your father," Romeo said, lower, so that the guards outside the door would not hear. They had just begun to wake from their drugged stupor, no doubt hoping that they wouldn't be punished for their collective lapse in loyalty and judgment.

"I know you did," Hamlet said with a nod. "And I know that you will not forsake it. Dark times are coming for us all, Romeo. I am glad beyond measure that you are willing to stand with me through them."

Romeo extended his hand to grip Hamlet's wrist. Hamlet returned the gesture. "You have my sword, and my service," Romeo said, reaffirming his vow.

"I'll work on getting you out of here," Hamlet promised. He hesitated before adding, "You will make powerful enemies."

"So?" Romeo lifted an eyebrow.

"Your very life may be at stake," Hamlet reminded him.

Romeo shrugged.

"You two. Your bravery will be the end of you," Friar Laurence warned.

Romeo released Hamlet's arm and reached for his empty sword belt, to buckle it on. He was, Hamlet realized, gearing up for battle even as he was imprisoned and disarmed. "That, my dear Friar, is entirely the point."

• • •

In the caverns below Elsinore, the corpseway whispered.

Claudius, bathed in its blue light, felt its power, and he did not quaver in his resolve.

The shadowy figure beside him held up his hands, drawing some of the shimmering azure from the surface of the portal.

"And you are certain?" Claudius asked the sorcerer.

The light took the shape of a figure, glimmering blue. A figure that looked very much like Claudius's nephew, Hamlet. A spectral sword pierced the vision, sprouting from the ghostly Hamlet's chest like some poisonous flower.

"You will rule not only Denmark, but any kingdom you desire, your majesty," the sorcerer promised.

Outside, the heavens raged, and a tempest stirred the sea.

GET TANGLED UP IN THESE ENTANGLED TEEN TITLES

SCINTILLATE BY TRACY CLARK

Cora Sandoval is suddenly seeing colorful light around people. Everyone, that is, except herself—instead, she glows a brilliant, sparkling silver. As she realizes the danger associated with these strange auras, Cora is inexplicably drawn to Finn, a gorgeous Irish exchange student who makes her feel safe. When Cora flees to Ireland, she discovers the meaning of her newfound powers and their role in a conspiracy spanning centuries—one that could change mankind forever…and end her life.

GRETA AND THE GOBLIN KING BY CHLOE JACOBS

While trying to save her brother from the witch three years ago, Greta was thrown into the fire herself, falling through a portal to a dangerous world where humans are the enemy, and every ogre, goblin, and ghoul has a dark side that comes out with the full moon. Greta's not the only one looking to get out of Mylena. The full moon is mere days away, and an ancient evil being knows she's the key to opening the portal. If Greta fails, she and the boys she finds stranded in the woods will die. If she succeeds, no world will be safe from what follows her back …

Get tangled up in these Entangled Teen titles

Naturals by Tiffany Truitt

Ripped away from those she loves most, Tess is heartbroken as her small band of travelers reaches the Isolationist camp in the mysterious and barren Middlelands. Desperate to be reunited with James, the forbidden chosen one who stole her heart, she wants nothing to do with the rough Isolationists, who are without allegiance in the war between the Westerners and Easterners. But having their protection, especially for someone as powerful as Tess, may come at a cost.

Everlast by Andria Buchanan

When Allie has the chance to work with her friends and some of the popular kids on an English project, she jumps at the chance to be noticed. And her plan would have worked out just fine...if they hadn't been sucked into a magical realm through a dusty old book of fairy tales in the middle of the library. Now, Allie and her classmates are stuck in Nerissette, a world where karma rules and your social status is determined by what you deserve. Which makes a misfit like Allie the Crown Princess, and her archrival the scullery maid.

GET TANGLED UP IN THESE ENTANGLED TEEN TITLES

INBETWEEN BY TARA FULLER

It's not easy being dead, especially for a reaper in love with Emma, a girl fate has put on his list not once, but twice. Finn will protect the girl he loves from the evil he accidentally unleashed, even if it means sacrificing the only thing he has left...his soul.

ORIGIN BY JENNIFER L. ARMENTROUT

Daemon will do anything to get Katy back. After the successful but disastrous raid on Mount Weather, he's facing the impossible. Katy is gone. Taken. Everything becomes about finding her. Taking out anyone who stands in his way? Done. Burning down the whole world to save her? Gladly. Exposing his alien race to the world? With pleasure. But the most dangerous foe has been there all along, and when the truths are exposed and the lies come crumbling down, which side will Daemon and Katy be standing on? And will they even be together?